Alien Desires

(Lovable Aliens #1)

Stacy McKitrick

Mythical Press * Dayton, Ohio

MYTHICAL PRESS * DAYTON, OHIO
www.mythicalpress.com

Cover designed by Covers by Stella
Edited by Michele Stegman and Stephanie McKitrick
Formatted by Enterprise Book Services
http://www.EnterpriseBookServices.com/

Published in the United States of America
First Electronic Edition: July 1, 2025
Print ISBN: 978-1-7331762-3-1

PROLOGUE

Calix 47825 sat in the dining hall with his fellow teachers at a long rectangular table, kept his elbows to himself, and picked at his lunch. His table faced rows of other long rectangular tables filled with students of varying ages. The din of conversations made his headache grow by the second, but if he ever told anyone about the constant pounding in his head he might never see another meal in District 10. People who complained about headaches were reassigned, not that anyone talked about such things. If they even noticed at all.

The only reason *he* had noticed was because a co-worker had promised to help with research on a class he was preparing. Before their scheduled meeting, the male went to the dispensary for extreme headaches. That was the last Calix saw of the male.

He did not wish to be reassigned. Not unless the reassignment came with a room of his own. Then he might reconsider. But not even physicians and travelers got a room of their own, so what hope did he have of getting one?

No hope. Not realistic. Might as well stay where he knew everything and everyone.

Bram 58236 leaned his bulky body across the table and practically yelled at Calix. "Can you resend me the file on our first travelers? I went to pull it up for class and it was gone. It got deleted somehow."

Calix rubbed his temple. "Every week you seem to lose a file. Is there a problem with your station?"

"No. I think there is a problem with my fingers. They are too big for the buttons and I manage to hit delete more times than save. Maybe I should request the buttons be farther apart. Or larger. I cannot be the only one with this problem." Bram studied his digits and they were rather large, thicker than Calix's.

But then every person at the table towered over Calix. Could they all have thick digits? One glance at the occupants nearby said no. "They are digital buttons. Why not just enlarge them?"

"I can do that?"

"A technician can show you how." And a technician probably had shown Bram how. The male had just forgotten. "Once I return to my classroom, I will resend the file."

"I would not have this issue if you posted your file in the directory."

"It is in the directory. I have told you this before. Under Calix 47825." How was it that Bram was a reliable teacher? Someone must have made a mistake when assigning him a vocation.

"Oh. Two five. I keep looking for five two. My pardon."

A clatter, crash, and scooting chairs caused Calix to spin around in his seat. Nothing was amiss in his aisle, but students in the seven- and eight-year range were standing at the table adjacent to his. Well, all but two. A male was unconscious on the floor and a female slumped over in her chair.

"The male was falling and grabbed the female," Bram said as he sliced up his protein. "Those two will miss class for a couple of days."

It never failed to have at least one accidental touching during a season, especially the younger students. They had been told numerous times that it was better to fall than brace. And while their clothing covered them from their necks to their toes, hands and faces were unprotected. Gloves would help, but were impractical. Every device needed the heat signature of their fingers to run. Better the students learned the hard way.

No touching.

A whistle blew. The students in the immediate area picked up their meals, assembled in a straight line, and followed the leader to another table, just like they were taught. Four laborers, wearing thick, padded gloves, hustled down the aisle. Two laborers rolled the fallen male onto a tarp and carried him away. The other two repeated the process on the female.

Calix straightened in his seat. The voices had never abated, even after the whistle blew. If only he could eat in his classroom. It was always quiet in there between classes. But food stayed in the dining hall. No exceptions.

Skipping meals was not an option, either. He had tried that a couple of times and it only made the headaches worse. So…get a headache while eating or get a headache from not eating? At least the headache from noise was short lived and not an all-day occurrence. Still, he spent as little time as necessary in the dining hall. On his last bite, he stood while still chewing, grabbed his tray, and headed for the disposal rack. A laborer stood in his way, holding a locator device.

"Calix 47825?"

"Yes." He never understood why he had to confirm what the laborer's device so clearly indicated, but that was not his job and he just did what he was taught.

"You are to report to Sentinel Gaylor within the hour regarding your request."

"Understood." Calix had put in a course request last week and was under the impression that requests took longer. Is that why the face-to-face? Had he left something out of his documentation? That was possible since this was the first time he initiated a request on a new subject matter.

He placed his tray in the disposal rack and took a pod to the administration building. Ahhh. He relaxed against the padded seat and relished the quiet trip. Maybe he should send in more requests if it meant he could ride the pod more often. The classroom, the dining hall, and his barracks were all within walking distance, so there was rarely a need to take the pod. Ten short minutes later he stepped off and headed for the sentinel's office. The door swooshed open upon his arrival and closed once he cleared the sensor.

He approached the receptionist's desk. "Calix 47825 reporting as requested."

The receptionist pushed a button on her station. "Proceed."

The door behind her swooshed open. As Calix entered the small room, Sentinel Gaylor rose from the chair behind his desk.

More peace and quiet. His headache was nearly gone. He could only imagine what living alone would be like. No more headaches. No more near bumpings. No more interrupted sleep. They were wistful dreams, though. A teacher would never achieve something grand enough to warrant their own quarters—only the higher-ups were eligible.

He nodded in greeting. "Calix 47825 reporting as requested."

"Yes, yes. It is good of you to arrive so promptly." The sentinel pointed to a seat in front of his desk. "Sit, sit. We have much to discuss."

Calix sat as told. "Did I leave something out of my request for teaching a class on failed missions?"

"Not at all." Sentinel Gaylor sat back in his chair. "How many of these kinds of failed missions have you uncovered in your research?"

"There are hundreds of failed missions. Which is why I thought—"

"No, no. My pardon. I mean, one of the failed missions you mention in your request has to do with discovering intelligent life on another planet. How many of *those* types of failed missions have you discovered?"

He had been surprised at that one. Finding intelligent life and it was a failed mission? Just what constituted a successful one? "Just the one. It is fascinating, is it not? The images—"

"Yes, yes. The images are extraordinary. They look just like us. Why have I not seen them before?"

"I assume because they are failed missions. Which is why I feel it is necessary to teach the students about these. We can learn so much—"

"And they call their planet Earth. The same as ours."

Being interrupted might have bothered him if it were anyone other than the sentinel. The sentinel was a busy person and Calix had to remember that. "I found that ironic, too. But then, one of their languages—and they have several—is very similar to ours. Makes me think we have more in common with them than I first thought. Except for the violence. The travelers of that time suspected they would all destroy each other over time." But would that really happen? People had to be smarter than that. Survival was natural. But maybe it was only natural for a society that was not violent.

The sentinel folded his hands on his desktop. "Do you suppose that happened? That their planet is no longer inhabited?"

"The whole planet? Probably not. There are many land masses separated by water and they were all populated."

"But the area the travelers visited. What about that?"

"I suppose anything is possible. It has been almost two centuries since our visit."

Sentinel Gaylor stared at his hands in thought. "That would be fortunate if they had."

Calix straightened. Had he stumbled on a solution or a problem? Or had he created an issue? "Fortunate?"

"You must not repeat what I tell you. It must be kept secret."

Something was wrong. No one kept secrets. It was one of their directives. "You want me to disobey Directive 1?"

"You will not be disobeying anything. You will be obeying me. Is that understood?"

Calix swallowed as heat rushed to his face. He had never been admonished by anyone before and to be admonished by the sentinel... "My pardon. I did not mean to imply— Yes. I understand." The sentinel's word was final. That was what they were taught. Maybe his memory was suffering as bad as Bram's.

Gaylor turned in his chair and stared out the small window. "Our Earth is in the path of a comet too large for us to maneuver."

He heard the words but they made no sense. "There is a comet...?"

"Headed toward Earth. Our Earth. Yes."

No, this was not possible. It must be centuries away. "How much time?"

"Seven years, seven months, one week, three days, and..." Gaylor glanced at the clock on the wall. "Seventeen hours."

"Seven years?" So short. Calix rubbed his chest. He stood. The room was shrinking. The air thinning. He could not catch his breath.

Sentinel Gaylor turned back to the room. "Calix. Sit. Breathe."

A command. He could follow a command. He sat. Took a breath. The tightness in his chest loosened. "What will happen to us?"

"That may be up to you."

"Me?" What could a teacher possibly offer in such a case as this? "I do not understand."

"We need you to travel to this other Earth. Earth 2, I believe you named it."

Calix had named it only to make his findings easier to understand, not to be considered for a mission. "I do not understand. I am a teacher. Not a traveler. I do not know how to operate—"

"You will be taught. I know you do not have to take this mission. That is your right since you are not a traveler. But you are the most suited to go there. You know their language, do you not?"

"Yes, the ones documented in detail, but still—"

"And your size. It is less likely to cause notice."

"Because I am short." Logical reasoning and one he could understand. If he were to blend in, size would make a difference. Knowing the language, too. But to travel to another world? He had never left Earth before. He had never left District 10. "Would I be traveling alone?"

"Yes. All the travelers are busy elsewhere and it would take too long to return here for training. We need you to leave by the end of next week."

"So soon? What about my classes?"

"The students will be reassigned. You will be rewarded for your help. I understand you still live in the barracks. Accept this mission, and you will gain your own quarters."

Had he heard correctly? His own quarters? Maybe he could do this. How hard was it to operate a ship anyway? The sentinel thought he could do it, so he must be able to do it. He would not have been selected otherwise. "What will this mission entail? Am I to find their leader—"

"No. We need you to observe only. If they have destroyed each other, if the land is uninhabited, your trip will be short. If they still exist, you will have a month to blend in with them. Live with them. We already know what they were like. We need to know what they are like now. Determine whether or not they can accept unification."

There was a new term. Must be a traveler thing. "Should I know what unification is?"

"It means they are welcoming to new people. Other life forms, like ourselves."

"And if they cannot welcome us? What should I do?"

"Nothing. We just need you to find out what life is like there now."

Calix nodded. He could not turn down such a mission. He must do what was best for the people. It was the way they were taught.

CHAPTER 1

Annie O'Shea squeezed the grab handle on the car door as her brother took another turn on the dark and wet road much too fast. She'd be lucky if she made it home alive. That's what she got for calling him for a ride home. That's what she got for living in the boonies.

That's what she got for spraining her ankle.

"If you don't slow down, we'll end up back in the emergency room," she said. That was if anyone discovered the wreck before morning.

The windshield wipers had their work cut out for them. Icy rain fell from an inky sky and, what the wipers missed, froze to the windshield. It sounded like someone was sanding down a rough block of wood.

Mac shook his head. "Please. I'm barely doing the limit."

"The speed limit was set for dry roads, not icy ones." And Mac's ancient Jeep Cherokee was lucky to drive on either. Maybe she should have called a taxi. Or Uber. Because heaven forbid her friend was home.

To be fair, the roads had been perfectly fine when she'd called Mac. It wasn't until he arrived at the hospital, after the sun set, that the freezing rain started. What little snow remained would have a nice crunchy crust come morning.

"We wouldn't be on this road if you lived in the city."

Too many people lived in Spokane. She liked her cabin, where it was peaceful. Secluded. No one bothered her up there. Especially during the winter.

"Or you could just slow down. Will you be able to move my car tomorrow? It's still at work."

"Where it will stay. It's not like you can drive anytime soon. How's your leg, anyway?"

Annie reached down and touched the big, clumsy boot that encased her right calf and foot. The pill the doc had given her seemed to be doing its job. The pain was down to a dull ache. "It's my ankle, and it feels okay now. This boot is gonna drive me nuts, though."

"Only because you can't drive with it. What the heck did you do, anyway? You're not usually a klutz."

No, she wasn't, but she wasn't about to tell her brother the truth. "It was stupid and I'd rather not say."

Stupid, because she had lost her temper. Again. Stupid, because she'd missed her intended target. Stupid, because for some reason she thought life should be fair. But life was so not fair.

Mac laughed. "Stupid? Who'd you get mad at this time?"

"Who said I got mad?"

"That boot. So, what's the plan? Don't expect me to haul your ass to and from work. I got better things to do."

Of course he did. He always had better things to do. Luckily, she didn't need his help. This time. "I can work from home." And thank goodness for that. She didn't have enough sick days to cover the amount of time it would take before she could drive again, and she certainly didn't need the expense of Uber. Because her brother had better things to do.

"Does the internet work there? I thought this solar storm was affecting everything."

That it was. Anything that utilized a satellite dish was down for the count. "Doesn't really matter. If I can't work from home, I can't work from work. Same internet."

"You'd think there were some preventive measures in place. Everything is fuckin' digital and one solar storm can take it all out?"

"It didn't take out everything. I got you on a landline didn't I?" Which probably only worked because they were in the same town.

"Once the satellites are back online, it'll all come back. Why do you care anyway? You work on cars. Why do you need the internet?"

"I miss my games."

"So take up Solitaire. I have a deck of cards at home." They had belonged to Grandma, God rest her soul. Annie couldn't bear to throw them away.

"Solitaire? Manually? That seems like an awful lot of work for something I can play on my phone."

"Are you kidding—" The car slid left of center and she squeezed harder on the grab handle. No way was she letting go. "Watch out, Mac."

"Will you stop? I have it under control."

Mac brought the vehicle back into their lane. Annie let out a breath. Icy roads were the worst. One wrong move and who knew where you'd end up? Either in the ditch waiting on a tow truck or on your ass heading for the emergency room.

She'd already done the latter and had no desire to experience the former.

A raccoon darted into the road, his eyes reflecting the headlights.

She closed her eyes. "Whatever you do, don't slam on the—"

Before she could spit out the word "brakes," her brother stepped on them. Hard. The back end swerved to the right. Mac cursed as they spun around. Annie's stomach lurched just like it had on the Tea Cups ride at Disneyland. The end result on that ride hadn't turned out well, either.

A loud thud reverberated from the back of the vehicle. Something hit them or they hit something. When the car came around, a dark shape lay on the side of the road. It looked like a log. She was pretty sure it was a log. *Please be a log.*

The tires crunched as they rolled through the snowy gravel on the side of the road. The bushes and plowed snow piles stopped their momentum. They were now pointed in the wrong direction and, in the light from the headlights, that log was looking more and more like a body.

"Oh my God, I think you hit someone." She opened the door and stepped outside, her medical boot no contest against the icy ground. She slipped and landed on her butt. "Shit!" This was not her day for walking.

The freezing water soaked her jeans and numbed her hands. Her gloves were tucked inside her coat pocket, all cozy and comfy where they were being totally useless. Well, at least she could tell the doctor she put ice on her ankle. She'd just leave out the part about walking in the freezing rain.

Mac crawled across the bench seat and poked his head out her door. "You okay?"

"Do I look okay?" Her stomach was half-way up her throat, her butt was freezing, and they might have just killed someone. "Get out here and help me up, will you?"

He managed to exit the vehicle without slipping. She grabbed onto his arms and slowly got her feet under her. Her pants were soaked and she shivered, but her attention was on that body.

"Come on." She pulled her fleece gloves out of their warm nest and slipped them on. Fleece—appropriate for cold weather, not rain. The instant she held onto the car for support, water seeped through the fabric. With her fingers getting colder by the second, she gingerly walked on the slippery road. Her boot was not made for the weather and her ankle throbbed. Just walking on it aggravated the injury. The doctor had said to stay off the stupid thing, and she would as soon as she got home.

She shuffled to the front of the car with Mac close behind. He was either afraid of letting her fall again or afraid of getting yelled at again. Either way, she was glad he was there.

The headlights illuminated enough to show the lump in the road was indeed a body.

"Oh, fuck me," Mac said. "Where did he come from?"

Good question. Had he fallen off the hill? She limped over to the shoulder and, with her injured foot, kicked at the snow-covered gravel. Good, not too icy. For some strange reason, snow always seemed to be less slippery than ice. She hurried toward what appeared to be a man lying facedown. And he was huge. The guy must eat his Wheaties or something.

"Help me turn him over."

Once they got him on his back, she whipped off one useless glove and put two fingers on the stranger's neck. Oh crap! No pulse? Or was she doing it wrong? Her fingers were so damn cold she was lucky to feel anything. She bent down on her left knee— which instantly became cold and wet—and placed her head on his chest. A nice, big, solid chest. Her head rose with his breaths and she heard a heartbeat. Relief washed over her.

"He's alive. You need to call 9-1-1."

"Yeah, right. With what signal?"

Crap. She forgot. No satellites, no cells. She brushed the gravel from the man's face and found blood oozing from his left temple. "He's hurt. Do you have a first aid kit in the car?"

"Yeah." Mac hurried back to the Cherokee as fast as the road allowed.

She placed her sodden glove on the wound and applied pressure. *Please let him be okay.* "Mac, hurry up with that kit!"

"I'm coming! Hold your horses."

The giant was dressed strangely. Instead of normal winter gear, he wore some kind of rodeo garb—suede with fringe. And his clothes were soaked through. Just how long had he been out here? Didn't he think to find shelter?

Mac slipped in the snow as he held out the kit. An umbrella would have been nice, too, but she knew better than to ask. Didn't really matter. With this rain, none of the bandages would stick. She searched the box for some gauze. "We have to take him to the hospital."

"Uh, no, we can't. Your place is closer anyways. Let's just take him there and see how he is."

Times like this she wondered if they had the same parents. "You've got to be kidding me. You just hit him with your car."

"We don't know that. He could have been here awhile. Maybe he passed out drunk. Or maybe that raccoon scared him and he ran into me."

She tore off a strip of gauze and wrapped it around the stranger's head, holding the glove in place. What Mac said were possible theories. "What does it matter? We still have to take him to the hospital."

"Annie… I can't." He ran a hand through his long, drippy locks. "If we take him, they'll probably call the police. Then we'll have to give a statement."

"Yeah, so?"

"Well…it's obvious you can't drive. And…well…I'm not supposed to. My license was suspended today."

"What!" She fisted her hand and counted to ten. Now was not the time to kick the crap out of her little brother. That could wait until she got home and had something harder than her foot. "Just when did you plan on telling me that?"

"After I took you home. I was getting ready to call you for a ride when you asked me for one."

Holy shit on a shingle. "We probably shouldn't even move him. What if we hurt him some more?"

"You were ready to take him to a hospital. How is taking him to your place any different?"

It was different because there were doctors and nurses at the hospital. But another hour drive? In this weather? They'd be lucky to make it without another accident. "Fine, we'll take him to my house. Just get him in the car."

"By myself? Have you seen how big he is? He's gotta be nearly a foot taller than me."

She was shivering from the cold, her wet pants no help in that department, and her ankle was objecting to all the activity it was forced into. All she wanted to do was get out of the rain, but she could see Mac's point. He was five-ten and worked on cars for a living. Not exactly a slouch, but no weightlifter, either. "Go move the car up here so we don't have to carry him so far. I hope no one drives by."

He snorted. "No one's come by yet, and why should they? They have better sense than to be out in this weather."

While he crunched his way to the vehicle, she searched the area for any belongings. Surely the guy had a coat or a bag or something. There, in the bushes, a black bag poked out. She tugged it free. Metal hit metal, but it wasn't all that heavy. She slung the bag over her shoulder and then went back to the man.

ID would be good, but his pants didn't appear to have any pockets, and she wasn't about to feel for any in the dark. Maybe he had something in his bag. She'd worry about that when the guy woke up.

She pointed at the man. "You better wake up."

Mac slowly drove the car up the shoulder, the branches scratching the driver's side of his pride and joy. Served him right. She couldn't believe he was driving on a suspended license. How the heck was she going to get around the next few weeks? Why'd she ever think she could rely on him?

Her light source disappeared altogether when he turned toward the road. After maneuvering back and forth, he parked alongside her, the front end partially blocking a lane. He activated the emergency flashers, got out, and opened the back door. At least they wouldn't have to walk on the icy road carrying the stranger.

"You grab under his arms and pull him in first, I'll carry his legs." Annie gave her brother a look to dare him to contradict her.

Wisely, he did as she said. Without a grumble, even.

Mac held the most weight, but her inability to use both feet for support made her job almost impossible. She grabbed under the man's knees and followed her brother to the car, keeping as much weight off her injured ankle as possible. But hopping in the ice-crusted snow was only asking for another fall, so she gritted her teeth each time that boot hit the ground.

Mac slid butt first into the back and pushed with his feet. Once they had the support of the seat bench, they were able to move the unconscious man inside the vehicle with a little more ease.

"I don't think he's going to fit," he said.

The big guy's legs hung out the door. She wasn't about to turn him into a pretzel.

"Sit him up, then," she said. "I'll sit back here and keep him from falling over." Any excuse to avoid walking around the vehicle. Not only would she get out of the rain sooner, she'd get to sit down sooner. Her ankle was screaming at her now. What she wouldn't give for another one of those pain pills. She tossed the man's bag on the floorboards.

Mac lifted the guy to a seated position, leaned over the seatback, and pulled a blanket from the back. "It's not clean, but maybe it'll warm him."

Him? Try her. She was freezing. Still, she at least had a coat—a soaking wet one, but one all the same—while this stranger had nothing. She took the blanket and wrapped it around his wide shoulders as Mac climbed out the passenger side and shut the door. She rested the man's shoulder against it. That should keep him from falling in her lap.

When Mac opened the driver's door, the dome light came on and lit up the stranger's bag. Stamped on the side in silver, block-type letters spelled CALIX, followed by some sequence of dots. His name or the make and model of whatever was in his bag? She went to reach for it when the light went out.

Should she ask Mac to turn the light back on? He'd only want to know why or argue about how it makes it hard for him to see out the windshield. Besides, it could wait until they got home. The stranger could end up having other injuries, and she wanted her brother to inspect him in the light sooner rather than later. The giant's heart was beating solidly, a reassurance that maybe he was okay. God, she hoped so. She didn't want Mac to get into trouble, but if this man didn't wake up soon, she'd be forced to get a neighbor involved. No one was dying in her home.

* * * *

"I tell you, something landed in the woods. Some kind of spaceship." Jay peered out his window with the phone pressed to his ear. The light he had seen streaking down from the sky had gone out hours ago, but this was the first time he'd finally gotten his call through without a message stating all lines were busy.

A long, drawn-out sigh came over the line. "Dad, did you forget to take your meds today?"

Meds, schmeds. Money was tight and food was more important. At least his stomach thought so. If he told David that, then he'd just go and buy them himself. Jay wasn't about to ask for no stinkin' charity. Besides, last he saw, high blood pressure and high cholesterol didn't cause a person to see things. "What has that got to do with the price of eggs? You need to come out here and investigate."

"I can't. I'm leaving for Seattle in the morning. Maybe when I get back. Okay?"

And there it was. The excuse. "Never mind. By then it'll probably be gone."

"Dad… Don't you think it's time you moved into the city? I'm worried about you being up there all by yourself."

"Hey, I've been taking care of myself for over fifty years. I can manage. I got Buster with me. He's a good watch dog." Jay patted the graying Rottweiler.

"Buster is ten years old. That doesn't make him good. That makes him old. Think about it, okay? I'll come by on Saturday and we'll talk."

Yeah, talk. Talk about moving to some old folks' home. That's all David ever wanted to do. Jay wasn't moving and he wasn't some old folk. Come morning, he and Buster would just take a walk in the woods and investigate. Something landed out there and he'd get the proof. That'll show them who wasn't old and crazy.

CHAPTER 2

Calix opened his eyes to darkness. Where was he? The last thing he remembered was falling. And what he landed on was not soft. Not like what he was lying on now. Was he on a bed? The mattress on his own bed had never been so soft, or so short—his feet were hanging over the end—but if not a bed, then what? From what little he could see, the ceiling indicated he was in a small room, not the large barracks he normally slept in, nor the small ship he had been living in for the last three months.

Before panic could set in, he took a deep breath and let it out slowly. Logic told him to go over what he remembered.

The ship. As he was entering the atmosphere, the dashboard had gone dark. Thankfully he was trained in how to land manually by observing the surface through the port holes. And thankfully he could still hide his ship. But had he landed at his destination?

He was beginning to doubt he had.

The outside. That was a shock to his system. When he had opened the outside door, he thought he had walked into a cold storage unit. It was freezing. Lots of freezing. Not only that, frozen water fell from the sky. Was that called snow? They rarely got rain on his planet and it was never frozen. If he had been smart, he would have worn all the garments he brought, but he did not wish to draw attention to himself. He dressed as they dressed. Or so he assumed. How did the people of this Earth survive in such cold with so little clothing? He did not recall the data stating Texas was cold. Or even mountainous.

Thus, he had traveled off course. But how far?

At least he found the answer to the population question. The people on Earth 2 had not destroyed each other. In fact, they appeared to be more technologically advanced than he thought possible. The satellites orbiting the planet confirmed that. So did the artificial lights.

But wherever he landed was not populous. Unless the wildlife had taken over, which he highly doubted. And that was something he was not prepared for.

Wildlife.

Some creature had startled him as he was climbing down the hill. He had lost his footing and fell. Onto something hard. He could not remember more.

Movement to his left caused him to turn his head. Stabbing pain radiated from his temple, worse than his normal headache. A headache he had been sure would disappear once he was alone. Turned out he was incorrect in that assessment. He went to rub the offending spot with his left hand, but something prevented his movement. Using his right hand, he pulled down the bedcovers and discovered an arm, a wrist, fingers. He jerked away and the arm slid off.

Where was the shock? Why was he awake? His head hurt, but that was all.

The owner of the arm moved. "Oh. Hey. You're up. Thank God."

A female. The owner was a female. He sat up and slid to the edge of the bed. Although he had studied their language, the words she spoke did not make sense. He understood up, though, and glanced toward the ceiling. He really could not see much. "My hay is where?"

After a click, a small lamp on a table at the other end of the bed illuminated the room. He blinked and squinted as his eyes adjusted. She was young—like him—and small. Smaller than any person he had ever encountered. Even the females on his planet stood as tall, if not taller than Calix. He was a giant beside her.

Her brown hair, so dark against her pale skin, might have reached her shoulders if not for sticking out in every direction. But it was her eyes that captured his attention. They were green. No one from his planet had green eyes.

"Not hay, h-a-y, but hey, h-e-y, as in hello? And up as in awake." Her lips curled upward at the corners. "I hope you don't think I was being forward sleeping with you, not that I was sleeping-sleeping with you. I was on the covers, not underneath. Heck, you could be a serial killer. It's just that you were shivering so badly and my brother is a bit homophobic. I just wanted to get you warm. You're not a serial killer, are you?"

Her voice was pleasing to listen to, but clearly their language had changed since the travelers visited this planet. Many of her words were unfamiliar and she spoke fast, but he understood her question. "I am not a killer."

"Oh good. Although, would you really admit such a thing? Guess I'll just have to take your word for it for now. Where do you live? Is it far?"

"Dis—" Wait. Did they even have districts on this planet? She probably meant city or territory. And since he had no idea where he landed… "Ummm…"

She rose to her knees and winced. "Okay, now you're scaring me. Are you in pain? Dizzy? Nauseous? How's your head feeling?"

His head. He was injured. He touched where the pain had come from earlier. Something plastic covered his temple and it hurt when he put pressure on it. "I hit my head?"

"Don't you remember?"

She was running her words again, but he caught her gist. "Not much. I fell. I think. Would you please direct me to your outhouse?"

"Outhouse?" Lines formed between her astonishing eyes for a moment then smoothed. "Oh. The bathroom is across the hall."

Did he use the wrong word? "I do not require a bath."

"Trust me. Across the hall." She pointed to the doorway. "You can walk, can't you?"

"We shall see." He shoved the bedcovers away and swung his legs to the side of the bed. The clothes on his body were not the clothes he had worn when he left the ship. These were soft, thin, and—he tugged at the material—pliable. Which was a good thing or they might not have fit at all.

"Those are my brother's. Yours were wet. And be careful standing. In case you get dizzy. From the head wound."

He nodded. She had a family member. Maybe he would be able to evaluate them. It would be a place to start. When he stood, he waited a few seconds. Nothing seemed amiss. But the ends of the leggings only reached his calves. "I take it your brother is small?"

Again, her lips did strange things. But she seemed…not angry. "Well, smaller than you…"

He turned toward the doorway—the short doorway. Was everyone on this planet smaller than him or just the inhabitants of this dwelling? In all the images he examined, not one included a traveler for comparison. They had only documented that the people were shorter than they were. Not much detail, but then they had thought their mission had failed.

And now he had to blend in. How would he do that if he towered over everyone?

* * * *

Oh. My. Gawwwd! Annie mouthed the words as the stranger left her bedroom and headed for the bathroom. That man was way hunkier awake than he ever was asleep. His sandy brown hair nearly covered the darkest purplish-blue eyes that had no right to be covered. She'd never seen eyes that color before. She could get lost in his gaze alone if it weren't for his body. That T-shirt showed every rippling muscle, and those sweatpants hugged his groin and butt leaving nothing to her imagination.

Holy shit on a shingle. She'd slept next to that. Well, not exactly slept. More like watched over him and kept him warm until she fell asleep.

Mac poked his head inside her room. "He's up?"

She sat on the edge of the bed and grabbed her robe. Her ankle was back to complaining. "Yes, and he seems fine, sort of. Said he fell—"

"He fell? He said that?"

"He doesn't remember everything but remembered falling. Which is when you could have hit him and he just doesn't remember that part. He talks funny, but it's possibly an accent and not associated with his head wound." For the life of her, she couldn't place it, not that she was any expert.

"Foreigner?"

She shrugged. "English isn't his first language. We should probably take him to the hospital. Get him checked out."

"I thought we went over this. What if he remembers me hitting him and tells them that? Didn't we commit a hit and run?"

"We may have hit him, but we didn't run. We brought him here."

"So…we kidnapped him. No… Hit-napped him."

Annie shook her head. The stuff that came out of her brother's mouth. "Hit-napped?"

"Yeah. Hit and then kidnapped him. Maybe it's not a thing, but I'm pretty sure we committed some kind of felony last night. We can't afford to have him talk to people. Not until we know more."

"Fine. We'll play it by ear." How the hell did she get into such a mess? Not only did she have to put up with her brother, now she was babysitting a total stranger? A hunk of a stranger, but still… She grabbed her crutches and stuck her uninjured foot into her slipper. While her bedroom was carpeted, the rest of the cabin was not and the wood floors were cold. She hobbled out to the kitchen as the crutches dug into her armpits.

"You know it's only, like, four in the morning, don't you?"

"It is?" The excitement of seeing the stranger alive and awake was enough to throw her internal clock off. "I'm up now. You want some coffee?"

Her boot rested on the heater grate, where she had left it in the hopes it would dry quicker. Standing on one foot and leaning against the wall, she tried slipping her injured foot inside the boot. But the boot was being very uncooperative. Or her foot was. She'd be lucky she didn't break her other ankle at this rate.

Apparently, Mac felt the same.

"What the hell do you think you're doing? There's a perfectly good chair in the room." And to prove his point, he wrapped his arm around her waist and dragged her to the dinette chair. "You should be resting that ankle. How do you expect to get better if you keep standing on it?" He then lifted her injured foot and gently placed it on the adjacent chair. "Gimme that boot."

She handed it over. "Since when did you get all motherly?"

"Since I need you well." He actually took care as he slipped the boot on her foot. The boot wasn't totally dry, but there wasn't much she could do about that. Except maybe put on another sock. And that wasn't happening anytime soon. Her ankle was back to throbbing and it wasn't time for more pain pills. Guess she would just suffer with the cold foot.

She leaned over and adjusted the Velcro straps. "You need me well? What for?"

"Really? I'm not supposed to drive. Until you're well and our guest finally leaves, you're stuck with me here."

Oh shit. She hadn't thought that far. Stuck with her brother until she could drive? That might be a week. Or longer. God, just shoot her now.

* * * *

Calix ducked his head in the bathroom doorway and then slowly straightened. He would have bumped it otherwise. Was he the tallest person on this planet or was this residence small? How would he ever blend in if he were a giant?

But the female did not seem concerned with his height. So it must be the residence.

He stepped into the outhouse—correction, bathroom—and searched for a light source. If the woman could light the other room, this one must also do the same. A switch by the door indicated "OFF". He flipped it up and a lamp above the reflective glass illuminated. The switch now indicated "ON".

A basin stood to the left, the sides littered with clips and bottles. Across the room was a tub behind a waterproof curtain.

He leaned down and looked into the reflective glass to examine his wound, but a beige-colored tape covered the spot. He yanked it from his temple. Burning pain spread and he nearly cried out loud. A cut, the length of his small finger, ran from the edge of his eye toward his ear. Blue and purple discolorations surrounded the wound and blood trickled down his cheek. Looking for something to clean up the mess, he found a box on the counter with the words "facial tissue" written on it. Must be for his face. Flimsy white material stuck out the top slit. He pulled the tissue and freed a small square. Another took its place.

Fascinating.

Calix folded the tissue and placed it over his wound as he inspected the bathroom. While he never used water to bathe, this was much improved from the facilities of their past. No wonder she looked at him in confusion when he asked about her outhouse. He was getting a good feel for this world. With their technology, maybe they would welcome his people.

But he could not rush into things. How many times had he been told to move slowly? Not something a traveler would need reminding of as they learned from a young age. Calix's training supported research and schooling, not travel and exploration.

After taking care of his needs, he turned out the light and headed toward the hallway. Bonk! His forehead hit the top frame of the door. Pain flared and he rubbed the offending spot. His head was getting quite a beating. *Must remember to bend down.* Something that was never an issue on his planet.

He managed to exit the bathroom without another incident. As he carefully walked toward the room he slept in, voices came from down the hallway. Not only voices, but a wonderful scent. It caused his stomach to rumble. Food, maybe?

The wound was still bleeding, so he continued holding the tissue to his temple as he followed the scent. He arrived at a large room with a hearth, but it was unlit. No cooking there.

"What did you go and do?"

The woman spoke from his left and rose from a chair. She wore a large black boot on one foot and a fuzzy pink shoe on her other, causing her to limp as she approached him. Before he could comment on her footwear, she grabbed his elbow and pulled him toward the table.

No touching! He jerked free and waited. His heart beat wildly, but he remained standing and awake. Why was that?

"I'm sorry, I didn't mean to startle you. But you're bleeding." She pointed to his head. "Mac, go get the bandages, would you?"

A man with the same coloring as the woman rushed toward the bathroom. Her brother? Family units did not exist on Calix's planet, but he understood a little from his research.

"I'm not going to hurt you," she said in a voice that strangely soothed him. She touched his arm again. He tensed, but since he remained aware and there was no pain—aside from his never-ending headache—he allowed her to lead him to the chair she had vacated. "Why'd you pull the bandage off?"

What a strange question. "I wanted to see the damage."

"Of course you did." She sat in the chair across from him and took the tissue. His blood had saturated the material and he had never seen so much of it at one time. She grabbed some kind of device that held other, larger tissues and pulled one out. After folding it, she placed it against his temple. "Hold this."

He did as he was told. This tissue was thicker and not nearly as soft. He wanted to ask what it was, but if it was an everyday item she might wonder why he was unfamiliar with it.

"Are you okay?" she asked. "You're not going to faint from the sight of your blood, are you?"

"My wound hurts, but it appears I will not pass out. Are you a physician?"

Her face softened and her lips turned up at the corners. "No. Not a physician. I just have a brother who got hurt. A lot. Patched him up so many times I lost count. By the way, my name's Annie. What's yours?"

She only offered her first name. He would do the same. "Calix."

"Oh, I saw that on your bag. That's an unusual name. Is it a family name?"

"No."

"Are you from around here? Is there someone I can call?"

"No. And no."

Mac returned with a red-and-white box. "I'm really sorry about your head. What the hell were you doing out there anyway? Don't you know you should make yourself visible when walking? I could have run over you."

Annie hit Mac with a fist to his arm. "Stop it. You make it sound like it was his fault. By the way, this is Calix. Calix, my inconsiderate brother, Mac."

Violence. Seemed they were still a violent people. Neither one carried guns on their person, but could very well have them stored elsewhere. Was his life in danger here? Should he find others to observe? If so, how? In a way, he got lucky someone took him in. And he did not relish having to go back out in that weather.

"I didn't mean to imply it was your fault," Mac said. "But next time, you might want to wear something, I don't know, reflective?"

"Like that would have prevented you from slamming on your brakes?" she said.

Mac's eyes widened. "I wasn't going to hit the raccoon. And if not for that animal, we might not have even seen him in the road. So there."

Raccoon? Was that the wildlife that had startled him? If he could get to a library, he could look it up. But asking them about wildlife was not a way to blend in.

Annie opened up the box. "That's true. He loves all living creatures. Dad couldn't even take him out hunting."

"Hey! You didn't like shooting deer any more than I did."

She pulled out a little bottle and some white fluffy material. "Guess we're both soft-hearted, then." After opening the bottle, she squirted the contents onto the fluff. The smell burned his nose. "Give me the napkin," she said, holding out her hand.

A napkin, not a tissue, yet both were basically the same material, just at different thicknesses and textures. Calix placed it in her extended hand. She then took the stinky wet fluff and pressed it against his skin.

"Oww!" Pain seared through his temple, worse than when he pulled off the bandage. He jerked back. What was she doing to him?

"I'm sorry. Guess I should have warned you. But I need you to hold still so I can clean it. It won't take long."

"She doesn't mean it," Mac said. "I think she enjoys this part."

"I only enjoy torturing you," she said to Mac. "I'm allowed," she whispered to Calix. "Because he's my little brother."

Little? Mac was more than a head taller than Annie. How did that make him little?

Annie went back to wiping at the wound. Calix did not wish to appear uncooperative—if someone gave him a command, he obeyed it—but whatever she was using on his skin hurt and he grit his teeth. Whenever he had to visit the dispensary, they always rendered him unconscious first. Maybe this was why. Who would want to go through this pain if they did not have to?

She pulled the fluff away and examined his wound. "It looks like you might have something embedded." After rummaging through the box, she selected tweezers. "This might hurt, but if you jump, I'll poke you. And if I leave it in, you can get an infection, which would be even worse. Can you hold still?"

Poking would most definitely hurt, but he did not wish to feel any worse. "Please be quick."

"I'll do my best."

Her poking did indeed hurt, but he was more focused on her touching than anything else. Her fingers were cool against his skin. Soft and gentle. Would be nice if his own people could touch. Instead, they would pass out. Wonder why that was? Was it the planet or some other anomaly?

"Got it!" she said as she examined the tweezers. "What the hell? I thought you might have had some gravel in there. This looks like some sort of computer chip. I guess you find all sorts of strange things out on the road."

He had no idea what a computer chip was—except that it might work on a computer and he was clearly not one of those—but it could be his locator chip. Every person from his planet had a device injected when young and were told it was for accountability. He had no idea where the physicians planted the device, though.

She applied pressure to his wound and attached another bandage. Something changed. Not counting the pain at the wound, that never-ending dull ache had disappeared. Was there something in that stinky stuff she used or could it have been his chip? Whatever the cause, he relished the absence and took a deep cleansing breath.

A wonderful scent filled the air. Not food. It was coming from Annie.

* * * *

Annie wrapped the chip in a napkin. Something wasn't right. How would that have gotten into Calix's head? Last time she noticed, the ground wasn't littered with computer chips. Neither was Mac's bumper.

"May I have it?" Calix held his hand out. A rather large hand. A hand without one callus on it. He must not perform physical work, although with a body like his, she found that hard to believe.

"Do you know what it is?" she asked.

"No, but it was in me so should it not belong to me?"

Well, with logic like that, she couldn't refute him. She placed the napkin in his palm. "You hungry?" She might be able to trick Mac into cooking. She'd die for one of his omelets.

Calix smiled. "I am. I thought I smelled something pleasing."

Goodness gracious! Besides having the whitest and straightest teeth she'd ever seen, his face transformed from serious hunk into puppy-dog cute. *Danger! Danger!* Anyone that gorgeous was probably stuck up and she needed to remember that. Plus, he was a stranger from who-knew-where. "I think you're the first person I've met who never smelled coffee before. But it does smell good, doesn't it? You want some while I fix you breakfast? I'm not a great cook—"

"Ha!" Mac said. "You aren't a cook at all." He nudged Calix in the shoulder. "Save yourself. Say no."

Ooh, she hooked the fish. Now she just had to reel him in. She stood and placed her hands on hips. "Hey! No one's died from my cooking."

"That we know of. Besides, you're supposed to stay *off* the foot. So sit."

Wow. Easier than she thought. Almost a letdown. She was prepared for several punches.

"You are injured?" Calix asked.

She settled back on the seat. Where did this guy come from if he never smelled coffee and he didn't recognize a medical boot? "Yeah. I sprained my ankle."

He glanced at her brother before turning those gorgeous eyes her way. "If you wanted to cook, could you not sit and do it?"

She leaned over and whispered. "Just between you and me, I wanted Mac to cook."

"Why did you not ask him?"

"Are you kidding me? He'd have said no. This works out so much better."

He furrowed his brow. "I do not understand. Are all…families like this?"

"Don't you have a family?"

"I…uh."

Great way to be sensitive, Annie. Not everyone was blessed with family. "Sorry, none of my business. But yeah, most family members probably squabble and coerce each other. At least the siblings usually do."

"Why is that?"

She shrugged. "Because they're there? Unconditional love, maybe? If you can't be mean to your brother, who can you be mean to?"

"Why would you want to be mean to anyone?"

"It's not like I'm really mean. He's my brother. It's expected of me." Damn, she really needed to change the subject. "Say, what were you doing out there last night anyway? You weren't exactly dressed for winter."

Again, he had that faraway look as if he was processing what she was saying. She prayed it was the language barrier and not due to any brain damage. His hair hung down over his forehead. Would he object if she brushed it away? She wanted to see all of his face. Oh God, what was she thinking? *Stanger, stranger, stranger!*

"I was traveling and I lost my way."

"On foot? Didn't you think to dress warmer?"

"I only walked part way. The weather caught me off guard."

That still didn't explain the strange wardrobe. "Where are you headed? Maybe we can help."

"San Antonio, Texas."

"San Antonio?" Mac piped in. "Dude, what'd you do? Take a wrong turn at Albuquerque?"

Calix's eyes widened. Damn Mac and his outbursts. The man simply didn't know when to shut up. She patted Calix's hand, hoping to reassure him, and this time he didn't cringe or pull away as he had before. Maybe he was getting used to her.

* * * *

Calix stared at Annie's hand as it touched his. Now that he knew he would remain conscious, he paid more attention to her ministrations. Her hands were soft, and a little cool, but got him warm in a hurry. Even his heart rate sped up. The experience nearly overwhelmed him. What must it feel like to touch all of her?

"Ignore Mac. He seems to forget people have to start out somewhere first. I can understand why you'd want to leave Washington this time of year. If I could afford it, I'd leave, too. What are your plans now?"

He closed his eyes. Did she mean Washington Territory? Maybe they had shortened the name. The weather made sense now. He had traveled north, toward the pole. He opened his eyes and could not look away from her astonishing eyes. And her hand was still touching his. "I do not know."

"Did your car break down? Should we call someone to get it?"

Car? The only car he recalled in their history was from a train. She made it sound more…individual. Must be some form of transportation, though. He had to be careful with his answer and not give too much away. "My ride ended. I walked toward the lights of the city."

"Were you hitchhiking?" She patted his hand. "Don't you have any money?"

He lowered his head. He had gold stored on the ship, where it would remain until he could determine how to use it. Gold was valuable before, he hoped it was the same now. And if it was, he needed to keep it safe. So, he told the truth as best as he could. "I do not have any money with me."

"Hey, you don't have to be embarrassed. We've all been there. They shouldn't have dropped you off on the mountain in the middle of a storm, though. Pretty heartless, if you ask me."

"It was my fault."

"That's not the point." She sat back. "So, who's in San Antonio? Family?"

He shook his head. "It sounded like a nice place to go. Warm."

"Yeah, we don't have much of that going around right now. I can't get you to San Antonio, but maybe we can get you back home. Is it far?"

"I have no home…here. I was…moving." Calix grimaced. Was that a valid excuse?

"You were moving without money?" Mac asked. "How?"

"Stop it," Annie said. "It's none of our business." Her lips turned up at the corners again as she faced Calix. "I don't think you should be alone until we're sure your head wound isn't serious. So it's okay if you stay here for the day. But you need to come up with a plan about leaving tomorrow. Do you understand?"

Calix nodded. He understood all too well. If only he could get to a library to see what his options were.

Mac carried two dishes over to their table and placed one in front of Calix. Yellow goo oozed from something that resembled mixed eggs. At least he thought they were eggs. But what was the goo? He bent down and sniffed. The smells caused his stomach to rumble and his mouth to water. His last hot meal had been on his Earth, just before he departed. The food on the ship, while nutritious, was cold and not always satisfying.

"It's only scrambled eggs and cheese. It won't bite." Annie picked up a fork and used the edge of the outer tine to cut a piece. When she poked the piece and inserted it into her mouth, she closed her eyes. "Damn, Mac. This is heavenly. Maybe you staying here won't be so bad."

Mac leaned down. "They'd be better if you had all the ingredients. I'm surprised you had the eggs."

Calix relaxed. He was right about the eggs, which meant the goo must be cheese, whatever that was. He mimicked Annie with the fork. The food was soft and did not require a knife. Similar flavor to his eggs, and the cheese was very tasty. When it seemed he would keep the food down, he ate every last bit.

"Too bad you didn't like it." Mac brought a cup with hot liquid.

"But I enjoyed it very much." Calix stared at his empty plate. Had he not eaten it all?

"I'm just yanking your chain. How do you take it?" Mac pointed to the cup.

Calix had no chain to yank. And take what? Better to decline than become a fool. He shook his head. He needed to research the planet since the language and items had changed more than he had anticipated. "Thank you for the meal. Once it is daylight, I would very much like to visit your library. Is it far?"

Annie poured some white liquid into her cup and the hot liquid inside turned to a light brown. "Ten miles. But I can't drive because of my foot and Mac's not supposed to drive."

"Hey! I can drive." Mac lowered his head and spoke softer. "I just have to be careful." He sat across the table from Calix.

Calix did not understand Mac's problem—all the more reason for the research. But ten miles was quite a distance in this cold weather. "Is there a livery close by? Maybe I can get a ride on a coach."

Mac's eyes bugged out. "Livery? Coach? Dude…where are you from?"

Not from around here, that was obvious. But from where? What place could he mention and not be questioned?

"Mac!" Annie narrowed her eyes at her brother.

"Sorry, but he sounds like he's from the past." His eyes widened. "Hey! Are you some kind of time traveler? Do you have a time machine?"

She slapped Mac on the back of the head. "Stop being an idiot. Last I heard, time machines didn't exist in the past."

"Okay, so maybe not a time machine. Maybe—"

"Stop it. Excuse my brother. He apparently lost his mind."

Calix sat frozen in his seat. His heart was beating faster than normal. Their fighting might not be a threat to him, but they seemed a threat to one another. He did not wish to witness that. He stood. "I can walk to the library if I dress properly. Do you have my satchels?"

Again, she stared at him as if he had used the wrong word. "You have more than one?"

CHAPTER 3

Calix placed his bag—not satchel—beside the couch. He should probably refrain from speaking until he could get to the library. But he could not walk to the library until he had the bag containing his wardrobe, which was most likely outside near where he was found. Annie assured him that they could take him to his other bag once the sun rose.

"Might as well sit and watch some TV while we're waiting." Mac patted the cushion beside him. "Looks like she got the cable back. Thank God."

Calix sat where indicated. Everything Mac said made no sense. He had read about their God, but TV? And cable? Unless Mac meant rope? Refraining from speaking was beginning to look impossible. So he said the only thing he could think of. "God provides you cable?"

Mac stared and his eyebrows rose. Calix silently moaned. Of course he had said the wrong thing.

"That's a good one," Mac said as he nudged Calix's arm with his elbow. "Wouldn't that be something?" He picked up a little black object with buttons and pointed it outward.

A large screen across the room lit up, showing a family unit seated around a table. Did people spy on one another? Calix searched the room for a camera, but could not identify any. What would one look like anyway? He had many questions. The sooner he could get to the library the better. They had been a great source of knowledge to the original landing party. In the meantime, he would enjoy spending more time with Annie.

"Will Annie be joining us?"

"Probably not. She told me she had work to do. I'll get her once it's light out so we can get your bag." Mac turned his body so it was facing Calix. "I don't mean to be rude, but where'd you get that outfit?"

Calix was wearing the clothing they had found him in, now dry. According to the documentation and images, this was what they wore in Texas in 1830. Had their clothing changed or was it different because of the temperature? Temperatures rarely fluctuated on his planet and their clothing never changed. He would have been better off if he had just worn his normal clothes. And he would definitely change into them once he retrieved his bag. "These were made for me."

"You like the western theme, huh? Me, I prefer my jeans and a soft T-shirt. So, what did you need at the library?"

"I need to research." Like, what was western theme? What was a T-shirt? Life on this planet had changed more than he anticipated.

"Why don't you just use the computer? Annie won't mind. She's got like three or four of these things lying around." Mac leaned over and lifted a metal object the size of a large book from the table in front of them. Opened it up. The alphabet, numbers, and symbols were printed on little buttons, in no particular order that Calix could see.

A computer on his planet computed numbers and data. How would that help him research? With the way Mac stared at him, he probably expected Calix would know what his computer was.

If only that were true. "I am not familiar with the term."

"Term? You mean computer?" Mac raised an eyebrow. "How about Internet. Google?" When Calix shook his head to both terms, Mac rolled his eyes. "How can you know what a livery and coach is, but not a…" He pushed his lips together. "Sorry. I guess you could say this computer contains an electronic library."

Calix grabbed the instrument and stared at it. Finally, something was going his way. "It does?"

"Yep." Mac pushed a button and the small screen lit up.

After being shown how to use the keys and access the Internet and Google, Calix was left on his own to research. It was so simple, too. For the first time since he arrived to this planet he relaxed.

* * * *

Annie stared at the open e-mail. Anger management classes! Were they kidding? She slapped her palm on the desktop. She didn't have any stinkin' anger issues. And anyone who said she did, she'd belt them one.

Oh, crap. She rubbed her stinging palm. Okay, maybe she had a tiny problem. But it wasn't her fault. Anyone would have done the same.

Damn that Logan Cartwright. Him and that fake charm of his. Her friend, Jen, had been swept off her feet. All because of a stupid company party. A party Annie thought would be fun. Now, because of that party, she was wearing a boot on her foot and forced to attend some stupid classes.

Logan would so pay for this.

But she had more pressing matters to attend to. A stranger needed her help and she wanted to help. Anger management-shmanagement. She could be a good person to good people. People like Logan deserved what they got. She clicked on the X to shut down the e-mail program, which didn't give her all that much satisfaction. They really needed to make it more satisfying. Like slamming a phone down. Although, nowadays, she couldn't even do that satisfactorily. It's like they took all the good stuff away when it went digital.

After a good long stretch, she opened the blinds. Damn Mac. He was supposed to get her when the sun came up. Light filtered through the trees and the snow glistened. With a layer of snow, ice, and more snow, how bad were the roads? She really hated going back out in that, but Calix needed his bag. How could she have been so stupid not to look for more than one?

She hobbled back to the living room, her ankle blessedly okay. Guess resting it and wearing the boot was actually working. Who knew?

The TV was on and the sound was turned down low, but no one was watching. Mac had fallen asleep with the remote in his hand. And instead of falling forward, he had slid sideways, Calix's body stopping him from going any further. Calix was also dead to the world, his head back against the cushion. One of her old laptops was in his lap.

He sure was a cutie, but he was also a stranger. A stranger she knew nothing about. Yet. And while she was basically holding him until she was certain he wouldn't report them to the cops, she had to face it: he was a stranger she wanted to get to know better.

A lot better.

She shook the shoulder that wasn't being used by her brother. His eyes fluttered open and she stepped back. When their gazes met, he smiled. Those wonderful purple eyes lit up and nearly stopped her heart.

Stranger, stranger, stranger!

She took a deep breath. "Time to wake up."

"I was asleep?" He paled and his smile disappeared when he saw Mac. Grabbing the laptop, he lurched off the couch.

Mac fell face first into the space Calix vacated, promptly waking up. "What the?"

The sudden movement must have been too much for Calix. His eyes rolled back. Annie rushed to his side, but was no match for his size and she managed to be more of a pillow than a wall. Her butt landed on the wood floor hard, jarring her spine. He landed on her stomach and practically knocked the air from her lungs.

As she lay there catching her breath, she couldn't help but smile. Holy shit on a shingle, but he was hard all over.

"Annie!" Mac said.

Calix rolled off her and grabbed his head with one hand while he held onto the laptop with the other. "I am sorry. Did I hurt you?"

That first breath burned, but she managed to get enough air to croak, "I'm fine." Slowly, she sat up. "You're not, though. Are you?"

He rubbed his temple, where the bandage covered his wound. "What happened?"

"You fainted."

Mac coughed. "Guys don't faint. He passed out."

"Whatever." Like that was a huge difference.

Mac guided Calix up by the upper arm. Calix's eyes widened, but he didn't bolt like he had earlier.

"Dude, you might want to get up slower next time. What with that head wound and all."

Once Calix stood, he shrugged free. "I suppose so."

He stared down at Annie and she smiled and waved as she went to stand. Her slipper made it difficult to get any traction on the wood floor and no way was she putting all her weight on the medical boot. He put the laptop on the coffee table and then reached for her. Oh wow, was he going to help her up? He seemed so averse to touching, but maybe he was feeling more at home here. She held her arms out, but instead of grabbing them, those big hands of his grabbed under her arms, his thumbs right over her nipples.

Too bad I'm wearing a bra. Man, when had she turned into a slut?

"Dude, what are you doing? That's my sister you're molesting."

No, not molesting. Far from it. Even with the T-shirt and bra blocking skin contact, her nipples hardened and sex clenched. This was what happened when a woman hadn't had sex in months. She was almost on her feet when Calix's eyes widened.

"I…uh." He stared at his hands as they covered her breasts, which were kind of squished together.

Made them look pretty perky. They sure made her feel perky.

He promptly released her.

She fell to the floor, landing on her bruised butt. Okay, now *that* hurt.

* * * *

"Damn it, Mac!" Annie yelled as she rubbed her bottom.

"What'd I do? He dropped you!"

Calix stepped back and ran a hand through his hair. He only wanted to help. He only wanted to blend in. Instead, he was doing everything wrong. "I apologize. I should not be here."

Annie's eyes widened. "No. Don't say that. It's not your fault."

Mac placed his hands on hips. "Oh. My. God. You've got the hots—"

"Shut up!" She raised her arm. "Someone help me. Please."

Before Mac had a chance to react, Calix extended his arm. It was the least he could do after falling on top of her and then dropping her. "Are you sure I did not hurt you?"

She took his hand and he grabbed her around the waist. She was soft, but her breasts were definitely softer, and apparently touching them was molesting. At least according to her brother. She did not seem to mind. So much he needed to learn.

As he brought her up, he noticed a difference in her scent. Before, he pictured flowers. Now, it was some kind of spice. Or spices. Whatever it was, his groin reacted and his heart rate sped.

Pain flashed in her eyes as she continued to rub her bottom. "I'm fine. Really." She turned toward Mac. "It's light enough now. You ready to go?"

When Calix released her, the stirring in his groin decreased and he missed it. He wanted to smell her some more. Was that good or bad? And was it just her or all humans? No one mentioned any alluring scent in all the documentation he had evaluated. He looked at Mac. Would he smell the same way?

"Yeah, but maybe you should stay here." Mac picked up a coat and slipped it on.

Calix took two steps toward Mac and sniffed the air discreetly. Still too far away to tell.

She glanced at him before returning her attention to her brother. "I'm not an invalid. I can still get around."

Mac placed his hands on his hips. "If you hadn't noticed, it snowed last night. How the heck do you think you'll get around with that boot?"

She curled her lips upward—which Calix now knew was a smile—and blinked her eyes several times. "You could carry me."

Mac's face screwed up as if he had eaten something bitter. "Oh hell no!"

With widened eyes, she shook all over. All while the most wonderful sound came from her mouth. But she must be ill. Or having a seizure.

"Oh my God! You should see your face. Hilarious!" Her words were uttered between gulping breaths.

But she said hilarious. That meant funny. Was she laughing? He had read about laughing, but did not quite understand it so he wondered if he would recognize it when it happened. He need not have worried. She sounded...delightful to his ears. In fact, the sound was contagious and he found himself laughing alongside her. Forget Mac. He wanted to be closer to her. "I could carry you."

Abruptly, her laughter stopped. She stared up at him with her eyes open wide.

Mac placed a hand on Calix's shoulder. "Don't encourage her. Please."

Taking advantage of his proximity, Calix sniffed again. Perspiration and chemicals. Nothing to trigger movement in his groin. Nothing pleasing to his nose.

"I was only joking," she said. "I can get a plastic bag." She smiled. "But, thank you."

He could stare at her eyes forever. Green became his favorite color.

"You might as well stay, Annie. It's not like you could help." Mac frowned at Calix. "You don't have a coat."

He did not want to leave if she was staying behind. "It does not matter. We can go later, when it is warmer. As long as I can use the computer, I do not need the library."

"Don't be ridiculous. You need your clothes." She looked sternly at Mac, causing him to shut his eyes.

"Fine," he said. Although his tone did not sound like he was fine. "You two stay here. I'll go get the bag."

"Then you'll have to go shopping for me, too," she said.

Calix did not want to be a bother and he certainly did not want them to fight. "You do not need to go out now. I can wait."

Mac glanced at Annie before turning his gaze toward Calix. "Believe me, this will be easier." He pulled out a ring of metal objects. Keys, maybe? "So what do you need?"

Annie went into the kitchen and started writing. He had studied the books on printing and cursive that the original travelers had obtained, but had never seen it in action. And without an implement on his planet, he had never attempted to copy the illustrations. Fascinated, he wished he could examine more closely, but that would only draw more attention to himself and he had drawn enough attention for one day.

Mac leaned over her shoulder. His eyes widened. "Oh hell no! I am not buying those!"

She smiled that same kind of smile she had when she got Mac to cook earlier. "Then I guess we're all going." She put the writing implement down. "I'll get a blanket for Calix. Why don't you just shovel a path to the car?"

As she passed Calix on her way down the hall, she blinked one eye at him. A wink! She winked at him. He smiled. She had no intention of being left behind, did she? Was she always so manipulative or just with her brother?

CHAPTER 4

The drive to the accident site might have been less awkward if someone spoke. Mac was still mad at her. His grip at ten and two and the thin line where his lips should be told her as much. But damn, first he was going to be alone with Calix and then he suggested leaving her alone with the man. Didn't her brother have any sense? Calix was a stranger. Sure, a stranger she kind of liked, but a stranger they wanted to keep an eye on. To make sure he couldn't implicate them in his kidnapping, if that's what they'd really done. So instead, she had made it uncomfortable for him to not take her—and it paid off.

Annie glanced back at their visitor. He paid her no mind as his attention was riveted to the outdoors. His eyes were wide in wonder and mouth slightly open in awe. And wow, what a mouth. Sure, her heart skipped a few beats when he smiled at her, and she nearly came in her pants when he had inadvertently grabbed her breasts, but what did she really know about him?

"You act like you've never seen snow."

Calix turned at her comment, and she zeroed in on those beautiful eyes of his. They seemed even more purple outside. "Not in daylight. It is so white."

"I thought you lived in Washington." Sure, the western part of the state didn't get as much, but they did get snow.

His jaw dropped, but before he could answer or avoid her question, Mac pulled a U-turn and stopped on the shoulder.

"I think this is the place." Mac put the car in park, leaving the engine running. "You," he pointed at her, "stay in the car." He talked over his shoulder. "Calix, get your blanket."

"Hey! You're not the boss of me," she said.

"Listen, I agreed to take you shopping. Nothing more. Now stay or I go back and you can forget about your supplies."

She didn't really need any of her feminine products, but Mac didn't need to know that. She only wanted Calix to get his belongings without either of them being left alone with him. Just because she was attracted to Calix, and so far he hadn't done anything worrisome, they probably shouldn't trust him. Yet. Until she knew more about Calix, it was best she and Mac stuck together. But Mac had no right to boss her around. She was the big sister, damn it.

She crossed her arms under her breasts and waited while the guys went out into the cold to retrieve Calix's bag. It shouldn't be too hard to find. He had been walking on the mountainous side of the road. If he had been on the other side, the cliff side…well, she shuddered to think where he might have ended.

She always thought her brother was a big guy, but standing next to Calix, he looked downright tiny. They pulled the bushes apart and peered through the branches. Mac pointed. Calix leaned over the hedge and then fell through. Snow billowed in the air. With Mac's help, he got back to his feet with the bag in his hand.

When they climbed back into the car, bringing the cold with them, she turned and smiled at Calix. But the smile held a short life. His bandage had come free and blood trickled down his left temple.

"Awww, man. You're bleeding again." She undid her belt and attempted to climb in the back between the seats, but her boot was being uncooperative and she might have kicked her brother a couple of times in her struggle.

And one of those kicks might have been unintentional.

"Will you stop?" Mac yanked her back onto her seat. "It's just a little blood. He'll live."

"I feel fine." Calix fingered the area, smearing blood on his face and fingers. When he started to wipe his fingers on his shirt, she stopped him.

"Don't. Here." She pulled a tissue from her pack and handed it over. "Wipe your fingers with this." Men! Honestly, they had no sense. She opened the door.

Mac grabbed her arm. "Whoa! Where do you think you're going?"

"To the back seat, where else?"

"Oh geez." He released her. "Be prepared to be mothered."

Mothered? Heck no. She just wanted to care for him. And sitting beside him would be a bonus. Maybe she didn't want to be left alone with him now, but how else was she going to get to know him? Or trust him? Because honestly, she wanted to do both, but in a safe, reasonable way.

She stepped out into the snow. Dang, she forgot how cold and wet that stuff was. Oh well, she'd just hold onto the car to keep from falling. But the car was cold and she no longer had her gloves—they were on her shopping list—so she hovered her hand over the vehicle in case. As she reached the door handle, she turned and grabbed for it. Whoop! Her feet decided to become traitors. She slipped and fell, hitting her head against the car. Pain exploded and her eyes watered. *Holy shit on a shingle.*

* * * *

With all the technologies that Calix discovered on the planet, Mac's car was a surprise. But then that explained the hard surface he had found earlier. The wheels needed something smooth to travel on.

This Earth was so different from his own. Snow, although too cold for him, covered the trees and road with a white blanket. And the trees were tall and green. Taller than any tree he had ever seen.

But when Annie questioned his origin, he had no answer. Where could he say he was from and not draw suspicion? Now it seemed maybe Annie had forgotten that conversation, and he was glad. He certainly was interested in learning what it was like to be mothered. Especially from her.

Was this Earth affecting him? He had never cared about another person before. Never noticed anyone's scent being different, either. He liked Annie's scent.

One moment she was at the door. The next she was gone. "Where did she go?" he asked.

"Ah, shit!" Mac opened his door.

Mac said a lot of words and phrases that made no sense, but the urgency in his voice spurred Calix into action. Leaving the blanket behind, he darted outside. Mac circled the front of the vehicle, Calix circled the rear. She lay in the snow holding her head. His heart pounded erratically at the sight.

"Annie!" He rushed to her and, making sure to stay away from her breasts, picked her up in his arms. She was light and fragile, even inside the big puffy coat she wore. He held her with care. He should have helped her climb between the seats, then she would not have been hurt. But he had been afraid of inadvertently crossing another taboo and having Mac yell at him again. Next time he would take the yelling if that meant Annie would not get hurt.

"I'm okay," she said. "You—"

"What the hell, Annie! Are you out of your mind?" Mac said.

Emotions Calix had never fully felt rose to the surface. He had known fear at losing opportunities, but not the ice-cold grip around his heart when he had seen her on the ground. He had known frustration when he had lost some research notes, but not the burning sensation that rippled through his body when Mac had yelled at Annie.

Calix stared at Mac. "You do not need to yell at her. She is injured. You should help her."

His words echoing down the street shocked him. He had never spoken so loudly. But he would not react. He would not show fear.

Mac held his palms out. "Whoa, big fella. Take it easy."

Was Mac afraid? Good. Maybe then he would see sense. Of course, it did not get past Calix that it took yelling to gain some respect, but maybe that was what it took to blend in.

"Calix?" Annie touched his cheek and he looked down at her. She smiled. No fear showed on her face. Only concern. "Hey. I'm okay. Really. Put me down before you hurt yourself."

He would not apologize for his outburst, even though he had no idea where it came from, but nodded at Annie as he lowered her legs to the ground. When she wavered, he picked her back up. "You are not well."

"I just slipped in the snow." She glanced at Mac. "Really."

Calix stared at her. She had been very good at tricking her brother before and he did not believe her now.

"Oh hell, put me in the car then. It's cold out here."

In that, he could agree with her. His fingers were getting stiff and numb.

Mac opened the door to the backseat area and Calix slipped her inside.

She scooted toward the center. "You, too," she said.

He climbed inside and shut the door. Before he had a chance to put on his seat belt, she was checking his bandage. Gently, he held her wrist and pulled her arm down. "I am fine. Please, let me see to your wound."

She opened her mouth to speak when Mac climbed inside and slammed his door. He turned in his seat to face them. "Am I going straight to the store or do I stop at the outpatient clinic?"

"I don't need to see a doctor. And I don't need you driving any more than necessary."

"Fine." Mac turned around and started the engine. He took off with a jerk and the back end of the vehicle slid as he turned the car around.

Snow was definitely slippery. Calix had discovered that when he went to retrieve his bag. But she was having trouble standing after her fall. "Are you sure you do not need to see a physician?"

"It's just a bump on the head. See for yourself." She tipped her head down, grabbed his hand and placed it where he felt a small rise. "I'm not even bleeding. Like you are."

So, bumps were okay, but bleeding was not? How was that so? He could stand. She could not. Her logic needed work.

But she was sitting now and seemed fine, so he let her go about her mothering.

He did not have a mother. Nor a father. In his earliest memories, he had been in a room with other children his age. Had he touched them? He could not remember.

In his research of this planet, fathers and mothers were married—or mated—to one another. Calix was not sure what mated was, only that it produced children. Fathers provided money and food and mothers took care of the home and children. Annie was mothering him. So did that make her the mother and Mac the father? But they were brother and sister. Did that make a difference?

His head hurt and it had nothing to do with his wound.

She bent around the back of the seat and picked up a white box with a red plus sign on top, but this one had the words "FIRST

AID". Did they get hurt so often they needed to carry bandages wherever they went? How violent had these people become?

When she opened the box, she frowned. "Shit. It's all wet. Guess I'll have to get more at the store." She pulled out a large white square and tore it on one side. She held up the loosely woven material and looked at him. "I'm just going to clean around the bandage for now. This shouldn't hurt. Okay?"

He nodded. She gently rubbed around his bandage. The wet, cold cloth scratched but did not hurt. Her fingers were light against his cheek as she held his face in place. All these years without touching a single soul and now he all he wanted was to touch her. Was it the planet that made him feel that way or something else?

"Are you in trouble? Are you running from somebody?"

He was in trouble, but not the way she thought. "I am not being chased."

"Then why won't you tell me where you're from?"

Maybe a traveler would be able to come up with a viable answer. He had never felt so out of his element. What could he tell her? The truth? Would she believe him? Sure, he was told not to tell anyone about his mission, but he was also not given instructions if he crashed his spacecraft. In the wrong region. He needed help and Annie might be able to help him. If he told her the truth. But just her. Not Mac. Not yet.

He brought his lips to her ear, rubbing his cheek next to hers. The touch thrilled him, better than all the other touches, and her scent enticed him. He almost forgot what he was going to say. "I will tell you where I am from when we are alone."

* * * *

Jay opened his eyes to the blinding sun. Damn it, he'd overslept. He had hoped to be outside by now. Something must be wrong with his mental alarm clock. That, or his clock decided a warm bed beat the cold outdoors. He refused to believe it had anything to do with getting old. He crawled out of bed and quickly got dressed.

Was he making a mistake going out there to search for whatever it was he'd seen? Sleep had cleared his head a bit. Then he recalled the conversation he'd had with David. Jay would never be trusted to live on his own if he didn't prove what he'd seen.

He popped two slices of bread in the toaster and poured a glass of milk. Coffee would have to wait. Besides, he might need it later to thaw out. He slathered peanut butter on his toast and wolfed it down. Then he drained his glass.

As he washed up, he peeked out the window. Damn snow. Well, at least he shouldn't get lost. He'd leave tracks behind and could follow them back home. Okay, so maybe the snow wasn't damned. He'd just have to dress more warmly.

Now, where was his scarf?

$$* * * *$$

As Mac drove them to the store, Annie touched the spot on her cheek Calix had brushed against. No whiskers had scratched her face—the man must not need to shave often—and his breath had tickled her ear, sending thrills down her spine. What might it feel like if he touched her everywhere?

Although…he pretty much had when he'd picked her up—and boy, what a thrill that was—and lifted her like she weighed nothing, or at least tons lighter than her actual weight. She had made a New Year's resolution to exercise more and lose the twenty-five, okay, thirty pounds she had gained since Thanksgiving two years ago, but that didn't look to be happening anytime soon. And why should she? Next to Calix, she felt almost tiny, and no one had ever made her feel like that before.

She shook her head. Daydreaming wouldn't get her anywhere. And it certainly wouldn't solve her problem with Calix.

Alone. He wanted her alone. Why? Where could he possibly come from that he didn't want Mac to hear? Then again, Mac had done nothing but make fun of where Calix was headed. Hell, she'd be cautious, too.

The SUV rocked as Mac turned into the store parking lot. It hadn't been cleared of snow and was packed down into small hills and gullies from everyone driving over it. Parking lanes were hidden and finding an open spot large enough between two vehicles was practically impossible. Of course, it didn't help that Mac was trying to get as close to the store as possible.

"Just park in the back. I'm not an invalid."

"So says you," Mac said. But he must have finally come to his senses and parked at the first open spot.

She slipped out her side of the vehicle and shut the door. At least her feet didn't sink in the packed snow. Would they let her walk? She really had just slipped.

"Do I need to get one of those electric carts?" Mac asked.

"I doubt they'd work in this mess. I'll be fine." She stood straight to prove her point. Giving Mac the stink-eye might have helped, too.

They managed to make it to the entrance without incident and she pulled out a shopping cart. She could lean on it and use it as a crutch since her ankle was starting to act up a bit. But if she even mentioned a twinge, she'd never hear the end of it. Thank goodness she could blame her limping on the boot and not any kind of pain.

Calix followed her and Mac around the store, acting as if he'd never been in one before. He pulled out nearly every box or can and read it. So when they approached the aisle containing the feminine products, she stopped. Mac had already seen fit to excuse himself. He probably never set foot down this aisle, the big chicken. So why did she have a problem with Calix accompanying her?

Calix read the sign and stared down the aisle. "Is that aisle for females only?"

Where did he come from and not know anything about a grocery store? "No, but the products are. Why don't you go wait with Mac?"

An older gentleman sauntered down that aisle and Calix followed. Okay, guess he was going to accompany her. How embarrassing could it get?

Calix pulled a packet of sanitary napkins from the shelf. "These appear to be different napkins than from the ones on your table."

She was wrong. Being interested was way worse than being disinterested. She plucked the package from his hand and replaced it. "Okay, I get that you don't have a sister. And your mother could have hidden these from you. But you must have had sex-ed."

"Sex-ed?"

"Education? About sex?" When he continued to stare at her like she was talking another language, she nudged him away. "Please. Go wait with Mac."

How could someone not have sex-ed? Home-schooled by a priest or something? Maybe. He did seem honestly curious, though. But he needed to leave. Now. And for once her brother saved the day.

"Dude, what are you doing?" Mac grabbed Calix by the elbow and dragged him away. "Don't let her rope you into anything that has to do with this aisle, you hear?"

"I do not understand," Calix said as he looked over his shoulder at her. Confusion flashed across his face.

Why did she get the feeling the questions were not going to end with that guy? She grabbed the items she'd claimed needing and headed for the checkout. Thankfully, Mac kept Calix by the doors.

As she placed the items on the conveyor belt, the bitch from hell—her cousin Portia—fell in line behind Annie.

"Well hello there," Portia said. "Why aren't you at work? It's not a holiday, is it?"

Why, of all the people to run into, it had to be Portia? Portia, who never passed up a chance to rub it in that she didn't have to work anymore because of her inheritance. Why the woman just didn't move was beyond Annie. Unless Portia just stuck around to brag. Yeah, that was most likely it.

Annie plastered the best honest-to-goodness smile she could conjure up. "I'm working from home until I can drive."

Portia stared at Annie's boot. "Oh dear. Did you go and fall down in the snow?"

That sick sing-song voice would be the end of Annie and give her a real reason to attend those anger management courses. "It was ice, actually." Kicking someone at a running start seemed like a good idea at the time. Note to self—be sure to hold onto something first. "So what brings you out in this weather? Couldn't find someone to run your errands for you?"

Because Portia and snow went together as well as…well, as well as Calix and snow. Annie glanced his way and smiled. If Mac had to hit someone on the road, he sure picked a good one. That man was fit for a romance cover and then some. But why was he staring at his feet?

"Oooh, who's that hunk with your brother?"

"What?" Annie turned toward where Portia had been standing not moments before. Her question apparently needed no answer. She was making a beeline to Calix.

No-no-no-no-no! Poor Calix didn't stand a chance against the vulture. He was a doomed kitten.

One customer stood between Annie and freedom to save Calix. The cashier called for a price check. Annie silently groaned.

* * * *

Calix stared at his feet. The store was a researcher's dream. He had never seen so many products in one place, and there seemed to be a product for everything. Even sex, whatever that was. Must be important. Or secret. Annie did not wish to discuss it out in the open. Maybe she would once they could speak alone. But the store…he could spend hours observing, if only he blended in better.

At least his footwear blended in. The boots had been stitched to match those shown on the images taken back in 1830. And with the cold and snow, apparently boots were essential. Still, now that he was able to observe how the local population dressed, he felt oddly out of place. No one else had fringe on their clothes. If he had money, he would purchase some new clothing, but he was sure gold would not do the trick. Everyone paid with a small card. And not even the same kind of card.

"Hey, Portia. What's up?"

Calix looked up at the sound of Mac's voice. A yellow-haired woman around the same height as Annie and wearing a bright pink coat that matched her lips approached them. She smiled broadly, showing off bright teeth. Her gaze zeroed in on him.

"Not much. Who's your friend?"

"This is Calix. He's…visiting."

Visiting. That was a strange word to use. Although Calix was grateful for being taken in after his fall, was he really a visitor? Maybe he was.

She stood in front of him and looked up, blinking several times. "Wow. You have the most amazing eyes. What color are they?"

Neither Mac nor Annie ever mentioned his eye color being unusual. As for the color, he went with the closest on the rainbow scale. "They are indigo."

"Oooh, how exotic." She licked her top lip and hummed. "So who are you visiting?"

Before Calix could answer, Mac did. "Duh. Who do you think he's visiting?"

Portia frowned. "Annie?" She said it as if it left a bad taste in her mouth. "How do you know her?"

She stood close enough for Calix to get a whiff of her scent. He had followed Annie all over the store and was so engrossed in the products he had forgotten about finding out if he would react the same to all females. And while this female smelled like a garden, she did nothing else for him. His groin remained unaffected and he had no desire to touch her.

But how would he answer Portia's question? He just went with the truth. "She found—"

"Through work," Mac interrupted. "Annie works with him. Calix, this is our cousin, Portia."

Okay, so Mac did not want Calix to tell the truth. So why was Mac lying? And what was a cousin again?

She smiled. "Oh, are you helping Annie with her job while she's convalescing?"

The lies did not sit right with Calix, but what right did he have to correct Mac? Calix's whole existence on this planet was a lie so he just nodded.

"Why the get-up?" She rubbed one hand over the sleeve of his shirt. "Don't get me wrong. I like it. Do you work at a rodeo, too?" She leaned in close, touching her breasts to him. "I bet you ride hard."

"Whoa, girl." Mac pulled her away from Calix. "This here is a family joint."

She narrowed her eyes at Mac then turned her attention back to Calix and smiled. "I'm sorry. I guess that was a little forward of me. I've just never seen anyone so handsome up close before. Have you ever modeled? Because you should. You'd be good at it."

"Are you asking to paint my portrait?" Calix asked. What else would he model for?

"Your portrait? Do you do nudes?"

"Ah look. Annie's done," Mac said. "We gotta go. See you later, Portia." He grabbed Calix by the elbow and pulled him out the exit. "Ignore her. She's nuts."

"Call me, Calix," she yelled. "They have my number."

Number? Why would he have to call her a number? With the frown on Annie's face, he could only assume a number was a bad thing.

When they reached the car, he risked asking Mac another stupid question, "Why did you lie to Portia?"

Annie opened the side door. "Who lied?"

"Mac did. He said I was here visiting you instead of telling her how you found me."

Mac's face turned red. "I panicked, okay? I told her he was working with you, Annie. Listen, Calix. Portia isn't the most discreet person. I figured she didn't need to know the truth. She would have bugged you more."

Calix understood panicking. It was what he was doing in the store. But why panic at all? Was Portia a threat to their existence?

"He's not wrong," Annie said. "She's very…nosey. Tries to get into everyone's business. It's better to let her think otherwise. Frankly, she's not a very trustworthy person."

"Is she a threat?" Calix could understand threats.

"Only to my sanity," she said. "She's just not a very nice person, okay? Don't worry about her. She's not important."

Everything was important to his mission. But why hide how they found him? Had they done something illegal? If so, he was okay with it. It was better than the alternative: being on his own.

CHAPTER 5

Annie was bushed. As if the trip to the grocery store wasn't enough, they had to stop at Mac's apartment—because he needed a change of clothing—and the thrift store to purchase Calix a coat. The man didn't even have one in his bag. If it weren't for the fact that Calix had promised to tell her where he came from once they were alone, she would have questioned him about his lack of warm clothing.

As they walked back to the car, she said to Calix, "I'm gonna sit up front with Mac, okay?"

He nodded and helped her inside. The man was certainly a gentleman.

As Calix walked around the car to sit behind Mac, Mac leaned over and whispered, "Tired of him already?"

"Don't be ridiculous. It's my ankle, okay?" Which was true enough. But in reality, she thought it best to keep her distance from Calix. The intense jealousy that had struck when her cousin had hit on him wasn't sitting well with her. Which was absurd. Why should she be jealous? Calix wasn't anything to her. Was he?

Her and her stupid heart. It never did see reason. Only one stinkin' day and already it was having feelings. Feelings for a stranger. A hunk of a stranger, but still... Would she never learn?

"Thank you again for the purchase of this outdoor garment," Calix said as he buckled his seat belt. "It is very warm and much better than the blanket."

"You're welcome. I'm just glad we could find something that fit." Because that had almost been a problem. Calix's shoulders were huge and most of the coats weren't.

"A woman in the store said she thought the last solar storm was an alien invasion."

The woman was also a little crazy, but Annie kept that to herself. "Some people have a wild imagination."

"Do you believe in life on other planets?" Calix asked.

She turned in her seat to face him. "Sure. You'd have to be pretty arrogant to think we're the only planet in this whole universe that sustains life."

"Including humanoids?"

"Dude, you're not one of those people who claim to be abducted, are you?" Mac asked.

Calix's eyes widened. "People are being abducted?"

Annie smacked her brother in the arm. "Will you stop?" She looked back at Calix. "No one's being abducted. Those are crazy people trying to get attention."

"So it is crazy to believe other humanoids exist?"

"No, of course not. Only if you believe they've already been here."

"Why do you say that?"

"Because distances in space are just too great. It would take several lifetimes to get here from another planet, even if they could find us."

"Based on your technology. But they could have faster ships."

Your technology? He was definitely raised by the Amish or something. Come to think of it, the Amish had accents, too. Could that be where he came from? "You know, I never thought of it that way."

"Do you think most people would be afraid of an alien? Would you?"

"Probably not. There certainly are enough science fiction books, TV shows, and movies out there. I'd like to think we're all kind of over the freaking-out part if any aliens were discovered."

"Unless those aliens had tentacles and wanted to eat us," Mac added. "Or take over our world."

Calix furrowed his brow.

"Don't worry." She reached over and patted his knee. "If there was an imminent alien invasion, the media would have spread the news for sure."

Mac laughed. "Got that shit right. The media knows everything. Even if it's wrong."

The rest of the drive was quiet, and when Mac finally pulled into the driveway, he held out his hand. "Keys. I gotta go."

"You couldn't do that at your apartment?" She dug the keys from her purse and he snatched them before she had a chance to hand them over.

He practically jumped from the car and dashed to the door.

"Is there a problem?" Calix asked.

"With my brother, who knows?" She grabbed her things and did her best not to limp to the door. Once she got inside, she'd take her pill. It was way past time.

She put her bag on the dining table, but instead of getting her pills, the chair called to her and she plopped into it. Really, she hadn't walked that far. When had she become such a wimp?

"Is your head bothering you?" he asked.

Now that he brought it up, she did have a small nagging headache. Of course, she attributed that to Portia, not her knock on the head. "Head is fine. Ankle, not so much."

And it wouldn't feel better until she took her meds. She started to rise when he touched her arm. "Sit. What do you need?"

He said it in a gentle, caring way, not in the demanding tone her brother had recently taken on. She told him and pointed where he could find her meds. Then she remembered his own injury. Shouldn't she be taking care of him? "How's your head feeling?"

"My wound does not bother me." He brought the pills and water to the table and placed them in front of her. "When can we talk alone?"

She really did want to find out where he was from and what his plans were, but why the secrecy? She palmed a honkin' big pill—800 mg of ibuprofen—and hoped she wouldn't choke on it. "Is there some reason you don't want Mac to know?"

"If you think he needs to know, I will share my information with him. But I would feel more comfortable talking to you first."

She swallowed her pill and it rubbed the sides of her throat on the way down. For a moment there she thought it might get stuck. The container said to take with food. Oh great. "I have to eat something. Since I'm at it, do you want a sandwich, too?"

She started to rise once again, and once again he placed his hand on her arm.

"I can make it," he said. "If you tell me how."

"That's not necessary. You know you aren't my servant, right?"

"You would not have stopped Mac if he offered."

"True. But he's my younger brother and, like all big sisters, it's my obligation to make him do stuff for me."

"So little means younger. And big older. Ahhh." He smiled and chuckled. Unlike the first time, this laugh was natural and she liked the way he sounded.

By the time Annie showed Calix where the ingredients were for sandwiches, Mac had returned from unloading the car and together the guys fixed lunch. She was beginning to think maybe being laid up wasn't such a bad thing. When else could she be waited on by her brother and not receive any wrath in accompaniment?

After lunch, the throbbing in her ankle was down to a nagging ache. Mac headed for the living room to watch TV.

She looked at Calix and tried to act as nonchalant as possible, just in case Mac overheard. "I have to run a program for work. Do you want to come back to my office or watch TV with Mac?"

Calix's eyebrows shot up and then he smiled. "I would like to see what you do if that is all right."

"Okay then." She stood, but Calix was by her side quickly and offered an arm to lean on. She still needed to clean his wound, but he wasn't fidgeting with it so maybe it bothered her more than it did him.

Together they walked back to her office. She closed the door before heading for her desk and indicated he could sit on the futon along the wall. She thought about using it as a bed for him, but now that she saw him sitting on it, realized the furniture was way too small for his big body. Mac could use it, instead, and Calix could use the couch.

Was a day long enough to trust Calix to go off on his own? He certainly wasn't looking to leave anytime soon. Why was that?

She logged in and started her program while Calix examined the futon.

"What is the function of this furniture?" He lifted the mattress and looked underneath the frame.

"Kind of a cross between a couch and bed. Called a futon. Haven't you seen them before?"

"No." He bounced on the mattress and smiled.

Almost everything fascinated him and, in that aspect, he seemed more like a child than someone from another country. If he was from another country. Maybe now she would find out why. "So, Calix. Where exactly do you hail from?"

He straightened up. A frown marred his beautiful face and his forehead was wrinkled in worry.

"It can't be that bad," she said. Unless he was some kind of fugitive. Hell, maybe she should have asked what kind of police record he had. Maybe she should have asked for his last name.

"Before I tell you, I want to say that I can show you proof of my origins and that I am not one of those crazy people looking for attention."

Proof of origins? Did he mean passport? And what crazy people? She certainly hoped he wasn't crazy. She was beginning to like the guy. What beginning to? She *did* like the guy.

He stood up and paced in front of the futon. "I am not from this planet."

No, she couldn't have heard him right. Not from this planet? And just like that her heart felt like it shriveled up and sank to the bottom of her stomach. He was nuts. That, or brain damaged. From the car accident.

Oh crap. They were so screwed.

* * * *

Jay tugged on his knit cap, making sure his ears were still covered. The icy wind whipped through the trees and pierced his jacket. Almost every part of his body felt numb, but not numb enough to ignore the cold. He'd thought the trees would help keep him warm. He'd thought wrong.

Buster jerked the leash and Jay stumbled ahead, narrowly avoiding a collision with a pine. Could he have been wrong? No way could a spaceship land in this dense forest. At least Buster was getting a good workout. It had been ages since the two of them had taken a hike and Jay was feeling every bit of that time. His legs and chest burned for oxygen.

Maybe he should give it up. He'd been walking for—he glanced at his watch—damn! Forty-five minutes? That's all? Okay. Maybe he could go a little further.

Buster stopped and barked.

"What is it, boy? You hear something?" All Jay could hear was the wheezing in his chest. Bears hibernated in the winter, didn't they?

The dog took off and the leash slipped through Jay's fingers.

"Shit. Buster! Get back here!" Following the animal's path, he ran as fast as his tired legs and the snow allowed and came to a small clearing. No bear, thank God. No spaceship, either.

Buster's barking echoed through the trees. Standing still, he continued barking at nothing in particular. Well, nothing Jay could see. Maybe there wasn't a spaceship, but something riled Buster. His hackles were up.

Jay walked up to his friend and petted his back. "Easy, fella. What is it?"

The hairs on the back of Jay's neck tingled, as if he were close to some electrical lines. He slowly stood and looked around when he noticed slight abnormalities in the surrounding area. A tree in the distance warped a bit on the side, as if he were looking through a ripple in a window. Jay walked a few steps. The ripple moved with him. What could cause that? It certainly wasn't any kind of heat signature. He extended an arm and took tentative steps forward. Shuffle, step. Shuffle, step. All the while his heart slammed inside his chest.

He touched something solid, even though his eyes told him there wasn't anything in front of him. Hot damn! He pumped a fist into the air. He found it. He actually found the spaceship. It was just cloaked, like those Klingon ships on *Star Trek*.

"Hello! Anybody here? I come in peace." He turned toward Buster and chuckled. "Listen to me. Talking to them like they understand."

Maybe there was a door he could knock on. Using both hands, he felt his way around. The surface appeared smooth through his gloves—he wasn't about to take them off and get frost bitten—until he reached an indentation similar to the door handle on his son's fancy SUV.

Jay pounded on the door. "Hello?"

It was quite possible the inhabitants had already left to explore, although there weren't any footprints besides his and Buster's. Of course, it hadn't started snowing until after Jay had gone to bed. Should he open the door? Apparently, these people had something to hide. If they weren't aliens, they could be some kind of spy instead. In that case, it was his duty to report this, and the more he knew the better. He hooked his fingers inside the indentation and pulled.

Warm air swooshed in his face as an opening appeared where there used to be a view of the trees. He went to peek inside when Buster scrambled on past.

"No, boy. Come back here." Jay climbed in after his furry friend and into the warm interior. The enclosure was no bigger than a broom closet. Some kind of security panel was embedded in the wall beside another door most likely leading to the rest of the ship. He knocked again, but got the same response as before—silence. "Ain't no one here, Buster."

He pulled out his camera and took pictures. Close-up didn't really show anything extraordinary. Maybe with the door open, an outdoor shot would be more convincing.

As he turned to leave, the outer door shut and lights blinked furiously, like some kind of silent alarm. Voices in a language he didn't understand spoke to him. Jay pushed on the door without success.

"Well, ain't this a fine mess I've gotten us into," he muttered.

* * * *

Calix's stomach felt like someone had twisted it inside out and that sandwich he had eaten—while very tasty—threatened to come up the way it went down. He must get her to believe, otherwise, he would have to leave. He was fairly certain she would not want to be associated with someone she thought was crazy.

And from what he had learned from the earlier travelers, crazy people were feared.

"What planet are you from?" Annie asked.

Her words were spoken very calm. He relaxed. Maybe this would go better than he hoped.

"My planet is located in a solar system in the galaxy your people know as Andromeda. Coincidentally, it is also named Earth."

"Andromeda? Isn't that like two million light years from here?"

"It is, but we have discovered…short cuts in the universe. And our craft can travel much faster than light."

"Short cuts? Like wormholes?"

"I am not familiar with that term. Do you know of one so I can confirm?"

She shook her head. "Stuff of theories only."

"These theories may be correct."

"So how did you find us? What is your mission? Are you planning on—?"

He raised his hand to stop her. "Your planet was discovered quite by accident, and my mission required me to go to the area labeled Texas Republic and observe the changes from our visit in 1830, except my ship malfunctioned and I ended up here instead."

"You were here in 1830? How old are you?"

"Not me. I am twenty-nine years old."

"Twenty-nine of whose years?"

"Both, actually. Your year is 365 and a quarter days, mine is 368 days. Minor differences, really."

"And how long is your day?"

"Not much different than yours. My planet is hotter, though. Water is scarce. We do not have snow." These were not the questions he expected, but then she was a technician, so it made sense. At least she had not tried to shoot him. If she even owned a gun. Maybe it was a good thing he had not landed in Texas.

"You're smiling," she said. "What'd I say that's amusing?"

He shook his head. "Just wondering if the people in Texas still shot first and asked questions later. I did not understand the phrase until now."

She laughed softly. "That was pretty much the whole western culture back then, I'm afraid. We are a little more civilized now."

"That is good to know. Do you believe me?"

"No."

That word took the life out of his legs and he landed hard on the futon. Now what would he do? With a malfunctioning ship, he was basically stranded.

"Maybe I should clarify," she said. He stared at her and hoped. "I have a hard time believing without seeing. You said you had proof?"

"Yes. My ship. It is in the woods not far from where you found me."

"You landed your ship? You didn't beam down here?"

"I do not know what beaming is." He would have to look that one up. Since she smiled, he suspected she was not being serious.

"How did you come to speak English? Any mind probing?"

Mind probing? That sounded…painful. "Do your people know how to mind probe?"

"Well, no."

What made her think of it, then? Maybe he should check out her science fiction books. "Neither does mine. The travelers who visited back in 1830 documented everything and brought back several books. Conversations were recorded. Lifestyles were recorded. The alphabet in Texas is similar to ours and was easiest for me to comprehend, so that is what I learned first. Everything I know came from the culture in 1830, and the few hours I spent on Google."

"So that's why you wanted to go to Texas?"

"It was. But I understand now that it would not matter where I landed."

"Why me? Why are you telling me? Shouldn't you talk to someone higher up? Someone in authority?"

"I am not supposed to tell anyone, but I am out of my element. I thought I could do this alone. I cannot. I need help. I trust you, Annie."

She cradled her face in her hands. Had he made a mistake telling her?

"That chip that came out of your head. It did come out of your head, didn't it?"

He nodded. "I believe it is my tracking indicator. All the people on my planet have one for accountability. I did not know where it was located, though."

"Tracking indicator? What kind of sick people are you? I wouldn't want anyone to know where I was at a moment's notice."

Her accusation gave him pause. Did she believe him? "How is my tracking indicator any different than that item you call a cellphone?"

She picked up the hand-held device. "At least I can turn this off. And not just anyone can call. They have to know my number, first."

"I am sure you can be accounted for. My people just do it more efficiently."

She mumbled words he did not understand while punching keys on her computer. He was glad he told her. It made it easier to ask questions without explaining why. Unless she decided to send him away or, worse, call the authorities. Then he would have to go back to his ship and figure out a way to get it fixed without her help.

A quick knock on the door preceded it being opened by Mac. He held his arm across his eyes. "I hope you two are decent."

"Of course we're decent," she said.

He lowered his arm. "Hey, you never know. Once I barged into Mom and Dad's room while they were—"

"Eeww, shut up, will you?" She covered her eyes. "What do you want?"

"Calix." Mac turned around. "Dude, your bag is beeping."

* * * *

Annie stood behind Calix as he crouched down and opened his bag. The muffled beeps turned into ear-piercing shrieks as he opened a large black box with a blinking red light. The sound was enough to bring back her headache.

"What is that thing?" she asked.

Calix glanced at Mac before turning his gaze on her. Oh crap. Did it have something to do with that ship he mentioned? And did she really believe his story?

God help her, she did.

"Damn, can you shut it off?" Mac said as he covered his ears.

Calix pulled out a device the size of a small cellphone and pushed a button, bringing the room back to a quiet zone. The silence hung in the air as if it had weight.

"That's worse than one of those car alarms," Mac said. "What the heck is that thing? Your alarm clock?"

"It is an alarm," Calix said. He stared at Annie as if it were her turn to speak.

She'd kept secrets from her brother before. Like the time she got detention for hitting Shelly Munoz. Annie had told everyone it was because Shelly had stolen her homework, which Shelly denied—and rightfully so. But Annie had done enough facial damage to keep the slut from going through with her plan: taking Mac to a high-profile party, adding him to her list of conquests, and then dumping his ass in front of everyone. He deserved better than being used, but probably wouldn't have seen it that way at the time.

She couldn't keep this secret, though. He was as involved as her, and if Calix needed her help, she needed Mac's.

Meeting Calix's gaze, she asked, "Is it bad?"

He nodded.

"What's bad?" Mac asked. "What's going on?"

She grabbed his coat and tossed it to him. "We'll tell you on the way. Good thing we bought Calix a coat. I have a feeling we're taking a walk in the woods."

CHAPTER 6

Mac followed Calix, who carried Annie piggyback-style as she explained it, traipsing through the snowy woods toward his spacecraft. His new coat, a wonderful shade of green that matched Annie's eyes, kept him warmer than he expected. Or maybe it was because he drew heat from Annie. But carrying her brought him more than warmth. There was something about her presence that made him feel such wonderful emotions. He wanted to understand and explore them more, and not necessarily through Google.

When Annie had told Mac everything, Calix had realized then that she had believed him. No more pretending. He could be himself and ask his questions. He had been pleased in the past, but not to the extent as he was now. Happy. Annie had said he looked happy. He supposed he was.

The tracking device was set for locating his ship. When the blinking light changed to a solid, it indicated the ship was within 50 meters. He halted. While footprints of the animal variety surrounding his ship did not concern him, the human variety did.

"Someone's been here," Annie said. "And they came from that way."

Mac examined the path that led from the woods. "Where'd they go? There's nothing here."

"My ship is camouflaged," Calix said.

"Like a cloak? You can cloak your spaceship? Man, that is soooo cool!" Mac was maybe too excited about aliens, but it was better than being afraid.

"If you look hard enough, you can probably see it. It is not a perfect system."

"Probably better than anything we can conjure up," Annie said. "You can put me down now, if you want."

Calix did not want, but since she had covered her injured foot with waterproof material and he needed the use of his arms, he let her go. She slid down his back, her warmth replaced with the cold wind.

"Be careful. Just because you cannot see it, does not mean it is not there." He held the tracking device out and pushed a button to locate the door.

"What is that thing?" Mac asked. "It looks like one of my game controllers."

"It helps me find the ship."

The light blinked as he hovered the device over what seemed like air to the unobservant. When the light became solid once again, he reached out and pulled open the door.

He still could not believe someone had found his ship and entered it. Yet, that was what the alarm had told him. And now the two bodies on the floor—one a human male, the other a dog—told him the same.

"Are they dead?" Annie placed two fingers alongside the man's neck.

"They should not be. They should be asleep."

Lights flashed and the warning system went off, asking for the code. Calix stepped inside and punched in the numbers 47825. The flashing stopped and was replaced with one steady beam overhead.

"Is that your language?" she asked. When he nodded, she smiled. "It almost sounds Latin. Doesn't it, Mac?"

"How the hell should I know? Do I look like I'm that smart?" He glanced around the enclosure. "You know, for a ship, it's kind of small."

"This is just the entryway. It prevents unwanted guests from entering."

"Wouldn't locking it from the outside also do that?" Mac asked.

"We do not have keys like you have for your car." Since entering the code, the inside door was now unlocked. Calix turned the lever and pushed, causing a swoosh of air to release. "Come on in."

"Oh wow," Mac said as he stepped inside. "It looks like a cockpit."

"What did you expect?" Annie asked. "The Enterprise?"

Annie always seemed to come up with a reference Calix did not understand. He really did need to do some more research. "What is the Enterprise?"

"The spaceship on an old television series," she said. "It's not real, though."

"Yeah, and they didn't have a bed on the bridge, either. You sleep in here, too?" Mac asked.

"Where else would I sleep? This is the only large room. The lavatory is small, as is the galley." His stash of gold was stored underneath the bed, but he did not think it was something to discuss at the time. Gold was a precious commodity on this planet. While he did not think Annie and Mac would try and take it from him, he thought it best to be prudent and keep it a secret.

"It looks very efficient." Annie turned toward the two sleeping bodies. "Are they going to be okay? What will you do with them?"

"I might be able to carry them back by following their tracks. But I cannot do it alone." He looked at Mac. "Could you carry the animal?"

"He's kind of big. Do you have something I can drag him with?"

Calix yanked the cover off his bed. "Will this work?"

"Yeah, it should be okay." Mac laid the cover beside the dog.

"What about me?" Annie asked. "You said you needed my help."

Calix smiled. He so enjoyed listening to her voice. "I do. I think the dashboard is malfunctioning. Do you think you could look at it while we are gone? It may only be a power issue, but I am not sure."

"You probably got hit with a solar flare. We've been having a major solar storm the last few days. If that's what happened, rebooting your system should set it right." She looked around the pilot's area. "Is there anything I should not touch?"

Calix pointed to a green button and the lever beside it. "If you accidentally start the engines, do not touch these, or you could find yourself in space."

She fisted her hands in front of her body with her thumbs upward. "Okay. Good to know."

She seemed to have hand gestures for everything, too. Or maybe everyone on this planet did. They were an interesting people and he looked forward to learning more.

Mac stood over the dog. "How long will they be asleep?"

"I do not know. If they regain consciousness before we get them back to wherever they came from, we will have to leave them."

"Are you going to wipe his memory?"

"Wipe?"

"Sorry. Erase. Erase his memory."

Annie had been searching under the console and looked up. "You can do that?"

"No," Calix said. "Why would his memory need to be erased?"

Mac placed his hands on his hips. "Do you have no concept of curiosity? He already knows this ship is here. He already knows how to get inside. Hell, he'll probably bring the news crew with him. This is a huge discovery."

"Mac is right," she said. "No matter where we leave him, he'll be back. So what can we do? Tie him up and keep him prisoner? That doesn't seem right."

It did not seem right to Calix either, but neither did being discovered. Before arriving on this planet, the concept of curiosity was unthinkable, as was love and hate. They really did not exist on his planet. But since arriving, since meeting Annie and Mac, he was starting to understand these emotions better because he was experiencing them. It was something his people would need to be aware of if in fact the atmosphere was the cause of these new-found emotions.

Unfortunately, that would not solve his current problem: how to keep the stranger from returning. If his ship worked, he would just move it. But if Annie could not fix the dashboard, the ship was stuck. If only he had more training as a traveler. If only he could contact his people. But as far as he could tell, even the transmitter was out. If what Annie said was true, that the outage was only temporary, it was possible he could just turn it back on. He walked over to the console and pushed the button. The transmitter lit up.

"Hey, looks like it's working now," Annie said.

"That's just the transmitter." He pushed the power button for the ship, hoping, but nothing happened. The ship was not working. Even though he was told not to contact home until his designated time, he really had no choice but to contact them now. "I need you to be quiet while I ask for guidance."

"Wow," Mac said. "You can contact your planet from here? That quickly?"

Calix wished there was a delay. Did he fail his mission? Would Sentinel Gaylor be disappointed? But for the security measures the ship held, they had to have expected something like this to happen.

Annie placed her hand on his upper arm. "Hey, it'll be okay. We'll be quiet. I take it you don't have video to worry about?"

"No. Video does not work in the transmitter." And he was grateful that he did not have to worry about that, too. He linked with his planet and called in his code.

"Greetings, Calix 47825," a male said in Calix's language. "This is Maxim 45555, head of communications. You are not expected to report in for another forty days. Is there a problem?"

"I need to speak with Sentinel Gaylor."

"If there is a problem—"

"I was told to only speak with Sentinel Gaylor."

"Understood. Hold while I get him." Several minutes passed before the male returned. "Calix, this is Sentinel Gaylor. Please state your business."

"May I talk freely?"

"You may. What do you wish to report?"

"A human and his animal found their way inside the ship. I need to know what the protocol is."

"Did you forget to camouflage?"

"No. But the people here question strange happenings. When I arrived, the dashboard malfunctioned and I was forced to land in unfamiliar territory. I can only assume the human came to investigate and found his way inside."

"Understood. These things happen. Proceed with Directive 23."

Directive 23? During his brief training, the thought of eliminating a risk had not bothered him. Now it made his stomach hurt. He turned toward Annie and Mac. They both smiled at him. Would they understand the need to exterminate the life of a man and his dog? If they did, would they have not suggested the same? There had to be another way.

"Is that really necessary?"

"Hold."

Had he said the wrong thing? Most likely. Had anyone ever questioned a directive? How much trouble was he in? He couldn't face Annie and Mac right now. They may think the conversation was over and if Sentinel Gaylor overheard… It was better to keep his back to them and hope for the best.

Time seemed to slow as he waited.

"Calix, we see your ship is offline, but should be online shortly. Were you injured in your landing? Your signal is weak."

Was that why he was put on hold? That would make sense. "Yes, I was injured. I hit my head. I believe my tracking indicator may have been dislodged. I carry it in my pocket just in case."

"How are you feeling?"

"I am well. No adverse reaction to injury or the atmosphere." Which was the truth. His reaction to this planet, while unfamiliar, was not in any way jeopardizing his life or his mission. So far.

"That is good to know. Please keep the indicator with you. But Calix, it is imperative you proceed with Directive 23. No one must know of our existence yet. That means disposal of the bodies. Do you understand?"

Not following orders would certainly jeopardize his mission. But that would mean lying. To the sentinel. "I understand."

"Good. Since you have run into some difficulties, you are to report back on your findings in ten days instead of forty. I will feel more confident knowing you are well and that your mission is going smoothly."

"I understand. My pardon, Sentinel, if I have erred in any way."

"You have not erred. These things happen, that is why we have Directives. I expect your report in ten days."

The transmitter light went out. Calix fingered the dashboard. His ship would eventually be functional, which meant he would be able to move it, so he did not need to follow the directive. But he had just lied to the sentinel and now he would have to lie to Annie and Mac. What was he becoming?

His stomach churned.

* * * *

Annie leaned back and smiled. Calix's language was beautiful. Although she couldn't understand him, the words flowed smoothly, almost like singing. If he spoke sweet nothings in her ear with his own language, she'd be goo in his arms.

Oh, who was she kidding? He could speak in Pig Latin and her reaction would be the same.

Calix had his back toward her, yet he was quiet. Had he finished his call? Could she speak now? Well, she certainly couldn't ask, now could she? But waiting like this was the pits.

After what seemed like an eternity, he turned around and smiled. Or rather, he forced a smile. And he didn't look at anyone in particular, like he was afraid to. "Good news. You do not need to fix my dashboard. The people on my planet are working on that now and it should be functional by the time we return."

"Wow," Mac said. "They can do that so far away? I'm impressed."

She would be impressed, too, except Calix didn't look like it was all good news. He was lying, she'd bet her life on it, and he was lousy at it, too. But what was he lying about? She glanced at the intruders. Could he be lying about them? "So we're still taking them back to wherever they came from?"

"Yes. I will be able to move the ship once it is back online, so there will be nothing for him to see if he does return. Would it be okay to land near your cabin? Will it be safe there?"

The solution sounded simple enough. Plus, she wouldn't have to figure out how to work alien electronics. She was good, but not that good. Still…she was getting a strange vibe from Calix. "There is an open field behind the tree line at the cabin. It'll be well hidden and no one should bother it there. At least not this time of year."

"Good." He finally made eye contact with Mac. "Let us take them, then, before they wake up."

She rose and limped over to him. The urge to run her hand across his face was strong, but she managed to fight it. "Calix? Is everything okay?"

Again, he smiled. And again, it seemed forced. "Everything is fine. But we must hurry. Please wait here. Use the chair or bed so you can rest your ankle. We will return as soon as possible."

There was lots of grunting and groaning—mostly from Mac—as they carried the intruders outside. Mac and Calix placed the dog onto the bed spread and then Mac showed Calix how to carry the man over his shoulder. Once they were gone, she settled inside and was greeted with silence. The interior of his ship wasn't much different than a studio apartment. Except the electronics were totally different. Instead of a TV or sound system, he had a dashboard with controls and levers.

Some items were labeled. The words made no sense, but the letters were similar. Wonder if they sounded the same? Maybe Calix could teach her.

Teach her? Holy shit on a shingle. He really was an alien.

So what were his plans? Why was he here? Was he planning on staying or only gathering information before he headed back to his own planet? And she got the distinct impression that Calix wasn't doing what whoever was on the other end of that call told him to do. And yet, what he was doing was the best solution. In her eyes, that made him a good guy.

She sat down on the bed. This was the kind of luck she had. The first guy she was really into since Denny, and who seemed to be into her, was an alien from another planet. Talk about a long-distance fiasco waiting to happen.

* * * *

Jay awoke with a start. Buster stared with those soulful eyes of his and wagged his tail.

"Hey, buddy." Jay petted the dog and looked up at the living room window. His living room? Wait a minute.

He bolted upright. How'd he get back to his cabin? He felt his chest, arms, legs, head. Especially his head. Had he been probed and then returned? The last thing he remembered was passing out in that spaceship.

"You okay, Buster?" He examined the dog, who seemed to be okay, since he took the examination to mean play time. Then again, what did Jay know about alien probes?

His legs seemed to be in working order and he walked over to the front door. Footprints were drying on the wood floor. *Jesus, Mary, and Joseph.* Someone, no, two someones had brought him and Buster back. But who? Or should he ask…what?

Except, if they were whats, they wore boots.

Jay still had his winter gear on. The leash was lying on the coffee table. He attached it to Buster's collar, found his camera, and grabbed another scarf. He might be thawed out now, but was sure to freeze by the time he finished with his trip. "Come on, boy. Time for another walk. Maybe they're still out there."

Going out to the spaceship was much easier this time. Most of the snow had been compacted as if the spaceship inhabitants had dragged him and Buster back to the cabin.

When Jay arrived back at where he'd found the spaceship, he cursed. The ship was gone. A huge spot free of snow was all that remained of its existence. He took several pictures.

They must be a friendly lot. They could have easily left him outside in the cold. Instead, they took him and Buster back to the house where it was warm.

Well, he had these pictures. The authorities wouldn't care, but if he could figure out how to put them on his Face-page-thingy, maybe someone would see them and be interested.

When he got home, he settled into his desk chair and shuffled through the computer file drawer looking for the Face-thing password.

CHAPTER 7

Calix sat on the couch in the darkened living room and unsnapped his pants. Annie was still at work in her office and Mac had left a few minutes before, grumbling about the lack of food in the house and why had they not bought some food at the grocery store. Annie had responded that there was plenty of food for her and maybe he should have thought about buying more. The argument ended with Mac leaving to go get a pizza—whatever that was—since no one would deliver to them. He had asked if Calix wanted to come, and in other circumstances he would have, but right now he had his own problem.

His penis ached and was hard. He hoped freeing it would bring relief. It did not.

When Mac and Calix had returned to the ship after their little trip through the woods, they found Annie asleep on his bed. Her vulnerability had stirred some kind of protective reaction deep inside him, yet no one threatened her. If anything, maybe he was the threat because all he wanted to do at that moment was lie beside her, feel the length of her body against his, and caress her soft breasts. Once that picture floated inside his head, his penis had grown hard and it remained so.

The office door opened, lighting up the hallway. Annie emerged. "How come you're sitting in the dark?"

Calix panicked. His highly sensitive body part would not go back into his pants and he was fairly certain he should not show it to her. He grabbed the coverlet from the back of the couch and placed it on his lap just as she turned on the lamp.

"What are you doing?" she asked.

"Nothing." He shook his head. As she stepped closer, his penis seemed to get harder. It ached for a release, but he had no idea what kind. He just knew it had nothing to do with his bladder and everything to do with her. None of the documents from 1830 indicated any of the travelers having problems with their body parts. Would she be able to help him or think him some kind of alien freak?

She walked around the table and sat down beside him. "It's not nothing. You look like you're in pain. Is your head bothering you?"

She pulled off the bandage and he relished the distraction. But her fingers were soft against his temple and he wondered what they might feel against his penis. Oh, bad thought. The thing actually jerked under the coverlet.

"It's not bleeding anymore. We'll leave the bandage off and let it get some air. Is it throbbing, though? Do you want some aspirin, medicine?"

Something was throbbing all right, and it was not his temple. "My head is fine."

She backed away and leaned against the arm of the couch. "Is it okay if I ask you some questions? About who you are? Ever since you told me where you're from, I've been wanting to talk."

He had wanted the same. Thought if they talked he might get the relief he desperately needed, but her work came first. He could not fault her there. "I would be glad to answer your questions if you could answer mine, too. Maybe we can take turns?"

She smiled. "Okay. I'll go first. But before I do, I have to say, these clothes suit you much better."

He had changed into his everyday clothes. "Thank you. They are more comfortable."

"So, do you have a girlfriend back home?"

"I have acquaintances. Some male, some female."

"That's not what I mean. Is there a woman you are intimate with? Someone you kiss, maybe?"

He had seen kissing—the touching of lips—on that television show he watched with Mac. "I do not understand intimate, but we cannot touch on our planet, so no kissing."

Her eyes widened. "Why not? Is it against your laws?"

"It is not a law. It is physical. If I were to touch another person on my planet, we would both feel a sharp pain and be rendered unconscious."

"What? Does that mean you go around wearing protective gear all day?"

"No. Protective gear would be cumbersome. We learn to not touch. My turn." He smiled at her confused look. "Why do your people kiss?"

She lowered her head and her face turned a shade pinker. "To show affection. But there are different types of kisses. Such as a kiss I would give Mac would be way more different than if I were to say…kiss you."

"Because he is your brother and I am a stranger?"

She shook her head. "Because he is my brother and you are someone I like who is not related to me."

Why did knowing she liked him make him feel all warm inside? His penis was still giving him fits, but right now he did not care. "How is not being related different?"

"People do not marry their relatives."

Calix understood what marriage was, between a mother and a father, but not why it was necessary. The travelers from 1830 could have documented it better. "So, how would you kiss your brother?"

"Well, if I wanted to kiss Mac, and I'm not saying I do because he'd probably belt me one, I'd kiss him like I do my mother. Like this." She placed her lips softly against his cheek and withdrew.

His heartbeat sped up and his penis jerked again. Somehow, he did not think Mac or her mother would have gotten the same reaction. He was not sure why he was getting this reaction either, but he liked the feel of her lips against his cheek and wanted more. "And how would you kiss someone you like, but was not related to?"

"More intimately. Like this." She held his face in her hands and placed her lips against his own. They were warm and soft. His heart pounded in his chest. Something inside of him wanted her closer and he held her head, too. She smelled like a warm night after a rare rain had cleaned the air.

She licked his lips, and when he slightly gasped, she licked him deeper, touching his own tongue. Flavors he had never experienced overwhelmed him and he copied her movements. He stuck his tongue in her mouth, so warm and tasty. This was nice. Then she sucked on it.

Something exploded from the tip of his penis. He jerked. Gasped for air. His penis no longer ached, but he breathed as if he had just finished using the exercise mat. He sank back against the couch and closed his eyes. His energy drained to practically nothing, yet he never felt better. How was that possible? And how had he never experienced it before?

He opened his eyes and found Annie touching her lips.

"Sorry. I mean, I didn't, um, just…sorry," she mumbled, nearly tripping over her medical boot in her haste to leave the room.

Strange. Had this kissing affected her body the same way? He would find out, just as soon as he could stand.

* * * *

Annie sat on her bed with her knees up to her chest. What had she just done? All she did was kiss him, but he acted as if he had an orgasm. Which was crazy. Or was it? He had been sitting in the dark and covered his lap with the afghan when she'd come into the room. If she didn't know any better, she'd say he was going through puberty, with no control whatsoever.

But damn. If her theory was correct—and she didn't doubt it was—she'd made him come. And he was certainly a virgin since there was no way the guy had sex when he couldn't even touch the people on his planet. Which meant he knew absolutely nothing about sex. Did that make her good or him easy? She wouldn't mind finding out, but only after Calix knew more. Should she teach him or should Mac?

Her cellphone went off and she pulled it from her pants pocket. *Logan.* She groaned and answered without bothering with the cheerful bit. "Office is closed. What do you want?"

"I'd watch that attitude if I were you," he said.

"And what are you going to do about it, huh?" If she had been smarter, she would have kicked him in the nuts, not his ass. Then her sprained ankle would be so worth it.

"Keep it up and you'll find out. I thought you were going to finish that program today."

"I did finish it. Don't you read your e-mails?" Granted, she had just finished the software program she'd been assigned and sent out the e-mail before shutting down for the day. But to imply she wasn't doing her job just irked her some more.

"I got it. Don't you install programs before you e-mail everyone?"

"What are you talking about? I installed it on the test box, just like I was supposed to. I even ran it myself. Maybe you looked in the wrong place."

"Or maybe you didn't do your job. Call me when you've installed it. You have two hours or I'm reporting you to the boss. I'm not going to be blamed for your error."

She snarled at her phone. She must remember never to set up a friend with a co-worker again. If she had ever seen this side of Logan, she would never have introduced him to Jen. He used to ooze charm, but apparently it had all oozed out.

She marched over to her office in a gimpy-but-angry kind of way. The boot made a loud bang every time it met the wooden floor. It wasn't until she got to her desk that she even remembered Calix was in the house.

God, she hoped he didn't think she was mad at him. She was kind of honored that he felt a sexual attraction toward her. He did feel that attraction, didn't he? Men, even virgins, didn't just come for anyone, did they? Calix wasn't some fourteen-year-old, he was twenty-nine. That made a difference. Didn't it?

She turned her computer back on and logged into the test box. Her program was missing. What the hell? Did that louse erase it? Where else could it have gone?

She went into her files and searched for her back-up copy. The file name was there, but the size was much too small. She opened the document in her notepad.

Gibberish. Line after line of gibberish. That son of a bitch. He'd corrupted her file. That would be the last time she didn't save something on her personal file. The boss always said it wasn't necessary, that if something happened to the employee, the rest of them needed access. At the time it had made sense. She picked up the empty mug and threw it against the wall. Ceramic pieces flew outward as it exploded upon impact. Logan was so going to pay for this. She didn't know how, but she would think of something.

Her door opened and Calix peeked inside, keeping the lower half of his body out of sight. Shielding or hiding? "Are you hurt?"

Great. If he stayed, she might just cry. And there was no way she would do that. She gritted her teeth. "I'm fine. Please go."

He looked at the mess on the floor and then back at her. "Did the cup insult you?"

She was about to ask if he was serious—because the guy was always serious—when he smiled. Holy crap, he'd cracked a joke. She tried to keep from smiling, but failed. Just like that, her anger dissipated. That was probably the first time she heard anything resembling a joke come out of his mouth. "Yes. Said I had bad breath."

"A highly punishable offense."

She nodded. "The worst."

"I will keep that in mind." He backed up briefly then returned. "You do not, though."

She looked up into his purplish-blue eyes. "I don't what?"

"Have bad breath." He smiled and closed the door upon his exit.

She silently laughed until it turned into sobs and the tears ran down her face. Anyone else would have yelled at her for losing her temper. Then again, Calix wasn't just anyone, now was he?

* * * *

Calix shut off the laptop and placed it on the table when he heard the car drive up. He took another glance around the couch just to be sure he did not miss a spot. Seemed he had only made a mess on the coverlet and water cleaned it just fine. He left the coverlet hanging over the rod in the bathroom.

After he had cleaned up, he did some research on the Internet. Using the words intimate and kissing, he'd discovered what he had was an erection. Something that led to sex, although he did not have sex with Annie. Not if the pictures were any indication. And there were a lot of pictures.

No, what he had was something called premature ejaculation. It even sounded awful. No wonder she had left the room so quickly.

Mac entered, carrying a square, shallow box in his arm. "Dinner's here!"

"You all eat without me," Annie yelled from her office.

The smells enticed Calix to approach Mac. His stomach rumbled.

"She's still working?" Mac put the box on the dining table.

"I do not know."

"I hope you like pepperoni." Mac opened the lid to the box. The aroma made Calix's mouth water. "I thought about asking you, but I guess all our food is new to you, huh?"

"There are some similarities. I have never had anything like that, though. What is it made of?"

Mac tore out a triangle piece and bit into the end. "Bread, cheese, tomato sauce. Dig in and try it. I kept it simple. Those round things are pepperoni. A type of meat."

Calix tore off a piece and sat down as he took a bite. The flavors were intense but tasty. Mac pulled paper towels from a roll and placed two sheets on the table, placing his pizza on one of them. He went back to the refrigerator and pulled out a can. "Want a beer? It's got alcohol in it. Do you know what that is?"

"If you mean liquor, then I understand, although I have never sampled any. I am willing to try it."

"That's the spirit. Nothing better than beer and pizza." Mac pulled another can out, along with two glasses, and brought them back to the table. Calix observed as Mac opened the can and poured the contents into the glass. Seemed easy enough and he mimicked the movements. The beverage had a strong odor, but the taste was not offensive.

Calix waited until he finished eating his pizza before he found the nerve to talk. "Something happened while you were gone and I am not sure what to make of it."

"Shoot. I mean, tell me what happened." Mac took a drink of his beer.

"Have you ever had premature ejaculation?"

Liquid spewed from Mac's lips and he coughed. "What the hell? Did you have sex with my sister?"

Calix laid his paper on the mess and it absorbed the yellow liquid. "No. I do not believe I did."

"Do you want to have sex with my sister?"

"I do not understand sex. I had an erection and then we kissed…"

Mac's face turned a funny shade of red and purple. "I'm gonna kill her!"

Alarmed, Calix stood. "You will not harm her. She has done nothing wrong."

Mac raised his hands, palms out. "I'm sorry. You're right. I didn't mean it the way it sounded. I love my sister and would never hurt her, okay? But sometimes she can get into some strange messes."

"And what mess has she gotten into now? I am the one who ejaculated prematurely. Not her."

Mac shook his head, went over to his bag, opened it, and pulled out a small, thin box. Then he walked over to the bookcase and, after looking at it for several seconds, pulled out two books. He placed all of these in front of Calix. The small box was labeled "Beach Babes From Beyond" and the books had pictures of half-naked couples doing a lot of touching.

Mac opened the box, which contained a small computer disk. "The movie on this DVD will show you how sex is performed, but not necessarily what it's all about, since it's basically soft porn. These books are romances that show what women hope sex is all about, but it's not really real, either."

"If these are not real, then why is there documentation?" And what was porn and romance?

Mac smiled. "This isn't documentation. It's entertainment. Fiction. But it should give you an idea of what sex is about. Better than any scientific documentation. Certainly a whole lot more fun to watch, too."

Apparently, he needed all the help he could get. "Would you watch this movie with me? In case I have questions?"

Mac sat and pulled off another slice of pizza. "Sure. As long as you promise not to mention premature ejaculation again."

Just as Calix had thought; what he had done was not a good thing at all. Else Mac would not mind discussing it.

* * * *

Annie picked up the cold piece of pizza and bit into it. Mac had brought in two pieces when he came to rip her a new one. Yeah, she probably shouldn't have kissed Calix, but how was she supposed to know he'd come in his pants? And did his actions mean he was interested in having sex with her? Or was it just another one of his fact-finding missions?

And exactly what kind of mission was the guy on anyway?

She was almost sorry she wasn't the one to explain sex to Calix, but at least he knew now. As much as Mac would be willing to say anyway.

Guys talked about that stuff together, right?

It had taken longer than two hours, but she finally managed to re-write the program and get it installed. This time she made sure to put a copy on a flash drive. She also copied all her other files onto a flash drive, just in case. "Fool me once, blah, blah, blah."

Man, if Logan could do these things to her in retaliation, how might he treat Jen? He'd already hit her once, what would stop him from hitting her again? Annie shuddered at the thought. She needed to have a real heart-to-heart with her friend and get her to press charges. Having a witness to the hit had to be enough.

Annie tossed her pizza crust on the plate and carried it out to the kitchen. When she passed the living room, the television was the only source of light. Mac was sleeping on the couch and Calix was watching a naked man oiling up a naked woman. Oh, God. Was this how Mac told Calix about sex? By giving him…porn?

"What are you doing?" she asked, then realized the stupidity of her question. At least Calix didn't have his hands down his pants, although he was sporting a rather large erection. Holy shit on a shingle. It had to be the light, right? No one was that big.

Calix turned and stared at her. "Researching. But I am confused. I watched this movie with Mac, but every time I had a question, he would drink another beer before answering. Once he went to sleep, I skimmed over this book, but now I only have more questions, so I thought I would watch the movie again."

She put the plate on the counter and limped over to Calix. Her brother was nuts, and she was nuts thinking Mac helped Calix. She took the remote from his hands and turned off the movie. The coffee table was littered with a half-dozen beer cans. Mac wasn't asleep; he'd passed out. She wanted to laugh. Just how many questions—or better yet, what kind—had Calix asked?

He stood. "Are you still mad at me?"

"Why would I be mad at you?" Oh, the stomping and throwing. "I'm not mad at you." She backed into the dining room and flipped on the light.

"Then if you were not mad at me, what made you angry earlier?"

She shook her head. No use going into the Logan debacle. She'd just get pissed all over again and she could think of better ways to spend the rest of the night. "It's not important. But help me understand. If your people don't touch, what did you do when your penis got hard?"

He approached her. "My penis has never gotten hard before."

Crap. Was that why his face never seemed to need a shave? Had he not gone through puberty? So why now? What was Earth doing to him? Better yet, what had Mac done to him?

"What you were watching wasn't real, you know that, don't you? Normal people don't have sex like that."

"So you are saying a woman does not enjoy it when a man touches her here?" He palmed her breast and she let out a little gasp.

"If the right man touches her, she enjoys it." Holy shit. She was certainly enjoying it.

"Is that the reaction of enjoyment?"

"It is." She took his hand in hers before he did any more touching. She might not be able to stop him the next time. "Are you thirsty? Would you like some water?"

"I would like to kiss you again." He cupped her face and planted his lips against hers.

She backed up a couple of steps and hit the wall. Now he had her pinned and she wasn't all that sure if it was a good thing or a bad thing. Her body screamed for his touch. Her mind was telling her to stop.

Whatever he had seen or read, he was a fast learner. He plunged his tongue into her mouth and she welcomed him. He tasted a little of beer. She wrapped her arms around his neck as his hands traveled down to her breasts and then around her waist. He pulled her close and she felt his erection against her belly. He hadn't gotten any smaller and he moaned at the contact.

She pulled away. "Calix, we need to stop."

Sadness filled his eyes. "Am I doing it wrong?"

Oh, hell no. "It's just that people who like each other usually wait until they've known each other a little longer before they have sex."

"You do not want my dick in your pussy?"

She was going to kill her brother. Seriously kill him. She placed her hand over Calix's mouth. "Okay, stop. Don't talk like that. It's crude, okay?"

He backed away, his face red. "I am sorry. I just thought…"

"This has nothing to do with me wanting you, okay? I like you, Calix. I just think we should wait. I mean, besides the fact your body is going through some serious changes, I don't even know how long you'll be here. Or why you're even on this planet. I'm not a one-night-stand kind of girl."

"It matters whether I stay or not?"

"Some people can have sex with strangers. I prefer to know the guy first and would like him to stick around."

He slunk over to the chair and sat. "I am sorry. I was only looking to get relief. When we kissed the last time, it worked. And when I asked Mac…" He glanced at the unconscious man. "He only drank more beers."

Dear God. What was she going to do with him? Then she saw the laptop on the table. She picked it up and handed it to him. "No more talking to Mac, okay? Look up masturbation. That may help you with your problem for now. And once you've taken care of yourself, once you've gotten relief, then we'll talk. I'll just wait for you in my room." She started to leave, then stopped. "Maybe try it in the shower, okay?"

Mac would wake up with one doozie of a headache. Served him right. Showing porn to a virgin. Did the guy have no sense at all?

CHAPTER 8

Calix awoke on the futon with a start. The room was still dark. Clock stated it was 4:12. He had been dreaming of Annie. Of having sex with her, just like the people did in that movie. And now his penis was harder than ever.

He had researched as she suggested. He had gone into the shower as she suggested. And he had masturbated, again as she suggested. While it brought some pleasure—and fascinated him as the semen shot out—it did not come close to the euphoria he felt when she had kissed him. Was it wrong to want that again?

After the shower, he had been anxious to talk with Annie some more, but found her already asleep on the bed. He had taken too much time and the disappointment burned in his chest. Not wishing to disturb her, he had turned off her lamp and went into her office.

Maybe the movie was not real, but the physical act seemed accurate. So he read one of Annie's books. While the story was not real, either, the physical act was the same. Where the two differed involved love. The movie never mentioned it, but it had been important in the book. He did not understand love or why it was important for relationships. Only that it was something Annie wanted. Kissing seemed to be involved. Getting to know one another, also. He wanted to experience both with her. Was that what she wanted, too?

He wanted to understand it all better. But his mind only wandered to Annie, which caused his penis to grow hard again.

Masturbating had not worked. He had thrown the book to the floor and decided sleep was his only recourse.

Mac slept on the couch so Calix slept on the futon. It was small and uncomfortable, but it had made his erection go away. At least until the dream.

That dream with Annie had felt real. He got up and went to her room, but she was still asleep. He brushed the hair away from her face. This planet had affected him in such a way he never thought was possible. To be able to touch her was a miracle. Going back home was not really feasible, since it would eventually be destroyed. Would his people think this planet was acceptable? Would they want to experience the emotions that now ran through him? Of course, none of that could happen if the people on this planet did not accept his people. He had to find a way to make that possible. He had only been here a day and already he did not wish to return to that old life. He wanted this new life. With her.

Leaning over her, he brushed his lips across her jaw. So soft and smooth. He inhaled her wonderful scent, ran his fingers through her silky hair. Urges he did not understand flowed through him and his penis throbbed. He did not want to bring himself relief. He wanted her to do it. To touch him.

But she had said she was not interested in a one-night-stand so he had looked that up, too. He was not interested in that either. The thought of never seeing her again caused a pain deep in his chest.

If he told her everything, would she accept him or reject him? He kissed her cheek. It was a chance he would take.

* * * *

Something soft touched her face and she opened her eyes to a darkened room. When had she turned out the light? Last she remembered, she'd been waiting on Calix. The bed rocked as someone sat beside her.

Not just someone. Calix. She turned on the lamp. There he was in all his glory. Damn, what a sight. No doubt about it, the light had not played tricks on her. He was a big guy everywhere and possessed all the right body parts. Nothing alien about him. "Why are you naked?"

"My erection will not go away and it is making my pants tight."

She smiled and soothingly rubbed his arm. "Masturbation didn't work?"

"It did for a little while. But your kissing made it so much better. Would you please kiss me and make it go away? I promise I will not be a one-night-stand."

She tossed the sheet over his groin area. Better to not even be tempted at what he was offering her. And, boy, was she tempted. "How can you promise that? Won't you be returning to your planet after your observation period?"

Still seemed strange his people had only sent one person to observe, but that's what he'd said and she had no reason not to believe him. Not after he'd shown her his ship.

"What if I said it was possible that I can stay?" he asked.

"Permanently?"

He nodded.

"But your mission…your people… Aren't they counting on you?"

"I believe my mission is complete. This planet of yours is wonderful. And that is what I will tell them." He caressed her cheek and she let him. "But I do not wish to return to a world without touching."

He did an excellent job of that, too. "I can understand that. I really can. But Calix, you've only been here for one day. What if it's not me affecting you? What if it's my planet? If we became intimate, close, I don't know if I could stand to see you attracted to everyone else."

He pulled his hand back. "I do not feel this way about Mac."

"Okay, then how about any woman? Maybe it's something else and not me that makes you feel this way."

"I did not feel anything toward Portia."

Wonderful words to hear, but… "How long did it take you to be interested in me?"

"You think I did not spend enough time with her to become interested?"

"I don't know. Shouldn't you observe some more before making a decision that will affect the rest of our lives?" Wow, listen to her. Sounding like a responsible adult. For once.

"You make a logical assumption. However, there was no documentation to indicate the people of your planet desired any of my people when they first visited this planet. So, it must be us, Annie."

She'd like to believe that. "How about an experiment, then? Would you be willing to test your conclusion?"

He leaned close to her and the sheet slid off him. "If that is what it takes to be with you, I will do it. What do you need me to do?"

Covering up would be a good start.

* * * *

Calix squirmed in the passenger seat of the vehicle as Mac drove into a parking area. The stiff fabric of the pants he wore—which Mac had called jeans—rubbed against his crotch. He preferred his softer pants, but Mac said he would blend in better if he dressed like everyone else, so they had stopped at some large store and Mac had purchased them, along with a long-sleeved shirt he called flannel. At least the shirt was soft.

Mac turned off the engine and grinned as he reached for the door handle. "You ready?"

A lighted sign hung over the opening to the building: Rusty's Tavern, Thursday Night—Ladies Night—Drinks Half Price. Annie seemed to think he needed to be around more women, and Mac had suggested this place. Calix would have felt better if Annie had come, but she said that would only ruin the experiment, that he needed to be alone and available.

"Exactly what am I to be ready for?" Calix stared out the window as a group of men entered the establishment. If it were Ladies Night, where were the females?

"Consider it research, okay? The women will come to you. Trust me. You only need to see if any of them interest you like Annie does."

Calix still did not believe Annie was right about the planet affecting him, but she wanted proof it did not. If getting the proof meant they could have a relationship, then he would get the proof.

"Why would they come to me? Is it because I am different? Is it because of your planet?"

"Nah. It's because you're a big, good-looking guy. Hell, if I was bent that way, I'd come to you." He opened the door. "Come on. Might as well have fun. I know I will."

Calix exited the car and followed Mac. This did not seem right. Portia could have worked just as well, but Annie had been against that. Said she did not want to get Portia's hopes crushed, yet she did not care if it happened to some stranger. How was that any different?

Music blared in his ears as they entered the darkened tavern. Calix had never heard music until Annie introduced it to him, and he had enjoyed listening to her collection of alternative rock. Whatever rock was, he did not know. But why play it so loud? Did these people have hearing problems? If they did not, after enough time in this establishment they would.

Each table had a small lamp in the center that barely lit the top. If not for the lighted bar in the back, Calix would have had problems maneuvering around the patrons.

Mac found a table close to the bar and indicated Calix sit. "I'll go get us some beers."

Even inside, the establishment consisted of more males than females. Is this how the people of this planet found a mate? The books never said. He had not found Annie this way. That was if he considered her a mate. He certainly would enjoy discovering what mating was all about if it involved Annie. But he was here for other purposes, and he just wanted to get it over with so he could go back to her. He scanned the area. One blonde, sitting with a brunette, spotted Calix and smiled.

A traveler would not have hesitated to acclimate himself with his surroundings and he should not, either. Even though this was Annie's idea, he still needed to observe the people of this planet since it was his job. He smiled and waved at the blonde. She immediately looked away. Had he done something wrong?

The brunette noticed the engagement with widened eyes.

Mac returned with two glasses of beer. "Seems you're already causing a stir. I have a feeling you'll be crushing a lot of hearts tonight."

"I do not wish to harm anyone."

Mac laughed and slapped him on the back. "That's not what I meant. They'll be disappointed if you aren't interested."

"Should I be interested?"

"I guess that's what we're here to find out." Mac took a swig of his beer. "Come on, don't look so glum. Now, who looks good to you?"

Calix glanced about the room. No one looked good to him. None of them were Annie. He should not have agreed. But how else was he going to get her to believe him?

Mouth dry, he downed the beer, and the fizzy liquid burned down to his stomach. He fought the belch that threatened to escape. Whenever Mac belched, Annie hit him, so Calix made sure not to do it. Next time he would drink it slower, but for some reason he was very thirsty.

"You know, that brunette over there is one hot lady and is giving you the eye," Mac said.

"You think she looks unwell, too? But how can you tell she has a fever?"

"Uh…no. Hot means good looking. Why do you think she looks sick?"

"Because she appears malnourished. The blonde beside her is healthier."

Mac raised an eyebrow and glanced quickly at the pair of women. "Really? So big is healthy to you?"

"She does not appear older than me."

"Big doesn't mean older. Big means large."

"But Annie is smaller than you, yet she claims to be your big sister."

Mac nodded. "That's because when she was younger, she was bigger, because she's older. Then puberty hit me and that was the end of her big regime. But when someone says they are the big sister or big brother, it means they are older. Otherwise, big is just…not small."

"Oh." There was so much yet to learn. "Well then, that blonde is not big. She is small."

"Well, yeah. Compared to you."

"No. Compared to the women I know."

Mac leaned across the table. "Uh, Calix? How large are the women…where you come from?"

He was apparently making an effort not to say planet, as it was agreed among the three of them that no one should know about Calix's origins. If anyone was to ask, Calix came from North Dakota because, according to Annie, no one came from there.

"They are short, like me, but less muscular."

Mac's eyes widened. "You're short? Holy shit. We must look like midgets to you."

"I have to admit, I have never felt so large before. I do not know what is worse, needing help to reach the top shelf where I came from, or forgetting to duck and hit my head on the archway at the cabin here. I forget a lot."

"I'm sure it'll become a habit soon enough."

A lady, who Mac said was a waitress, stopped by their table. He asked for two more beers, and when she returned with them, he paid her with paper money and told her to keep the change. Currency apparently came in many different varieties and none of them gold. Somehow Calix would have to convert it over.

"Why don't we go over and introduce ourselves? You take the blonde and I'll take the brunette."

"Where will we take them?"

Mac shook his head and picked up his beer. "I meant talk. You talk to the blonde. See if she affects you any. Okay?"

One person was as good as another. He took a deep breath and mentally recited the lines Mac and Annie suggested he use. Why he was nervous, he did not know. According to Annie, he did not look any different than the men of this planet. Even naked. Which was nice to know if he should ever be without his clothes.

They got up and walked over to the women. The blonde's eyes widened and she smiled.

"Hello. My name is Calix. This is my cousin, Mac. Can we buy you two a drink?"

"Calix?" The brunette asked. "That's an unusual name."

"It's an old family name," Mac said.

The blonde elbowed the brunette. "My name is Miranda. This is my friend, Justine."

Mac sat beside Justine and engaged her in conversation.

Calix inhaled. Miranda smelled nice, some floral scent, but nothing in his groin stirred. Her voice was pleasant, but did nothing to make his heart race. If he touched her without a reaction, would that mean it was not the planet affecting him? He extended his hand, like he was taught. "It is very nice to meet you."

Miranda's face reddened when she shook his hand. He did not get the same rush like he did whenever he touched Annie. Maybe this experiment would be okay.

CHAPTER 9

The two ladies excused themselves; said they'd be right back.

Mac could not believe his luck. That Annie had insisted he take Calix out was one thing. That Calix wasn't interested in Justine was the best news yet. Mac couldn't stop grinning. That woman was a knock-out and she seemed to like him just fine, too.

Calix leaned toward Mac. "I wish to leave."

"Bathroom's in the back."

"Not relieve myself. Leave. Go back to Annie."

Mac stopped grinning. "I can't believe it. You basically have your pick of the room and you want to go home? Are you nuts?"

Calix stood. "I am only here because Annie wanted to know if I was attracted to all females. Neither Miranda nor Justine affects me like Annie does. I have also not been affected by those women you call waitresses. So why not leave?"

Mac slumped in disappointment. "Ah, come on, man. At least help me hook up. I've been dry for a month."

"I do not know what you just said, but if it means I have to be involved with Miranda or any other woman, then I will not do it. If you want to stay, then stay. I can find my way back."

Oh hell. Annie would skin him alive if he did that. Which meant only one thing. Lie. It was a rotten thing to do, but what choice did he have? "If you leave so soon, Annie will just send you out again."

Calix's eyes widened. His face might have paled a little, too. "She will?" When Mac nodded, Calix frowned and returned to his seat. "But it is too loud here. My head is hurting."

Okay, loud Mac could fix. Anything to stay with Justine. "Then we'll go someplace quieter. I'm sure the girls will go for that. And then Annie will think you've tried everything and not make you go through this again."

Because, clearly, Calix did not want to do this again. The guy just didn't realize how attractive the women here found him. To have his pick of women and then pick Annie? Maybe Mac had hit him in the head with his car after all.

"What kind of quiet place?" Calix asked.

"The Donut Shack is down the street. It's pretty quiet. I'll even buy you a donut, a sweet treat. What do you say?"

Calix nodded. "I would not mind trying a new food."

"That's the spirit."

Once this night was through, Mac would definitely get Justine's number. Because when he asked if they'd rather go someplace quieter, she was all for it. If Annie weren't his sister, he'd kiss her.

* * * *

Calix added cream and sugar to his coffee and stirred. The cream made interesting swirling shapes before the liquid turned light brown. Yet he continued to stir and stare. This was his third cup. Or was it his fifth? He lost count.

"You okay, buddy?" Mac asked.

Mac had good ideas. Like picking out the donut shop. It was quiet, just like he had said it would be. And like sitting at the square table so they could sit together on one corner and the women together on the opposite corner. And like knowing what to put into coffee. Calix had tried it black, but it was bitter that way. Mac suggested the cream and sugar and that was when Calix started devouring them.

"We do not have coffee back home. Nor sugar." There was no drink that stimulated the body such as this one did to his. He could probably climb a building. As long as the building stood still. Right now, everything seemed to be moving.

"You don't?" Miranda asked.

"It's a religious thing," Mac said. "I think maybe you've had too much." He reached for Calix's mug, but Calix pulled it away.

"I am not done drinking it." He looked at the women. "I like you. You are very nice. But I like you like Mac. Not like Annie." Because Annie was different. The planet had nothing to do with it. Thinking of her made his penis hard. And drinking coffee kept it that way. Or was it the donuts? He did not know. At least he knew how to get relief, even though he would rather have Annie do the relieving.

"Who's Annie?" Justine asked.

"My sister. He has a little crush."

"I do not wish to squish her. I wish to—"

Mac grabbed Calix by the face. "Come on. Let's get you to the restroom. Excuse us, ladies."

"Yes. I could use the restroom." Calix stood and the room spun. He grabbed the back of the chair.

Mac rushed beside him. "Did you eat too many donuts?"

Calix smiled. Donuts. What a wonderful creation. "We must take some home. I like the ones with the sprinkles the best. Did you like the sprinkles? They are so tasty."

"They are pretty good. But maybe you need to lay off if you're not feeling well. Can't have you upchucking in the car." Mac continued to hold Calix around the waist as they stumbled across the room.

"What is upchuck—oh, you mean vomiting. I do not feel the need to upchuck. What I need is Annie, but she is not here."

"What do you mean you need… Ah, geez. Quit thinking about her, then."

"I tried. So I ate donuts and drank coffee. I think they made it worse, but I cannot seem to stop. They are so good. We need to take some of those donuts home."

"So you said."

Had he? His thoughts were a jumbled mess. Between his dizziness and erection, he had trouble focusing. Maybe if he was more comfortable. He started to adjust his penis when Mac jerked his arm away.

"Do not touch it in public, you hear me?" Mac hissed. "The last thing we need is to get arrested."

"It aches, Mac."

"I know, buddy, but you gotta lay off."

The floor moved in the wrong direction, but when Calix tried to right himself, Mac steered him back toward the table.

"Is the restroom not the other way?" Calix asked.

"I think it's time I got you home."

Home. With Annie. Calix smiled. "Do not forget the donuts."

* * * *

Annie flipped through the stations. Nothing on TV interested her and she turned it off. She should just go to bed. Mac and Calix could be out for hours.

Oh why did she suggest Calix see other women? Was she nuts? He was like a Greek God of lust. One look and women would fall all over him. Hadn't she?

She prayed he wouldn't do any more than kiss another woman. To let their chemistry be just between them and not have anything to do with the planet. Because she'd been stupid. So, so stupid. So what if he was an alien? He had wanted her. Her! Wasn't a moment of goodness better than no moment at all?

She picked up the book Calix had been reading. Oh sweet mother. If he tried to emulate the hero in this book, she could be in for one wild ride. If she remembered correctly, the sex had been pretty hot and explicit. Maybe she should hide her books.

Then again, maybe she should have him read them all. Or better yet, teach him. He'd probably have no problem fulfilling her fantasies. Provided she hadn't already ruined any chance of them being together.

The sound of an engine propelled her up and she dashed to the front window. Her heart leapt with joy when Mac's Cherokee came into view. Whatever caused them to return early, she didn't care. Calix was home. She yanked the front door open just as he tumbled out of the car and into the snow.

"Are you okay?" She hadn't wrapped her boot in plastic, and the moment she stepped into the slush, her toes froze, but seeing Calix on the ground urged her forward. What the hell had Mac done? They were supposed to check out the girls, not drink into a stupor.

She stupidly extended her arm, like she could actually help him up. He locked onto her hand and pulled, sending her down on top of one solid hunk of man.

His laughter floated in the air as he hugged her tight with one arm and nuzzled her neck. "Annie, Annie, Annie."

If she weren't on the verge of freezing, she'd be a puddle of goo in his arms. He seemed pleased to see her, with the way he kept saying her name over and over. Too bad he was out of it.

She looked up at her brother as he rounded the front of the vehicle. "What the hell, Mac? You weren't supposed to get him drunk."

"He only had one beer."

"One beer did this to him?"

"Uh, no. One beer did nothing to him. He started acting like this after the six or seven cups of coffee. Or the donuts. Or maybe the mixture of the two. Who knows?"

Now that he mentioned it, a sweet smell of coffee emanated from Calix as he continued to kiss her neck and say her name. Damn, he was getting better, too. Desirous shivers ran through her body. How many women had he kissed tonight?

Calix cupped her breast in that meaty hand of his and she gasped. She'd always wondered what it would be like to make love outside in the woods, but not with her brother standing two feet away and certainly not in the dead of winter.

"Hey, buddy." Mac pried Calix's arm from Annie and then helped her stand.

She missed the warmth of Calix's body, but limped her way back to the porch to get out of the snow. However, Calix was still sitting in it. His butt had to be numb by now.

Mac stood in front of Calix with his hands on hips. "What'd I tell you not to do in public?"

Calix started to stand, holding his crotch, which bulged considerably, but his foot slipped and he fell back on the snow. Had he been holding it the whole time? "Not to touch my penis." He looked down at his hand as if it were someone else's. "Are we still in public?"

"Consider me public, okay?"

Calix removed his hand from his crotch and fisted a thumb up sign. "Mac equals public. Got it." He turned those purplish-blue eyes toward her. "Annie. Can you help me get relief?"

"Okay, that's my cue to leave. I have to be at work tomorrow anyway and I can walk from my place." Mac leaned toward her. "I think we both know you're okay with him, don't we?"

She had to agree he was right in that regard. She honestly didn't think Calix would ever hurt her. Not on purpose, anyway. "What happened with the experiment?"

"All he did was talk about you. And apparently thought about you a lot, too. The waitresses did nothing for him. Justine did nothing for him. He liked Miranda, but as a person. She did nothing for him. And before the coffee drinking, he was prepared to come back here, but I talked him into going someplace quieter and, for you, he went, giving it one last shot. At least I got a date out of the whole thing. I see Justine tomorrow night."

Were two women enough to consider an experiment successful? Was it possible their attraction for one another was simply that? An attraction and not some planetary mojo? Oh, what did she care? If he wanted to be hers, then she'd take him.

Mac went behind Calix and lifted him by the shoulders. "You gotta help me, buddy."

Calix grabbed onto the car and hauled himself up. He swayed on his feet.

"Let's get you on the couch, okay?" Mac placed an arm around Calix's waist and ushered him into the cabin.

Annie placed some plastic and an afghan on the couch so Calix wouldn't get it wet. The last thing she needed was a mildew-y smell in the house. As she turned around to close the door, she noticed Calix's jeans. Sure, he looked pretty damn good in his polyester-like pants, but somehow the jeans made him more…yum. She nearly had an orgasm just looking at his butt.

After settling on the couch, Calix looked up at her and smiled. "Mac said I drank too much coffee, but it was good and I could not stop. Are you mad at me?"

He was like a little kid—although that neck nuzzling he had done earlier was nothing kid-like—and she fought back a laugh. She shook her head. "Did you have a good time?"

"I was not until the donuts. Did we bring any with us? They were very tasty. I would like another one."

"Sorry, buddy." Mac patted Calix on the shoulder. "I think you had enough for one night. I'll bring some fresh tomorrow. Okay?"

That seemed to satisfy Calix as he smiled and leaned his head back against the cushion.

Mac lightly punched Annie in the shoulder. "You and your stupid experiment. I'll come by after work tomorrow and bring dinner. See you then. Goodnight, Calix."

Calix lifted his hand in a wave, but his head remained back on the cushion and his eyes were closed.

Annie sat on the couch. "You tired?"

"No. I feel like I could run miles and then climb a building after. But if I open my eyes, the room moves." He reached out and found her hand. "Is Mac gone?"

"Yes."

"Good." He placed his free hand over his crotch and adjusted himself. He sighed and then opened his eyes. "I am sorry. You are not considered public, are you?"

She chuckled. "No. Doesn't mean I want to watch you masturbate, either." Which was probably a lie, but if he thought he could do it in front of her... Oh, who was she kidding? Her hands itched to touch him.

"I am not sure how I like masturbating. Everything I read said sex is between two partners. I want you to be my partner." He took her hand and placed it on his chest. "My heart is beating fast."

"That's probably the caffeine." She went on to explain how coffee affects most humans.

He shook his head. "I think it beats fast for you. It always does when I think of you." He turned his head and opened his eyes a crack. "May I kiss you?"

"Do you want to kiss me because you think you'll get relief down there or because you just want to kiss me?" Like it really mattered to her. She wouldn't have stopped him if he just kissed, but maybe it was better for him if he knew why he was doing it. And a little better for her heart, which was already on the verge of being lost.

"I will not lie. I do want relief, but I also know that kissing will not necessarily bring it. In fact, it could make it worse. I would like to kiss you because I like kissing you."

"Did you kiss Miranda tonight?"

He frowned. "No. But she kissed me on the cheek."

Oh thank God! "Why didn't you kiss her?"

"Because I did not want to."

"But you like kissing, right? Why wouldn't you try with her?"

He paused and his breathing became more rapid. "Because she is not you. I am sorry. I did not go into this experiment with as much anticipation as you needed. If I failed, it is because I only want to be with you. No one else has made me feel the things I feel when I am with you."

She felt like pounding her fist against her forehead and berating herself for being an idiot. Because she was one. Life should be lived, not tip-toed around. And here was this wonderful, albeit alien, guy who liked being with her. She touched his cheek and he opened his eyes a crack.

"Yes, you may." He raised his eyebrows in question and she elaborated. "Kiss me, that is."

He grinned and put his hand behind her neck. Pulling her forward, he kissed her. She opened her mouth to him and he devoured her like a man seeking water in a desert. He tasted of coffee and sugar. This was no kid, but a man with passion. A passion for her. She wrapped her arms around his neck and molded herself to him, already wet with desire.

He moaned and pulled away. "I did not understand the phrase when I read it in one of your books, but I do now. Your scent undoes me."

She was pretty much undone herself. But the couch didn't feel right. Not for a first time. Not for him. Before he could go any further, she placed her arms on his shoulders and stopped the kiss that nearly rocked her socks off. "Let's go to my bed, where it's more comfortable."

"Are you sure?"

"Yes."

Before she could stand, he was up and scooped her into his arms. But he must have forgotten about his dizziness and swayed on his feet. Afraid she'd end up on the floor, she suggested they walk together, him at her back, holding her shoulders. When they made it to her room, she sat on the bed and he knelt in front of her. He gently removed the boot from her foot, but looked lost when it came to what to do next.

She'd never deflowered a virgin before and kind of liked the power she had over him. He certainly wouldn't have any bad habits, and if he did anything wrong, well, she only had herself to blame. But was she doing the right thing? She'd like to think she was. He would eventually learn about sex. Better to learn in a safe environment where he wouldn't be hurt. And she would never hurt him.

* * * *

Calix stared at Annie. He had never really paid much attention to the female race. Someone was either pleasing to look at or they were not; however, their looks did not stop him from conversing. Annie was more than pleasing to his eyes. She was more beautiful than any woman he had ever met.

"Take off your clothes and lie down beside me." She stretched out on her bed.

"Should you not be undressed?"

"Patience."

The bulge in his pants made moving painful in a good way, but the spinning of the room made him move slowly. He wished he had not drunk all that coffee or eaten those donuts.

Once undressed and blissfully unrestrictive, he settled beside her. She stared at his penis, which only made him harder.

"Have you been like this all night?"

"Yes. I could not stop thinking about you."

She turned on her side and rubbed her hand on his chest. "In what way? The ways you read about in that book?"

It was hard to concentrate on her questions. Between the coffees, donuts, and her touch, it required more strength to focus on her words. Oh, but to have her touch him all over... No, he must concentrate. She was going to help him. "The book and the movie."

"You want to experience sex? With me?"

"Yes, very much so. But you need to be undressed." He reached for her sweatshirt.

She grabbed his hands, stopping his actions. "Yes, I do. But I think you're a little too excited."

"You mean have premature ejaculation?" He was fairly certain that would occur if she touched his penis right now. He ached for her touch, for release, but did not wish to disappoint her.

"You don't worry about that, okay?" She brushed his hair back from his forehead and smiled. "I'm going to touch you now. If you feel the need to come—ejaculate—then do it. Enjoy it. Okay? I won't get mad." Her hand rested lightly on his extended penis.

Pleasure at the touch tightened his testicles and he pointed his toes. So much better than his own hand. "Oh, Annie. Do not stop. That feels good."

Which was quite an understatement. He just had nothing to compare it to. Her hand was soft, warm, exciting. He relished the sensations she brought forward. And then...

She squeezed his penis.

He grabbed the bed covers and closed his eyes. Waves of pleasure spread out from his groin and his world exploded. He had found release from his own hand before, but not with this kind of intensity. He cried out her name as each wave hit him. She held his penis and rubbed it up and down. If she was trying to keep the mess to a minimum, it was not working. The slickness of her hand only prolonged the waves, not that he wanted it to stop. It felt like he was spraying the room. The energy seeped out of his body with each squirt of semen.

Her lips touched his ear and she whispered, "Did you enjoy that?"

"Oh yes, Annie. More than anything, but—"

"No buts. Let's clean you up, okay?" She kissed his cheek.

Were they finished? What about her?

She rolled over and pulled some tissues from the box on the nightstand. After wiping her hands, she pulled some more tissues. He hadn't realized how sensitive his penis had gotten until she touched it while wiping away the mess he'd made. Electric shocks ran through his body and he hissed. Would it be like this every time?

"I'm sorry," she said. "I should have had a warm wash cloth. I forgot how sensitive it could be after coming. Next time I'll be more prepared."

It was nice that she thought there would be a next time. But he was confused. "Are we finished? I did not give you any pleasure."

She smiled and kissed him lightly on the lips. "We are definitely not finished. But don't you feel better now? A little less…urgent?"

"I do, but what does that have to do with you?"

"I need you to take your time. Focused on more than your erection. Okay? What you are experiencing now, our male species goes through at a much younger age. I don't expect you to have control when all you want to do is come. Once you get more control, we can move onto the next step. In the meantime, I can teach you about safe sex and show you what pleases me. That's if you still want to."

He stared into her entrancing green eyes. With her, he could be a better man. "I would like nothing more than to please you."

Her smile brought him joy.

CHAPTER 10

Doug Lazar clicked through the pictures and stifled a yawn. Is this what his job boiled down to? Picture after picture of bogus alien sightings? Where was the adventure? The excitement?

Ever since he was a kid, UFOs and space had enthralled him. When he discovered the Department of Homeland Security had a secret division designed to investigate alien encounters, he thought he'd died and gone to heaven. But if he had known the division consisted of a skeleton crew—basically him and John—and boring computer searches, he might have reconsidered.

This was worse than *The X-Files*. At least Scully and Mulder got to go places.

He clicked onto the next site and stopped. Not the typical kind of picture he'd been viewing. He'd lost count of the number of photos showing "unexplained" lights in the sky—when they were easily explained—or of alien creatures tied up. If the photographers were going to use a costume, they should at least make it look realistic or at least make sure the human parts were unidentifiable.

However, this shot was of a meadow of sorts, covered in snow, except for one huge circular spot, the size of a studio apartment, in the middle. Nice touch using the Rottweiler as a reference. Something had been there before snow fell and it had to have flown away after, since there was no sign of it being lifted, dragged or driven through the snow. Even the trees and brush in the distance were undisturbed.

He clicked on the details of the photo. Taken by Jay Bryant in Spokane, Washington, just two days ago. He read the write-up of what the man encountered. Doug printed the pictures, along with the information.

He checked the appropriate government sites. Nothing going on in Spokane or even all of the Pacific Northwest.

It was probably just another bogus alien sighting, but that didn't mean the evidence was bogus. Spies, aliens, it didn't matter. Something had left that spot and it didn't belong to the government.

But man, if it were an actual alien? He could see having a real adventure then.

* * * *

Calix was tempted to put his fist through the monitor. For the past two days he had come to his ship hoping to discover some kind of information regarding unification. Did it really exist? This planet was the only other planet his people had discovered that had sentient life and they had basically forgotten it. Did unification exist back then? Or was this planet not worth the trouble?

Now that his planet was in trouble, his people could not be picky, now could they? What might happen if the people on this planet did not want his people to move here? Would there be an all-out war? If so, the people on this planet did not have a chance. They did not possess the technology to win that kind of war. But would his people really resort to that kind of destruction?

No, no, no. His people were peaceful. They did not fight. He was just feeling... What was he feeling? Annie would be able to tell him, but then he would have to confide in her and he wanted more information before he did that.

If only he could find absolute proof of what his people would do. But how would they label it? That was his problem. It could be labeled something innocuous, something the documenter or their manager would understand. Because no one else would care. He certainly had not cared when he was a teacher. He had been told what to teach. He had been given the documentation. The only reason he had found the failed mission of Earth 2 was because a student had asked about failed missions. It was that question that had made him think that the failed missions should have been discussed as much as the successful ones.

Mac had called it curiosity. Was Calix now curious or had he always been that way, but it was buried? Had that student uncovered it? It was what got him interested in finding new topics to teach. No other teachers were interested in that. They taught what they were told to teach.

And now he was on a different planet and his curiosity increased. Had this planet brought his curiosity more to the surface? Or… He touched his temple. Could it be… He pulled the tracking indicator out of his pocket and just stared at it.

The inner door slammed shut and the alarm went off. He stuffed the chip back in his pocket.

"Calix?"

Annie. He pushed the override button, re-opening the inner door and halting the gas that would have rendered her unconscious.

"What are you doing here?" While he was happy to see her, she should not be walking through the woods in her condition. What if she had reinjured her ankle? Who would have known she was out here? Before he could voice his concern, she wrapped her arms around his neck and pulled him down for a kiss. He yielded and immersed himself into the softness of her lips against his. Relished the hint of chocolate on her tongue. He liked the way she said hello.

"I missed you. What have you been doing out here all morning?" She eyed her laptop, which sat on the console. "Am I that noisy you have to come out here for some peace?"

"Noisy? Never. You were busy working and I came out here to see if I could transfer some information to your laptop to review in the comfort of your home, but I am not having any luck." He hugged her, molding her soft body up against him. She had said she liked being held. He certainly enjoyed holding her.

"What kind of information?"

A reason for his existence? He most likely would not find that in the files. "About my mission."

"You know, you've never told me what that is exactly."

Because he had doubts. "First, tell me why you risked reinjuring yourself to visit me."

She pulled away and limped to the console, wincing and removing her coat in the process. "It's not like I haven't ventured out into these woods before. I know what I'm doing." She stared at the monitor. "Is that your language or some strange code?"

Just as he suspected, she had reinjured herself. Her limp had been nearly unnoticeable yesterday and this morning. He tossed her coat on the bed and scooped her up. She uttered a surprised squeal, but did not protest. Instead, she wrapped her arms around his neck and smiled. He sat in the chair with her in his lap, which may have been a mistake. He was already growing hard for her. "That is my language, but also strange code. The words do not make sense to me."

"That's because you're not a computer geek." She looked at the screen. "So what's the problem?"

"I believe it is a connectivity issue, but it is not important. Now that you are finished with your work, I am finished, too." He nuzzled her neck. Her scent made him wild. For the last two days she had pleasured him and shown him what she liked, but they still did not have sex. She had insisted he wear a condom, but every time she touched him to slip one on, he would lose control. She had said it would happen soon, that he was getting better. And he was, but he was also feeling a new emotion—impatience. He would get that condom on. "Is Mac home? If not, I'd like to go back and try again."

"You *are* a man, always willing to try again." She wriggled her butt against his erection, and he smiled at his control. "He's not home, but I don't want to go back."

Disappointment gripped his heart. His failures must have been too much for her. "You have changed your mind."

She freed the bottom of his shirt and pulled it up, rubbing her hands over his chest. He gasped. Would he ever get used to the sensations she caused? He hoped not. But why was she touching him if she did not wish to go back and try again?

"No, silly. It means I brought the condoms with me."

"Oh." His heart lightened and he could not stop grinning. She had not given up on him. He would make sure to do it right this time. He kissed her and played with her tongue while she ran her fingers through his hair. She made his body tingle. In a good way.

"You are such a good kisser. I could kiss you all day."

"I enjoy it very much, too. But I would like to experience more."

"I know you do. I want that, too. I think I've been going about it all wrong. So today I won't touch you when you put on the condom. Okay?"

He still did not believe he needed to wear the condom. She had been adamant he use one, saying it protected against disease and unwanted pregnancy. He only saw it as a barrier between them, since he did not have any disease and breeding did not occur on his planet. But whatever made her happy, made him happy, so he obliged.

"Let's get rid of this." She pulled the shirt over his head. "Now, your turn."

She raised her arms and smiled. The past two times she had gotten herself undressed. This was a first for him. With confident hands, he removed her top.

"You are wearing a red bra today?" The last two times they had been white.

"I wish I had a green one. I know how much you like that color."

"Because it is the color of your eyes."

She caressed his cheek. "Oh, Calix. You say the sweetest things. Now, show me what you learned."

He would show her and make her proud.

* * * *

Annie stared into Calix's eyes. The purplish-blue had practically taken over the pupil.

She knew the last couple of days had been frustrating for him. Who knew a condom would be so difficult to put on, or maybe he was just so sensitive that any amount of pressure was enough to make him blow. Hadn't stopped her from showing him what she liked, though. And frankly, he was a better student without the raging hard-on. But she wanted more than his finger probably just as much as he wanted to be more than a finger to her.

"Annie." He held her head and ran his thumbs across her cheeks, an action she enjoyed very much. "You are so soft."

"And you are strong." She ran her hands along his pecs. Man, was he strong.

His lips brushed across hers, teasing her. He claimed her with a hungry kiss, thrusting his tongue in and exploring her mouth. Ooh, damn. He'd gotten better. Much better. She wrapped her arms around his neck as he ran a hand up under her bra. There was something sexy about having one breast freed. Her nipple hardened at his touch and the lower half of her body clenched. He kneaded the nub just the way she liked.

Yep. He was an A-plus student. She was twisted like a pretzel and wanted to face him so she swung her leg around, straddling him. His erection pressed right up into her crotch. Mistake or not? He seemed to be holding his own, so maybe he had better control than she gave him credit for. She let up a little, just in case.

He took the nipple into his mouth. Sweet Jesus, she was in heaven. He flicked it with his tongue and she grabbed his head so he wouldn't leave. Could she come from this alone? Never had before, but there was always a first time, right?

Grasping her hips, he ground into her while he continued to suck on her nipple. She was wet with desire. Her skin was on fire. She removed the bra and tossed it away. "Oh, baby. We need to get naked. Now."

Calix continued sucking on her breast. Laving the nipple. But she wanted more.

She grabbed his head and dislodged him. "Did you hear me? Naked. On the bed. Now."

And if he didn't take her there, she'd just have to drag him herself, sore ankle or not.

* * * *

Calix smiled. Today, according to Annie, he would lose his virginity, but he would not lose control.

He kissed her again, tasting her full sweetness while he stood. She wrapped her legs around his waist, making it easier to carry her. Or was it? His penis was pressing up against her crotch, which hugged it and rubbed it. Seemed the condom was not his only issue. Taking deep breaths, he focused on getting them to the bed.

Thankfully unimpeded, his shin bumped against the bed. He lowered her onto the semi-soft mattress.

She grabbed the waistband of his jeans, bringing him back to the here and now, and pulled him closer. When he went to unbutton, she slapped his hand away and ran her fingers down the length of his hardness. His testicles tightened and he inhaled through his teeth. *He would not fail. He would not fail.* If he repeated it over in his head, maybe he would succeed.

She leaned back on her arms. "I'm sorry, I keep forgetting, but it's your fault. You just seem so…experienced. Go ahead and undress. I'll stop playing."

"Is playing part of sex?"

"Yes. It's what we've been doing. But I promised I wouldn't touch you this time."

"Because I am a virgin."

"Which we want to remedy today. Right? I just hope you like it."

He could not imagine not liking sex. So far it was quite enjoyable. He kicked off his shoes and quickly undressed. He then gently removed her boot and shoe while she unbuttoned her jeans. Arching her back, she slid the pants down over her hips revealing a patch of dark hair covering her sex.

His heart hammered in his chest and his penis jerked. Control. He must keep it. For her.

She slid over and patted the bed. He climbed in beside her, intending to mount her, when she handed him the condom.

He moaned. The final test. He had hoped she had forgotten.

"If you don't want to do this—"

He snatched the packet from her fingers, cutting off her sentence but eliciting laughter from her. He could do this. Just because the other four times he tried putting the condom on initiated his ejaculation did not mean this time would bring about the same result.

He tore open the packet and slowly rolled the cold, slimy thing over his penis. Maybe because it was colder this time, or maybe he had more control, he managed to keep from ejaculating, although the rubber was tight in a pleasing way. So far, so good, although his control was slowly fading. He started to roll on top of her when she placed her hands on his chest.

"Let me on top, okay?"

"Why?"

"Well, you're kind of big and a little anxious."

"You think I will hurt you?"

"Not on purpose, no. Let me show you how it's done this first time, okay?"

He did not wish to hurt her so he nodded. She straddled him, but he still had not entered her.

She leaned down and kissed him lightly. "I like it when you touch my breasts."

And he liked touching her breasts. But her body shook with little tremors. Was she just as nervous as he was? How could that be? She had had sex before. He ran his hands over her smooth thighs, up along her curvy hips, and ended at the two soft mounds. When he rubbed his thumbs over the tips, she closed her eyes and moaned. The tremors disappeared.

"Yes, like that." Slowly, she raised her hips, held his penis—something he tried not to focus on, but it felt so, so good—and guided him into her.

Pressure built as she lowered down around him. He nearly fisted his hands, squeezing her breasts, but stopped before he caused her any pain.

Pleasure at the tightness and warmth surrounding his penis nearly sent his heart shooting out of his chest. She rose and lowered, creating a friction of sorts, and the more he toyed with her nipples, the more she moaned. In all the practices they had partaken in, she had always been silent while he nearly screamed his head off. He was sure he had done something wrong when maybe she just needed more than a finger.

Once he understood the technique of the mating ritual, he slid his hands down to her hips and held her as he pumped into her. Her eyes squeezed shut and her breathing became labored. Sort of how he reacted when he came close to ejaculating. He continued the rhythm of sliding in and out, reveling in the tightness, but wishing for more skin. More moisture.

Suddenly, he felt more of her. More heat. More friction. Wetness.

No wonder the men of this planet sought out sex. Why were they not doing it all the time?

She screamed and her sex convulsed around his erection as she shuddered. The constant squeezing and the contact—he was sure they were now skin to skin—was all it took for his own release. He lost control as explosion after explosion of pleasure shot out of him. Something primal filled him and he screamed her name over and over.

She had told him she was afraid he might not like it. She had nothing to fear.

* * * *

Annie collapsed onto Calix's chest as the last bit of her orgasm crashed through her in wave after wave. He held her tight as he cried out her name. Something she was coming to love hearing him do.

But dang, she'd never had sex so explosive like that. Had never come so hard or so quickly. Past boyfriends always had their work cut out for them. Heck, she had to do most of the helping. But Calix, he was different. He treated her as if she were important. As if her feelings mattered. And here he was, a virgin. Well, used to be. God, could he get any better? If so, she just might die from the sheer enjoyment of it all.

He rolled over on top of her. "Now that we have mated, does this make us married?"

Oh, the things he discovered blew her mind. "No, Mr. Alien. We just had sex. We didn't get married."

"Just sex?" He furrowed his brow. "Not mated?"

She rubbed the wrinkles away. "Well, no, not *just* sex. Really great sex. Mind-blowing sex. But marriage is different, and while we technically mated, we're not mated to one another." Gee, what books had he read? Her paranormal ones? "Do you understand?"

"I thought marriage is another word for mated."

"Not really. Marriage is a declaration of love between two people. To be there for each other. Forever. It doesn't usually occur until the people have known each other, like for a year. Doesn't stop people from having sex, though. That's just the physical act. The mating. It's when you have sex with someone you like, that it becomes special. It was special for me, but we are not married. Okay?"

"I understand. It was special for me, too." He pulled out.

No, not yet. She wasn't ready. Just like that, she missed his warmth.

"Guess I made a bit of a mess." He plucked the remnants of his condom—his burst condom—off his penis.

Her heart nearly stopped. "Oh no. No, no, no!"

His eyes widened. "Did I hurt you?"

"No, but—"

"So my semen is not dangerous to you?"

"No, of course not." Except…he was an alien. Could he have any diseases? And then she had missed taking her pill for two days in all the excitement of his arrival, not to mention how lax she'd been since Denny left. What if? "That condom was supposed to prevent pregnancy and disease."

"Are you sick?" he asked.

"No, but—"

"Neither am I, so do not worry. I cannot get you pregnant." He went into the small lavatory.

What did he mean by that? Did they have birth control for the men on his planet?

He climbed back into the bed and pulled her close.

She loved being in his arms, but her mind was reeling. "Are you sterile?"

"I do not understand the question."

"How do you know you can't get me pregnant?"

"We do not breed like your people do." He kissed her along her jaw. "I want to have sex with you again. May I be on top this time?" His mouth moved over hers before she could answer him.

She wanted nothing more than to have him again. Especially since he knew what to expect now. Sterile or not sterile, the ruined condom kind of spoiled her mood. She placed her arms on his shoulders and he stopped. "I'm still a little confused about the not-getting-me-pregnant part."

He rolled off her and sat up. "Since my people do not touch, we do not have sex. New life is created in the laboratory."

"But how do they get the eggs and sperm? You need those for creating life."

"I do not know."

"What about your animals? How do they procreate?"

"All new life is created in the laboratory. There is no breeding. It is not like it is on your planet."

Maybe not, but the same ingredients were needed. Weren't they? "How often do you see a physician? How do they touch you?"

"I am required to visit a physician once a year. I suppose they wear gloves."

"You suppose? You don't know?"

"I am rendered unconscious."

"Why knock you out if they wear gloves?"

"I was told it makes the experience pain free. And it does. I never feel any different after."

Or, it was their way of taking something without the donor realizing it. Holy shit on a shingle. His sperm was swimming upstream looking for something they never had a taste of before: her egg. She prayed the birth control pills had kicked in. She prayed she wasn't ovulating.

She'd never thought she'd have kids, always figured she wouldn't—they just seemed so messy. But having them with a husband was one thing. Having them with a guy who could literally blast off into outer space was another.

"Annie, your planet is different than mine. I have never felt the things I feel as I do here. I have never wanted to be with a woman before I came here. Your planet has awakened me."

Or that accident did. Oh shit. "What about that chip you lost? Is it possible it's more than a tracking indicator?"

He fingered his wound. "In what way?"

"In a way that your sexual desires are curbed."

He appeared thoughtful, maybe she got through to him. "No. If that were true, then..."

"Then what?"

"Nothing. It is this planet. I am sure of it."

"So, you're saying the same thing happened to your people when they visited back in 1830?" She kind of hoped it had. She hated to see him disillusioned.

He got up and went over to the chair at the console and sat down. "There is no documentation to indicate it had." He stared at the monitor with the foreign words. Suddenly, he grabbed it and screamed, "Why can I not find it? Why?"

Something was wrong if he felt the need to yell at a piece of equipment. She hopped on her good foot over to him and held his arms to get him to release the screen. He had cracked the casing. "What is it you're trying to find? Maybe I can help."

His eyes watered as he stared at her. He grabbed her face. "I do not want to go back and I do not want to lose you."

Her heart felt tons lighter knowing he wanted to stay. With her. But he was afraid of something. "What's the matter?"

He kissed her. Hard. As if she was going to bolt or something. As if that were even possible. His tongue probed her mouth and before she knew it, he lifted her by her thighs and carried her back to the bed. His erection was back big time, but she wasn't going to let him distract her with sex. Regardless of how much she wanted him.

She scooted back and held her hand out. "Calix. I'm saying no right now. Do you understand what I mean?"

"I just wanted one last time before…" He lowered his head. "I am sorry."

Before what? She reached out and touched his arm. "Hey, I'm not saying no forever. You need to talk to me. Sex isn't the answer for everything. Forget what Mac told you."

A small smile formed. "He has not told me anything. He does not like to discuss sex."

Probably just as well. He'd just give Calix another movie. "So, tell me what your mission here is."

Calix stared at her with those purplish-blue eyes of his. Fear made them seem lighter somehow. "I was to observe and report back my findings."

"So you've said before. Why observe?"

"In about seven years, my home planet will be destroyed by a comet."

What? She covered her mouth as she gasped for air. A whole planet destroyed? Would that mean Calix would be destroyed, too? No wonder he didn't want to go back. She wouldn't either. "Oh my God. Isn't there anything your people can do to stop the comet?"

He shook his head. "We do not have the ability to move something so large."

Who did? "Are you here to see if Earth is a suitable planet to inhabit?"

He shook his head. "We already know we can live here. I am here to determine whether or not your people will accept us."

Well, he was in for a surprise. If America had issues with foreigners entering the country, what might they think of actual aliens wanting to move in? "If we do not agree, what happens? War?"

He stared at her. "More like annihilation."

"What? You can do that?"

"I believe so. I just cannot find the documentation to prove my theory."

"But why would they want to annihilate us?"

He stood and she realized he was still naked. It took all her effort to listen and not stare as he paced inside the small ship. "Do you not kill bugs that are unwanted in your house? Or even outside? Have they done anything to you to warrant such behavior? No. Yet you kill them anyway. But if there was hope you could work together with the bugs, live in peace and harmony, would you then spare their lives?"

She pulled the cover over her body to keep from shivering. He would have to bring up bugs. She hated those suckers and shuddered at the thought of living in a house full of them. But she got his point. "I suppose."

"I do not believe my people wish to annihilate anyone."

Well that was good. She certainly didn't want to be annihilated. "Okay, say our people accept you. Then what?"

"That is what I am trying to discover. I was told it was called unification, but the meaning I was given was vague. I do not know how it is achieved. It is somewhere in those files. I am sure of it. Nothing is hidden in our world, because no one has enough curiosity to wonder about it. If it did not affect my job, I did...not...care." He sat on the bed beside her and touched the scar where the chip had been. "But I care now. Why?"

She rose to her knees and hugged him. His arms tentatively came around her and he buried his head into her neck.

"What are you going to tell them?"

"I do not know. I have to report in next Saturday."

She pulled away and held his face. "That gives us a week to figure something out."

"How come you are not angry with me?"

"For what? Doing your job?" She shook her head. "So...I might have a small anger issue." She stopped at the raising of his eyebrows. "Okay, I have anger issues, but not with you. You bring out the nice in me."

"I like you nice." He smiled and stared at her lips before leaning in for a kiss. As he explored her mouth, he lowered her down to the bed. His erection returned.

She should stop him and get a condom, but heck, his seed was already swimming around in her. If she was ovulating this minute, a condom would be useless. But next time, yeah, next time she would make sure there were some close at hand.

CHAPTER 11

Calix continued to search for unification with no luck. There had to be a better way of locating the information he needed.

"That has got to be the craziest bathroom I've ever used," Annie said upon exiting the lavatory. "Who thought you could be clean without water? I am clean, aren't I?"

"Probably cleaner than water can get you." He looked up from the ship's monitor. How was it that one person could make his life so wonderful? He not only enjoyed her company, but the sex was unbelievable. Once he realized he wouldn't hurt her and did not have the barrier of the condom, their mating had only intensified. He liked being on top and in control, especially when he was able to get her to orgasm twice before his own release. And now that he was no longer a virgin, he looked forward to playing without any more premature ejaculations.

He might not be married, or mated, to Annie, but he felt a connection with her he had never felt with anyone else. Not just touching, either. Although, he could touch her forever and still not get enough.

Staring at her now, standing so close to the bed, research was the last thing he wanted to do. Time was running out, though. He—no, they—needed a plan before he was to report back to his planet.

"No luck yet?" She leaned over him and looked at the monitor.

Her scent filled him with desire once again. He grabbed her hips and settled her on his lap.

"I think I've created a monster," she said, but made no move to leave.

"I just wish you could help me. This is becoming…frustrating." Actually, it was already frustrating. He had never had such problems searching for data before. But then, he had known exactly what to look for.

"Do you have a search function?"

"Yes, but I cannot get it to work."

"Maybe you're searching for the wrong words. Have you tried searching for 'procedure' or 'process'?"

He had not. But when she went to get up, he extended his arms on either side of her and placed his fingers on the keyboard, in essence trapping her.

"Sneaky," she said. "You could have just asked me to stay."

He thought of the times she had tricked her brother into getting her way and finally understood. "Ah, but this is so much better."

Her laughter reverberated through him as she leaned back against his chest. "You won't get an argument out of me."

He entered 'procedure' and so many documentations appeared on the screen he had to scroll several times to even see them all. He smiled. He could not believe how simple that was. As he quickly scanned the list, he found a couple of sources that could possibly be what he needed, but he paused his scanning on one particular documentation. It was on reproduction.

She had been outwardly upset when the condom broke. Even his reassurance about getting her pregnant did not seem to cause her any relief. Later, when he was alone, he would check out that source. But not now. He did not want her around to misjudge his reaction.

"Have you found what you're looking for?"

"I hope so." He selected one of the sources on unification and was bombarded with screen after screen of data. It would take him several hours to read through it all. If it was even the correct documentation.

"Maybe I should leave you to your reading."

He shook his head. "I do not wish to read all this here. It is much more comfortable back at the cabin."

"But I thought you couldn't copy—"

"I forgot I had this." While he had been looking for something that might transfer the data to her laptop—not that he expected he would, but he had to at least try—he had found something better. Something that *would* work. "I will be able to transfer the files to this portable reader. It will probably take several hours to download everything, but once I do, I will be able to read it back at the cabin." He hugged her close. "Thank you for helping me find the files."

"Hey, I didn't do anything. You'd have figured it out eventually."

"Maybe." He plugged in the device and selected everything. He clicked on the transfer button. So easy. If only he had found that device sooner, but better late than never. "It says it will take a few hours to complete. In the meantime…" He nuzzled her neck and inhaled her wonderful scent. She tipped her head sideways to give him better access. He had been semi-hard while she sat on his lap, but now his erection strained to be released. He tugged on her chin and turned her head so he had better access to her lips. The kiss had barely started when she pulled away.

"Calix, not here."

"But we are alone."

"I know, but the condoms are at the cabin. We'll just have to go back there."

He had no problem going back to the cabin, but he did not like the condom. "But we did not use one the last time."

She cupped his face in her hands. "That was my mistake. I should have said no. Calix, I'm sorry. I don't want to get pregnant, and unless you can show me proof that you're sterile, then you'll just have to wear a condom."

He glanced at the monitor. Was the proof he needed in that file? And was not wearing a condom really that important? No, it was not. As much as he disliked it, if wearing the condom made her happy and at ease, he would do it for her.

* * * *

Buster lifted his head and barked. That only meant one thing.

Jay turned off the tap on the kitchen sink and listened. Sure enough, a car was driving up the lane. He placed the clean plate in the dish drain and wiped his hands on the dry towel hanging on the oven door.

By the time he reached the big window, Buster had his paws on the sill and continued to bark.

Jay patted the old dog's head. "You can hush, now. I see them."

Buster apparently didn't care, or he was informing the neighbors. What few remained in the winter.

Two men drove up in a black Chrysler 300 and pulled alongside Jay's old Ford Bronco.

Jay grabbed his coat and walked out to the porch, keeping Buster inside the house. The dog apparently found the slight impolite and voiced his opinion about the whole matter. The barking turned into a wail.

An icy wind whipped across the yard and Jay huddled inside his coat. By the afternoon, the brilliant blue sky would be a thing of the past and the muddy driveway would look clean with fresh snow. At least, that was what the weather girl predicted.

The driver, a dark-haired, college-aged yuppie, stepped out of the vehicle. The man clearly didn't have any sense or his car was super warm. He did not wear any kind of outerwear. Just a black business suit. "Are you Jay Bryant?"

"Who wants to know?" Jay nearly chuckled. He'd always wanted to say that.

The other occupant, a man a few years older, seemed to have more sense. He exited the vehicle wearing a blue knit cap and a thick overcoat. So much for having a super-warm car.

The driver answered, "I'm Doug Lazur. From Homeland Security. We talked on the phone."

Jay stared at the other gentleman. "And your friend?"

"My partner, John Harper. Can we come in? It's kind of cold out here."

"Are you really here about the aliens?"

Doug flashed a model's smile. "That's what we're trying to find out."

Jay nodded. Or they were here to punk him or some such thing. "You got badges?"

They both pulled out identification, and Jay stepped down to get a better look. Seemed real enough, but what did he know? People could fake things nowadays.

"Homeland Security, eh? They have a division on aliens now?"

"We do, but it's not common knowledge. Most people don't believe in extraterrestrials, but you do, don't you, Mr. Bryant?"

That he did, but he didn't go blabbing about it. Probably why Homeland Security didn't either. Some people might not take a fancy that their tax dollars were going into alien research.

John went to the trunk and pulled out something resembling a large tackle box.

"Wrong time of year to be fishing, don't you think?" Jay asked.

"Depends on what you're fishing for." Doug walked up the steps and stared at the window. He smelled too fresh, like one of those dryer sheets. "Is your dog going to be a problem?"

Buster was jumping and barking, making a spectacle.

"Nah. He's just mad he couldn't come outside." Jay reached for the doorknob.

"Wait!" Doug pulled Jay's hand down. "We need to dust for fingerprints."

"Fingerprints? You have a database of alien fingerprints?"

Doug laughed. "Well, no. But we need to eliminate a possible human interaction."

"That ship wasn't created by any human on this planet. And the language wasn't any of ours, either."

"And how do you know this? Have you seen all our space shuttles? Have you heard all of our languages?"

Jay couldn't say he had, but it sure looked and sounded alien. But then, so would Russian. "I guess I see your point."

He let Doug open the door with his gloved hands. Buster quieted and sat, eyeing each person as they entered the cabin. Doug gave the dog plenty of leeway, while John just plowed right on in.

Jay wasn't sure what he got himself into, but if these guys could prove aliens landed on their planet, he was all for it.

* * * *

Sitting on her bed recovering from another mind-blowing sexual encounter, Annie reached over to her nightstand and picked up the box of condoms. Just as she thought, the expiration date was years away. So why did the stupid things keep breaking?

"Damn it!" She threw the box against the wall. Condoms flew in every direction, littering her bedroom floor.

That little outburst was enough to bring Calix from the bathroom. He sat on the bed and held her. "It is my fault. I am sorry. Please do not be mad."

Bitter laughter erupted from her mouth and she buried her face in her hands. It wasn't his fault any more than it was hers. Damn. Did they make them in super big and super strong? Did it really matter? There was no way she would chance that again. As much as it disappointed her, sex would be put on hold until her next cycle or he found proof of his sterilization. If she had to wait for her cycle and it came like it always did, then it wouldn't matter. The pills were working. And if her cycle didn't come… Well, she just wouldn't think about that unless she had to. One week wasn't long. Oh, who was she kidding. The next week would feel like an eternity.

She lowered her hands and tried to offer a smile, even though her heart wasn't in it. "I'm sorry. I didn't mean to blow up at you like that. It's just the odds of breaking two condoms…"

He pulled her down onto the bed and held her close. Alternating between her arm and back, he massaged the grump right out of her. For someone who hadn't touched in the first twenty-nine years of his life, he did a pretty good job of touching now. Almost like he knew what she needed. And she needed this. She needed him.

"Is it children you do not want, or just my children?"

That question blew her mind, especially after all his denials. "You said you couldn't have kids."

"I believe I cannot, but you apparently believe I can."

Had she hurt his feelings or was he really trying to understand? "I'm not ready to be a mother. Don't know if I ever will be."

"It has nothing to do with me being from another planet?"

"Hard to say. I've never been with an alien before you." She laughed, but he must not have gotten the joke since he just stared at her and cocked his head. "Seriously, we've known each other less than a week. It's too soon to plan a family."

"So it is time you need?"

"I told you about marriage. I would like that first. I would like a forever. But you can't give that to me, now, can you?"

He tilted her chin up so she would look at him. "Annie, I am not going back."

The intensity of his gaze bore into her very soul. She'd love nothing more than to have him stay. To get to know him better. Maybe have a life with him? Yeah, as if that would ever happen. He was from another world! She needed to stop being delusional. "That doesn't mean you'd stay here, either, does it? What if your people find another suitable planet? One that was uninhabited. Wouldn't you go back to them? They're your people."

Before he had a chance to answer, someone knocked on the front door. Great timing. Who the heck would drive all the way up here without calling first? If it was Mac, he would have just let himself in, probably all the way into her bedroom if he wasn't thinking. She sat up to get her robe, but her boot was across the room.

"I will see who it is." Calix grabbed his pants and quickly slipped them on, zipping up as he walked out the door.

The room became cold without him in it. She scooted to the edge of the bed and stood, gingerly putting weight on her sore ankle. Pain shot up her leg. For someone who was supposed to be taking it easy, she had done everything but. Traipsing through the woods earlier had been a mistake, but she wasn't about to tell him. He hadn't let her do much walking after that anyway.

"Well, hello!" That sing-song voice carried all the way down the hall. "Calix, right?"

Shit, shit, shit! What the heck did Portia want?

* * * *

Calix let Portia into the cabin and quickly closed the door. He had come out here without his shirt on and the frigid wind cut into his skin.

"I will tell Annie you are here." He turned toward the hall.

She grabbed his arm and stopped him. "Don't rush away. I'm sure she heard me anyway. So, you guys are working on a Saturday, huh? If I'd have known this was your work attire, I'd have been up here much sooner."

A strong floral scent assaulted him and he wrinkled his nose. She ran a finger down his chest and tugged at his waistband. While her touch did not cause him pain, he recoiled all the same. For some reason he did not want her to touch him. Plus, she just smelled wrong. He grabbed her wrist and pulled it away.

Portia pouted. "Don't tell me she got her hooks into you already. But then, I haven't met a man who didn't like a little extra on the side. I won't tell her, I promise," she whispered as she cupped his testicles.

He gasped at the touch. Why was she doing that? Did she wish to have sex with him? He backed away quickly, disconnecting her hold, but not before his penis reacted. Could it be Annie was right in a different way? Maybe he wasn't drawn to women; the women were drawn to him. Was that why Annie liked him? And Miranda? Now Portia? Should he have given more time to that experiment?

When Annie emerged from the hall, he turned to hide his semi-erection.

"Wow! Someone just got out of bed, didn't they?" Portia raised an eyebrow at Calix. "Exactly what kind of work do you do? And can you do it at my place?"

He glanced Annie's way, keeping his erection hidden. She had on her jeans and a blue sweater, but her hair was pointing every which way.

"Nice, Portia. He's not a whore."

"I never said he was."

"What do you want?" Annie placed her hands on her hips.

"Is that any way to treat a cousin who came up here to help?" Portia slipped her coat off and held it out. She wore jeans similar to Annie's and a red, fuzzy sweater. "There's apparently a big storm on the way and Mac asked if I would take you shopping. I asked him why he just didn't do it, but he was a little…indisposed." She glanced briefly at him before returning her attention to Annie. "I guess it's going around, huh?"

He shot another glance Annie's way. Her face reddened, but she did not take Portia's coat. "That's very nice of you, but I think I'll be okay. I wish you had called first."

"I did. Your phone dead or something?"

"What?" Annie rushed back to her office, limping along the way.

He knew she had been using her ankle too often. Had he been to blame, wanting sex all the time? Somehow he would get her to rest. The sex could wait.

Portia stood closer to him. "I didn't see a car out front. Do you need a ride home?"

"No. My place is not far." That was the standard answer Annie and Mac had said to give, and in truth his ship was not that far.

"Oh. How can you stand living out here? It's so…rough." Her eyes lit up and she placed her hands on his chest. "Is that the way you like it? 'Cause I can be rough."

He did not understand her, but could not very well tell her that. He assumed it had something to do with sex, though. Mac had mentioned that Portia was hungry for men. At first Calix had thought she ate them, but Mac went on to explain some women crave sex more than others. Which was probably why she grabbed him the way she had. "I do not wish to have sex with you. I like Annie."

She backed away and headed for the kitchen. "Sure you do. Don't all men? But when she gets bored with you and tosses you on the side of the road like she has the others, call me. I don't mind leftovers."

Others? What others?

She opened the refrigerator, freezer, and then several cupboards. When Annie returned, Portia said, "Girl, I think you might want to reconsider my offer. Your supplies are…lacking."

"Fine, fine, fine!" Annie said. "We'll go to the store. Calix, in case you forgot, your coat is in my office."

He had not forgotten, but did not wish to accompany Portia anywhere. "I will just stay here and work on that…project I need to finish." Hopefully she understood which project he was talking about, and he could probably get a lot read while she was gone.

Annie looked at him with sadness in her eyes and she opened her mouth to most likely speak when Portia exclaimed, "No working on a Saturday. You'll have all the time to work after the snow gets here. Besides, don't you need food, too?"

"He does," Annie said. "We won't be long. Besides, I'm sure the download hasn't finished yet. You can access it when we get back. I'm sure it will be done by then."

Seemed he was going to the store. With Portia. A weight settled on his shoulders as he went to get his coat. And shirt.

* * * *

Sitting on the couch, Jay held Buster by the collar. Not that the dog was trying to get at the two agents. But Agent Lazur had insisted Jay subdue the dog and holding him seemed like a quieter option. Agent Harper stared at a hand-held contraption that was supposed to identify who, if anyone, the prints they found on the doorknob belonged to. Taking fingerprints seemed like a waste of time, but it was their time, not his. What else was he going to do? He'd already gone shopping. All he had left to do was wait for the snow to arrive.

"Got a hit," John said. "Do you know an Eric McClelland O'Shea?"

Jay shook his head. "Got a picture?" When John turned the contraption around, a grainy image appeared. The man was young and his hair a bit on the long side, but no one Jay had ever seen. "You're saying he was in my house?"

John nodded.

Well, damn. O'Shea wasn't an alien. What the heck did he find in the woods then?

"Don't lose hope," Doug said. "We still have the other unidentifiable set. It's possible your alien has a human accomplice, that's all."

"And if their fingerprints show up on some other thingamabob, what then?"

"Then our job is done and someone else takes over."

"What do you mean? Who? Why?"

"Mr. Bryant," Doug said as he stood in front of Jay, a safe distance from the dog. "If a ship as you described actually landed in your woods, then that means someone has the ability to fly around without detection. If it's an alien, that's our division. If it's a spy, that is a huge national security issue and someone else's department. Now, why don't you take us to that site?"

Jay grabbed the leash and hooked it on Buster's collar. As he slipped on his coat, he stared at the two men. John was dressed okay, but Doug... "You might want to bundle up some. It's not exactly around the corner."

Heck, he wasn't exactly thrilled about going back out there, either. The wind had kicked up a notch. They'd be lucky to get back before the first flakes fell.

After Doug grabbed a coat from the car, Jay led them down the path. The footprints were still visible in spots and John took pictures on the way. If these guys had waited another day, he may have never been able to lead them to it. He got lucky stumbling upon it the first time. The second time he had a trail to follow.

Buster watered many a tree on their walk. The trees kept some of the wind to a minimum, but cold was cold and Jay's face numbed. His scarf was no match for Mother Nature.

Doug gasped when they arrived at the site. Enough snow remained indicating something had sat in that spot before it snowed and left after. The flattened grass and leaves also helped with that assessment. John took picture after picture.

"Did you walk over there?" Doug pointed to the trail of footprints on the other side of the open spot.

"No."

"What's that way?" John asked.

"The road?" Jay shrugged. "It's not like I've been out here before. Do you need me anymore? I need to get out of this cold. My old bones can't take much more." Old age certainly sucked. He really wanted to stick around, but it wasn't worth his health.

Doug waved him away. "Sure, sure. We can find our way back. Thanks again for showing us."

"Well, don't take too long. A storm is coming and you don't want to be stuck out here."

"Point taken."

Jay and Buster left the two men to their work, or whatever it was they were doing. He wasn't sure what good any of it would do. It wasn't like the ship was actually there to board. But he'd done his duty and reported it. That's about all he could do. At least they didn't think he was some kind of nut.

* * * *

Everyone was taking the coming storm seriously since the little store Annie normally used was pretty much cleaned out. Portia had to drive them into Spokane.

Annie slipped out of Portia's SUV and regretted not taking any pain medication before they left. Pain shot up through her leg all the way to her butt. After shopping in this monster of a store, she'd be lucky if she didn't fall down.

"You should not be walking, should you?" Calix asked.

His voice startled her. He hadn't spoken a word during the whole trip. In fact, as soon as she had returned from plugging in her cellphone, he'd been quiet and reserved. She'd love to find out what Portia had said to him, but her cousin hadn't given them a moment alone. It had to be bad if Calix didn't even want to take the trip out here. And she would have begged him to reconsider if her cousin hadn't spoken up. For once she was happy the harpy had interfered.

"Should we get one of those handicap carts?" Portia asked.

Annie was about to decline the offer, but once Calix discovered what they were, he insisted she use one. Well, more like blackmailed, although he probably didn't realize he'd done that. Would he really have carried her through the whole store? She wouldn't put it past him.

The three of them meandered through the aisles: her in the electric cart, Calix pushing the grocery cart, and Portia admiring the view. After perusing the third aisle in relative silence, Portia's cellphone went off and she stopped to take the call. Annie put some distance between them, grabbed Calix's arm, and pulled him down. "Did Portia say something to you?"

"About what?"

"About anything. You're acting strange. You haven't pulled one item off the shelf, and you were quiet on the drive here. What's the matter?"

He glanced back at her cousin. "Nothing. I am trying to blend in."

Like hell it was nothing. "Come on. What'd she say to you?" When he refused to answer, she asked for his help instead. There was one thing she desperately wanted to buy, but without any prying eyes. "Do me a favor, then? When we get to the feminine products aisle, please take Portia away."

"You need more sex products?"

"That aisle isn't for sex." What the heck had Mac told him? Calix looked confused and she promised to explain later. "Can you do it for me? Please? I'll get you some donuts."

As he contemplated her request, she was sure her plea had worked. He leaned down. "I am afraid to talk with her around. I do not want to give myself away."

She'd like to believe that's all it was, but when Portia came up to them and put her arm across Calix's back, he straightened and became stiff.

"Now, now. No funny business here," Portia said. "What else do you need?"

What Annie needed was some more free time with Calix, but since that didn't seem to be available, she continued on her way through the store to end the nightmare. Nothing she picked off the shelf was good enough. Portia would put it back and pick another brand, or find another size that was a better value. Annie just wanted to leave. Portia wanted to stock Annie's cupboards.

As they completed another aisle, a little girl came squealing around the corner and collided into Calix. He crouched down and smiled. "Hello."

The toddler giggled.

"What is on your face?"

"Come here, sweetie." Annie examined the child's face. "It's jam." She pulled a tissue from her purse and cleaned up the mess.

"You okay?" The little girl nodded and giggled between gasps. "Where's your mommy?"

"Apparently not paying attention to her child," Portia said.

A woman well into her pregnancy wobbled into view. "Annabelle! Don't ever run off like that again." She stutter-stepped when she saw Calix and her jaw dropped when she got a good look at his face. "Oh my," she muttered. Annie nearly laughed. He certainly had that effect on women.

The mother took her child's hand. "I'm so sorry about her. I just can't seem to chase her down like I used to."

Calix stared at the woman's stomach, his eyes wide. He probably didn't know she was pregnant and thankfully kept quiet.

"It's no wonder. I'm just glad she didn't hurt herself. When are you due?" Annie asked, hoping Calix would figure it out eventually.

The woman rubbed her belly. "Next month. I'm ready, too. I think he's going to be a future soccer player. Thanks for catching her for me."

As soon as the woman and her daughter were out of sight, Portia snorted. "You'd think she had better sense than to bring a child along in her condition."

Annie always thought her cousin was uncaring, now she could add heartless to the list. "Maybe she didn't have any choice."

"Sure she did. We all have a choice."

Yeah, but sometimes the choices weren't all that easy.

Portia wrapped her arm through Calix's. "I noticed you haven't bought anything. Aren't you going to stock your kitchen?"

"I do not have one." His eyes widened. Poor guy probably thought he blundered again.

Annie came to his rescue. "He means his is being remodeled. He's been using mine until it's finished."

"Oh, so you're visiting Annie a lot, then? Not that I mind, but how come Mac didn't have you take Annie to the store? I assume you have a car at your home."

Calix opened his mouth then closed it. He stared at Annie pleading for help with his eyes.

"His car is in the shop. Mac has been helping us both out."

"Oh. Well, if you ever need a ride anywhere else, you can always call me. I don't mind at all." Portia smiled sweetly, nearly causing Annie's gag reflex to kick in.

They had passed the feminine products section when they approached the aisle containing books and magazines. Calix turned to Portia. "Would you help me pick out a book to read?"

Boy, did Portia eat that up. Her face lit up as if it was Christmas morning and she discovered all the presents under the tree were hers. She looped her arm through his. "Sure. You got any favorite authors?"

Annie almost felt guilty, but Calix, bless his heart, came through, and she would reward him later. She quickly drove to her destination, found her item, and stashed it under the eggs. Since Portia had some of her own items to purchase, she most likely wouldn't be hanging around when it got rung up.

By the time they reached the cashiers, Annie's little cart and Calix's big one were filled to the top. Way more than she would have bought, but Portia did make a valid point. Calix's size alone made it appear he ate a lot, and maybe he could. Annie just hadn't seen him chow down like someone his size was apt to do. Yet.

She was thankful Mac had seen fit to get her to the store before the storm, but she was through with spending any more time with Portia. Calix had kept his distance from her cousin for the most part, but then he was also doing the same to her. Annie knew one way to get him alone again.

"Since we're in town, do you mind driving me to my car? I had to leave it at work after the accident, and if it's going to snow a lot, I'd rather have it at my place. And this way, you won't have to drive us all the way back to the cabin."

"But how are you going to drive it home?" Portia asked, staring at her boot.

"Calix can drive it."

He turned from perusing the magazine rack. "I can?"

No, he couldn't, but Portia didn't need to know that. Annie would explain it to him later. "Sure. It's not a stick."

"Do you really think that's wise?" Portia said. "I'm sure the battery has died."

"It hasn't been out there that long. And if it is dead, I'll get a jump."

Portia pouted. This clearly wasn't in her agenda. "Are you okay with it, Calix?"

When was she going to get the hint that he wasn't interested? And thank God for that. Annie wasn't sure she could compete with Portia. That woman probably worked out in a gym.

"I can drive it," he said.

Bless Calix and that alien heart of his. Annie smiled as they unloaded their groceries onto the belt. Portia took her meager items to the fast check line and neither she nor Calix noticed the item Annie kept underneath the eggs.

CHAPTER 12

Calix sat in the back seat of Portia's car. Portia had tried to get him to sit up front, but he had declined, using Annie's sore ankle as an excuse. It was safer to sit in the back. He did not want Portia to grab him again.

She drove where Annie indicated, beside a snow-covered car in a nearly empty parking lot. If this was Annie's car, it was small. Large or small, Calix was excited at the chance to drive one of these cars. He had watched Mac enough times and it had seemed easy enough.

Annie slid out of her seat and winced when her feet hit the ground. Once they got back home, he would insist she stay off her foot for the rest of the day. And while she was resting, he would go back to his ship and collect his files. He did not want to talk to Annie until he had all his answers. And he should not have delayed his researching. Sex was definitely a distraction; one he could not afford any longer.

She pushed a button on a little black device similar to the one Portia had to unlock her vehicle. Red and yellow lights from within the snow-covered mound blinked on and off. With gloved hands, Annie brushed the crusty snow from the side of the vehicle and tugged on the handle. The door did not open. "Damn it. I think it's frozen shut." She looked at Calix and pleaded with her eyes. "Would you try, please?"

His fingers were already getting stiff from the cold, but he nodded anyway. The sooner she got off that foot, the better. When he reached out with ungloved hands, she handed him her scarf to use as protection.

He tugged several times before he heard a cracking noise. Had he broken it? No, it was only the ice. He tugged harder. The door opened quicker than he expected and he lost his balance. If not for Annie pushing on his back, he would have fallen on his bottom or maybe on top of her.

She uttered a cheer, climbed inside and stared the engine, which groaned and took several seconds before it sounded like other cars. "Whew, that was close." She turned some knobs on the dash. "The heater will eventually kick in. Which will make it easier to clean off the snow. I popped…" She looked at him and smiled. "I mean unlatched the trunk, but I'm guessing it's frozen stuck, too. See if you can pry it open, okay?"

Neither Mac's nor Portia's vehicles had a trunk that he was aware of. Where would it be anyway? Before he could ask for the location, she pointed toward the back and indicated he should lift upward. Using the scarf, he brushed the snow aside and found a lever. After two tugs, and a lot of crackling noises, it opened. Ah, a little storage area.

Portia handed him a bag. "I still don't see why I can't take you home and help you unload there. It'll take forever to thaw this car enough to drive."

Calix agreed with Portia, but for some reason Annie wanted her own car. Could it be she did not wish to be near Portia any longer? Had she seen Portia grab his penis earlier? Probably not. If she had, she would have said something by now.

Annie climbed out of her car and approached the back of Portia's car, limping and wincing. "It won't take that long. Honestly, Portia, I would think you'd be glad to get home before the storm hits. I'd rather have my car at home than buried even deeper here."

Watching her fight the pain was too much for him to witness any longer. Doing his best to act and sound like Mac, he pointed at her. "You. Sit. In car. I will take care of this."

Annie smiled and brought her fingers to her temple. "Yes, sir."

Finally, she did as he requested. He must remember to use that tone of voice in the future.

As Calix transferred their bags, the wind picked up and numbed his face. When they had driven to the store, he couldn't keep his eyes off the brilliant blue sky. Now he marveled at the thick grey clouds that hung overhead, a rare sight on his planet. To think the moisture from those would turn into snow. He anticipated the experience.

Annie thanked Portia for her help, and if he only listened to her voice, he would think she meant it. Her words rang sincere. But her actions told him, and maybe Portia, something entirely different. Her hug was light and stiff and her smile did not crinkle the sides of her eyes the way they did when she smiled at him. Even Portia acted the same way. Neither one of them appeared unhappy to depart. Did the people of this planet always say one thing and mean another? And why had the travelers not noticed it in their previous visit?

Then again, had he not done the same on his own planet in regards to his headaches? Maybe they were not so different after all.

Annie started scraping the ice off the windows, keeping the weight off her right foot. It pained him each time she winced. He had thought this whole trip was unnecessary, but once they arrived at the store and he saw that they were not the only ones stocking up on food, he began to understand. Traveling in snow would be difficult, and just because these people lived in this area did not mean the weather did not affect them.

He took the tool from her hand and opened the driver's door. Apparently sounding like Mac did not work. "Please sit and rest your ankle. I can do this."

"Yeah, I guess I better if I expect to drive this thing home."

"What do you mean? I am driving."

"I only told Portia that so she would drop us off."

He would not let her drive in her condition, but how could he persuade her in the same manner she always persuaded her brother? Could he do it without her realizing what he was doing?

"So, now are you going to tell me what Portia said to you?" She had yet to sit, instead she leaned against the open driver's door.

"I will tell you when we are home and out of the pending storm. Now sit in the car and shut the door. You are letting all the heat out."

"Oooh, bossy. I kind of like that in you." She smiled and tried to maneuver her booted foot inside, but the pedals were in the way.

"A smarter woman would know when she was defeated. I find it hard to believe you will be able to manage the pedals."

She chuckled. "Yeah, that is a problem. Guess I'll just have to take the boot off."

"That is not what I—"

"Well, well, well. I thought you were incapacitated."

The male's voice seemed to come out of nowhere and interrupted Calix. He turned around. A man, about Annie's age, with short dark-brown hair, had come from the building where Annie worked.

The man must have also surprised Annie as she momentarily froze before turning around to face the speaker. "I am incapacitated, you dolt."

Calix inched closer to Annie, just in case someone started hitting. Neither person looked pleased to see the other.

"Hey, watch it, or maybe I'll report you for harassment. Oh wait. I already did."

"Very funny, Logan. What are you doing here? Don't you have an animal to kick or something?"

Logan. Annie had mentioned a Logan from her office. Someone she was forced to work with. The puffy coat he wore made it hard to determine his upper-body physique, but he stood taller than Mac by two inches at least, and his legs appeared muscular in the jeans he wore. And while he wasn't holding any kind of weapon, he frowned at Annie, making Calix wonder if Logan was a threat to her.

Logan glanced at Calix briefly. "If I recall, you're the one who kicks. Not me."

"Well, at least when I kick, the kickee deserves it."

Logan's eyes narrowed, and he took two steps toward her and stopped. "You know what? You and your ho of a friend aren't worth it."

"You son of a bitch!" Annie fisted her hands and rushed toward Logan. Calix grabbed her around the waist.

"Yeah, you better hold her back," Logan said. "Next time I'll call the cops."

"Yeah, go ahead. Call for help. I'll be sure to tell everyone you couldn't handle an injured woman on your own."

"I don't know how injured you are if you can drive. Maybe HR should know you're faking your injury."

Calix had no idea who HR was, but wanted to come to her defense about the injury. It was clear she was hurt. But if this was the way he got to drive, he would just stay quiet.

"I'm not driving, you idiot. I was just unlocking the car." And as if to prove her point, she pushed a button inside the door and limped over to the passenger side, where she stuck her tongue out at him.

"Classy. Enjoy your anger management classes, O'Shea." Logan stomped away but did not go far. His car was in the next row.

* * * *

Drumming her fingers on the door, Annie sat in the passenger seat of the idling car and waited until Logan drove away. Ooooh, how she hated that man. She wouldn't put it past the bastard to report her appearance to the boss.

"You were going to fight him?" Calix asked.

She supposed it did look that way. And maybe she would have. If not for Calix. "Not on purpose. My luck, I would have just gotten hurt again. Thanks for stopping me. He just makes me so mad, though."

"You should not be mad, Annie. I like you better when you are happy."

"Yeah? Me, too." Logan drove off and she grabbed the door handle. "Okay, let's change places."

Looking more squished than he needed, because she hadn't shown him how to scoot the seat back, Calix held onto the steering wheel. "No. I will drive."

"I only sat here because I wouldn't put it past Logan to turn me in for faking my injury." Being set up for anger management courses was bad enough. She certainly didn't want to lose her job.

Her boss had already warned her that if she couldn't get along with Logan she was gone. Didn't seem fair that he took Logan's side over hers, but then he always took the men's side.

"But you are not faking. You are hurt. Which means I drive." Calix grabbed the gear shift between the seats and tried to move it, but since he wasn't pushing the button to dislodge it out of park, the gear stayed in place.

Annie reached over and pulled the keys from the ignition, killing the engine. "If you'd rather sit here and freeze, fine. But you're not driving. It's bad enough Mac is driving without a license. At least he knows the rules of the road and how to operate a car."

"It does not seem that difficult to operate. I put this lever in the D spot and step on the right pedal to move forward and the left—"

"Fine," she interrupted, impressed he'd been paying attention. Then again, wasn't that why he was on this planet? To observe? "But you still don't know the rules of the road. And driving in bad weather is not for inexperienced drivers. Do you really want to get pulled over by the police?"

He shook his head. "So, you are saying if I know these rules of the road, you would let me drive?"

Was that what she was saying? Of course, he didn't want to get in trouble any more than she did, and he would probably be more cautious than her brother. Calix flew a freakin' spaceship, how difficult would a car be for him? "Yes, that's what I'm saying."

"Then I will learn these rules." He placed his hand on her arm. "Are you sure you can drive?"

"I won't lie to you, my ankle hurts. But it doesn't take that much pressure to work the pedals and I'll be careful. Trust me. It'll be okay." She hoped.

She was about to open her door when he grabbed her arm. "You stay here. I will come get you."

Again with the order. She wasn't helpless. She started to argue with him, then thought better of it. If it got him to relinquish the driving, she could be quiet. Besides, it would be easier to remove the medical boot without the steering wheel getting in the way.

She loosened the straps, pulled the boot off, and tossed it in the back seat. A shoe would have come in handy, but it wasn't like she hadn't driven barefoot before, and she did have on her fuzzy sock, which was currently down below her heel. It had gotten all scrunched in that damn boot. She went to pull it up and stopped. Oh crap. Her ankle had swollen up twice its size and was turning kind of purple. Teach her not to ice it and keep it elevated. No wonder it was throbbing. If Calix saw that, he'd never let her drive. She pulled the sock up, trying not to wince through the pain and thankful it covered her injury.

He came around and scooped her out of the seat. His arms were strong and she loved it when he held her. Being transported this way had its perks.

Once he had her situated behind the wheel and headed to the passenger side, Annie gently pressed down on the gas pedal. Her ankle didn't hurt any worse than walking with the boot on. She pushed on the brake and nearly went through the roof. Okay, she would just use her left foot for the brake. She could do this.

She showed Calix how to slide the seat back, but even with it as far as it could go he still looked squished. Guess Honda Civics weren't made for giants.

After starting the engine, she slowly drove out of the parking lot. *Please keep the raccoons from crossing in front of me*, she prayed.

The light ahead was red, so she applied pressure to the brake. Wrong foot, wrong foot! Shooting pain wrapped around her ankle and she gritted her teeth. The light turned green before she came to a complete stop. She breathed easier and relaxed her grip on the steering wheel as she drove through the intersection. She really didn't want to do that again.

"You are hurting. Annie, let me drive. You can tell me the rules as we go."

Crap. How much had he seen? The gritting of her teeth or the gripping of the steering wheel? Whatever. "I'm fine. Don't worry, okay?" She wanted to wipe that stern expression off his face and knew one way to do it. "So tell me what Portia said to you."

"No."

No? He'd never said that before. It must be bad if he wasn't sharing. She turned to face him. "Damn it, Calix. Why won't you—"

His eyes widened. "Watch out."

A car came from the left, cutting her off as it pulled into her lane. Out of habit, she used her right foot and slammed on the brakes. Tires squealed and the most excruciating pain flared up her leg. She cried out in agony. Every profanity she had ever heard flew from her mouth while tears streamed down her face. She pulled over, put the car in park, and laid her head on the steering wheel. Breathing might be good, but she was afraid to move.

"Annie!"

Her ankle hadn't hurt this bad when she first injured it. But then, she had been in shock at the time. She wished shock would visit her again. She wished she'd just pass out. Anything to dull the pain.

Her door opened and Calix unbelted her. With a gentleness she didn't deserve, he carried her back to the passenger side and belted her in. He wiped the tears from her face. "I will take care of you."

She believed him, too.

* * * *

Calix had never seen Annie in so much pain before. Her face was practically white and her breathing was erratic. He would get her home as soon as he could.

He had observed enough to push the seat back and put the car in gear. The tiny pedals might be a problem with his huge feet, but he would just be careful.

He made it through the city and turned on the road leading to her cabin. The driving became easier. Five miles out and the first flakes hit the windshield.

"Turn on the wipers." She pointed to the lever on the steering column.

All in all, driving the vehicle was simple. Learning the rules should be easy, too. He probably knew most of them anyway. He would not let her drive again, not until she was healthy.

The snow fell heavier, making it harder to see the road. What used to be fascination turned into frustration. Snow was pretty, but it was also dangerous. The vehicle slid a couple of times and he slowed down.

The turn for her driveway came out of nowhere and he skidded past it. After making sure no one was behind him, he reversed the car slowly. Gravel crunched as he drove on. Relief came out in one breath as her cabin came into sight. He made it. So had Mac.

Calix parked beside Mac's car, put the lever in the P spot, and turned off the engine. He rushed to Annie's side. As he unbuckled her belt, Mac came outside. "What the hell? You don't like me driving—" His eyes widened when Calix lifted Annie up. "What happened?"

Annie wrapped her arms around his neck and rested her head against his shoulder. She felt good in his arms.

"She reinjured her ankle. Would you please get the groceries from the trunk?" His finger was through the key ring and Mac took it from him.

"They'll keep in this weather. Let me get some ice for her ankle. You okay, sis?"

She shook her head.

Calix entered the house and strode to her room. As he settled her on the bed, he noticed every movement she made caused her face to wince. If he could make her pain his own, he would.

Mac came in with a blue item, placed a glass of water on the bedside table, and handed her a small container. "Here ya go."

She took the pills and sat up. When he slipped her sock off, she cried out.

"What are you doing to her?" Calix demanded.

"It's okay," she said. "He's putting ice on it."

"That will make it better?"

She nodded.

"Dang, Annie," Mac said. "It's really swollen. Shouldn't you go to the doctor?"

"With this storm coming? No way. Just wrap it."

He wrapped the blue item around her ankle. "You got something I can tie around this?"

"T-shirt. Middle drawer." She opened the container and poured out a pill. "I have to take this with food."

"I can get it." Calix knew just what to bring her, too. He grabbed the keys Mac had placed on the counter and rushed outside, forgetting about the snow. He slid several feet, but kept his balance. One day he would like to examine snow more closely, but today was not that day. After searching through several bags, he found the box he was looking for. He returned to her bedroom, holding a donut.

Tears formed in her eyes and she bit her bottom lip. "You're giving up one of your donuts for me?"

"I'll leave you two alone." Mac closed the door behind him.

Calix was confused. Did she or did she not like the donut? "If you do not like this, I can get you something else."

"No, don't. I love it. Thank you." She took the donut, pulled off a chunk, and placed it in her mouth. "You did good, getting us here. I should have known you'd be okay with driving."

"You are not driving until you are better."

"Don't worry, I don't plan on it. I don't think it will matter much anyway. If it snows as much as they say, we'll be stuck here for a while."

"Will I be able to get to my ship?"

"Eventually."

Eventually might be too long. His information was in the ship. He glanced at her bedside clock. Had enough time passed? He could not remember.

"What's the matter?" she asked.

"My downloads. I need to get back to the ship."

"Calix, it's snowing. If it comes down any heavier, you can get lost out there."

And this whole planet—as well as Annie—could be lost if he did nothing. His intuition might be wrong, but what if it was right?

He shook his head. "I will give you my chip. My tracking device will lead me back to it. But I need that data."

"Fine, but be careful. And bundle up. It's not like I can come out there and find you."

He crouched beside her and took her free hand. "I do not want you leaving this bed."

She touched his cheek. "I promise I'll stay put if you promise not to be long."

"Then I will be as quick as possible." He pulled the chip from his pocket and placed it in her palm. She was the one person he could trust more than anyone not to lose it. And the one person he wanted to come back to.

* * * *

Annie finished her donut and took her pill. Calix's chip lay on the nightstand. What kind of society tracked their people as if they were property? And if they all came to this planet, would they expect the same of her people? She shuddered at the thought. Maybe Calix shouldn't even be carrying that chip anymore. He should just get rid of it.

Of course, if he damaged it, would that only alert his people to come looking for him, or worse, just send another scout to Texas? Crap. She didn't want that to happen. Not until she knew more. She had to trust Calix knew what he was doing.

Her ankle only throbbed as long as she kept it still. If she moved, well… She didn't want to see if she could reach the ceiling. She fluffed her pillow behind her back and grabbed the paperback from the nightstand. At least she didn't have to put the groceries away. She hated doing that.

Holy shit on a shingle. The groceries! She dropped the book on the bed and started to swing her legs around. Sharp pain flared with that little movement and she jumped. Damn ankle.

She slowly moved back into a more comfortable position. Getting out of bed was out of the question. She hung her head in defeat. So much for hiding her purchase.

Mac appeared at her door. "You had sex with him, didn't you?"

Oh, crap. She didn't need to ask how he knew that. Better he found it than Calix. She held out her hand.

He entered the room and slapped the pregnancy test in her palm. "Shouldn't you have thought about this before deflowering the guy?"

"It's not like I didn't use protection. I can't help it if the protection broke." Oh God, was she really having this conversation with her brother?

"I thought you were on the pill."

"I am. I just forgot a couple of days." Every month for the past six. Yeah, she would have made a lousy Boy Scout.

He sat on the edge of the bed, and she gripped the bedcovers. Was every little movement going to cause her pain? All because she had wanted to drive?

"Geez, Annie. What the hell were you thinking? He's a virgin."

"Was."

"No. Is. He doesn't understand about love. He barely understands sex."

Calix understood more than Mac realized, but she didn't think now was a good time to bring that up. "I'm not going to hurt him. I like him."

Mac leaned close. "I'm not worried about him, doofus. I'm worried about you. I'm afraid this will end up like Denny."

He would have to bring up her ex-fiancé, the jerk who had left her when all she'd done was answer his question honestly. Was not wanting four or five kids so wrong? He had acted as if she'd cut off his balls and then wouldn't even discuss a family after that. At least she'd found out before the wedding. So what if she had been an emotional mess when he left? "It won't. How do you know I'm not using him for sex, huh?"

"Because that's not you. Be careful, sis. You don't really know him or what he's capable of."

"I thought you liked him."

"I do, but that's not the point, is it?"

No. The point was she was falling deep for Calix, and now she might be pregnant and he probably wouldn't be around to help. That's not the kind of life she envisioned. But Mac was wrong about one thing. Calix did understand about love. Hadn't he brought her a donut?

CHAPTER 13

The words could not be any clearer, yet Calix felt the need to rub his eyes. He had been sitting in his ship, waiting for the final files to download—about another hour's worth—when he decided to read one of the files to pass the time.

The file on reproduction.

Actually, it was more like a user manual.

There were records on every individual indicating parentage so that the sperm of one donor was unrelated to the egg of the other. Not all sperm and eggs collected were used, but taken yearly from each person, between the ages of 17 and 30, during their annual physicals.

He skimmed the part that explained the process. To think some person held his penis and… He shuddered. No wonder he had been rendered unconscious.

He was about to exit the site when he came upon a section on lineage. If Calix wanted to know his "family" history—who sired him and who he sired—he only needed to enter his name and search for the records. And he was about to do just that when Annie came to mind.

How mad would she be when he told her the truth? Or maybe she already suspected and was afraid to tell him how naïve he was. Why else would she be mad when the condom broke? He could very well be having a child with her now. And while that seemed to upset her, it made him smile. He liked to think there was a part of him in her. A part of them together.

Would he feel the same way if he found out he had a child back home? He entered his name in the search box.

No offspring were listed, but he only had three samples on file, not twelve. He selected his history. He had fertilized nine eggs, all destroyed. Five had been the wrong sex needed at that time and the rest had been the correct sex, but rejected due to DNA results. No other information was given. A sense of loss filled him. Nine lives that would never be.

He hovered the indicator over the lineage link. Did he want to know who sired him? Would he even know who the people were? Probably not, but he might as well get all the information, he was already here. He clicked on the link and two names appeared.

They should have been unfamiliar names. Just two unknown people a lab decided to put together. And while the female was unknown to Calix, the male was not.

His sire was Sentinel Gaylor.

Fatherhood on his planet meant nothing, but Calix touched the screen where Gaylor's name was listed. Most likely, Gaylor had no clue they were related. Even if he had, the data would still be available. Calix's people did not so much as lie about anything, they just did not care. Why else would he be able to access the data so easily? They did not need to hide that which no one cared to find.

His people thought they had a perfect society. He thought so too at one time. But at what cost? The cost of freedom? The cost of life?

One of his classmates had complained about headaches and was never seen again. Whatever happened to him? Calix entered the name.

Terminated.

Hard to tell whether from natural causes or not, since all deaths were marked as such. But the date of termination confirmed it. He had not been transferred to another area or to another profession. He had been killed. For a headache! And most likely the chip had caused it. Did this mean if a person could not tolerate the chip, they were destroyed?

And he had told them he had lost his chip. In an accident. They still did not know about the headaches. Would that matter? Would they just try to replace it?

Did he want it replaced?

He touched his left temple. Could that chip be more than a locator like Annie said? He went to search when the computer beeped, indicating the downloads were completed. The search could wait. He disconnected the cable attaching the portable reader to the main file server.

Information could be sorted later. Now he needed to get back to the cabin, and Annie. He still wasn't sure if she liked him for him or because he was emitting something all women on this planet found irresistible. Could it be that the chip blocked whatever it was? Is that why the travelers in 1830 did not document any changes to their body? They had not documented any unusual attraction toward them from the inhabitants, either. They all had their chips, or so he assumed. Would that have made a difference? His head hurt trying to sort it all out.

He placed the reader into his bag and closed it. When he opened the door, the frigid wind blew in some flakes. No one on his planet would believe ice falling from the sky. His planet was just too hot. He could use some of that heat right about now, though. He huddled inside his coat, secured his hood, and slung the bag over his shoulder.

The anticipated storm seemed to be in full force and the setting sun made the air colder. Wind whipped across the trees. In the clearing, the snow blew sideways. The footsteps he had made coming out to his ship were long gone. He pulled out Annie's cellphone and selected Mac's number. She had insisted he call when he left so they knew when to expect him. At the time he thought it was unnecessary, but now he could see the logic behind her concern.

"Calix?" Mac answered.

"Yes. I am leaving the ship now. How is Annie?"

"Driving me nuts, of course. Be careful. It's pretty nasty out there."

Nasty. That was a good word for it. He assured Mac he would be fine and disconnected the call.

He pocketed the cell and pulled out his locator device. Annie's coordinates illuminated. He pointed the device until it indicated the correct direction.

The snow covered his boots. His steps were sluggish. Snow looked fluffy, but he might as well be walking though deep sand for all the traction he could get. He was panting and his face was numb by the time he reached the tree line. He had left his scarf in the ship, but going back for it did not seem like such a good idea.

His steps were no easier through the forest, even though the snow was not as deep. The tree cover made the impending night even darker. They also did nothing to keep the wind from penetrating his jacket and pants. He was glad he had worn the jeans as they were thicker. Still, he had never felt so cold in all his life.

He approached the clearing to the cabin and stopped. The sun had set, if it could have been seen through the cloud cover to begin with, and he faced a wall of snow as it blew sideways. The air almost seemed to glow as the snow reflected all available light, not that there was much to reflect. If not for his indicator, he would have no idea which way to go.

He pulled the hood tighter around his face, bracing himself against the bitter wind while continuing on his journey to Annie. The snow cover fooled him and he stepped into a hole. As he fell to the ground, his pack slammed against his back. The indicator flew from his hands.

He spit out ice. Surrounded by flying flakes, he pawed through the fallen snow with numb fingers. Where was the indicator? If he lost it, how would he find his way back to Annie? How would he even survive out here?

* * * *

Annie hobbled into the kitchen on her crutches. She'd tried to put on the medical boot, but would need several more pills before she would attempt that again, not that her ankle was feeling too chipper being bounced around, either. But she just couldn't lie still any longer.

"What are you doing out of bed?" Mac said.

"I'm worried about Calix. Shouldn't he be back by now?" She clomped her way to the back door and stared out at blackness. Calix could be two feet away and she probably wouldn't even see him. She turned on the security light and it slowly illuminated the wall of sideway snow. She still couldn't see very far. Oh, why did she let him go out in that? The stupid files could have waited.

"He just called ten minutes ago. Give the guy a chance. It's not exactly spring out there."

And Mac didn't think to turn on the light? She all but bit her tongue. "He's not used to this weather. Shouldn't we go out looking for him?"

"Are you high?" He frowned and shook his head. "Forget what I think. Calix would have a fit if he knew you were out in that." He wrapped his arm around her waist, grabbed her crutches and tossed them aside.

"What are you doing?"

"Putting you back to bed where you belong."

He picked her up, but without the ease Calix always had. Apparently, Mac could feel the extra poundage she carried. His legs wobbled.

"Put me down. You're going to hurt yourself."

Mac's phone went off, saving her from further argument. He placed her on a kitchen chair and pulled out his cell. "You okay, buddy?"

Buddy? That could be anyone. Mac never called his friends by their names. Did he have something against using first names? Or did he just not want her to know who was calling?

"Let me check." He lowered the phone. "Calix lost his locator device in the snow. Do you have something loud he can follow?"

Okay, so maybe he had something against first names. "The car horn?"

"Yeah, think again. Besides the house blocking the sound, I'm not going out in that."

"The generator?"

"I'd rather save that for when we need it."

"Picky, picky. How about the lawn mower? It's in the back porch storage room."

"Does it have gas?" When she nodded, he put the phone back up to his ear. "Listen for a motor. And look for the light. That should help guide you."

She reached her hand out and wiggled her fingers for the cell, but Mac put it in his pocket. "Hey! I wanted to talk to him."

"You can talk to him when he gets back." He rushed putting on his winter gear and went out the back. Frigid air whipped around her in the brief moment the door was open, forming goosebumps on her arm.

She turned the chair around so she could watch Mac. Lucky for him, the shed holding the yard equipment was situated at the end of the covered porch and he wouldn't have to trudge through snow to get to it. It took a couple of pulls to get the motor running, but unfortunately, it wouldn't stay running unless someone held the handle down. Before she could yell that bit of advice, Mac figured it out on his own. He found some rope, secured the handle, and started the motor up again.

It didn't sound all that loud through the door, but was louder when he opened it to come back inside. Hopefully, Calix could hear the motor through all that snow. Snow had a tendency to muffle sounds.

"Okay, time to get you back to your room," Mac said as he removed his coat.

"Why? He might need some help."

"Which is exactly why you're going back. He won't want your help if he thinks he's hurting you. And if he sees you, he might not admit to anything. If you want what's best for him, you'll do this." He picked her up and carried her on wobbly legs to her prison.

Really, he was going to give himself a hernia or something if he didn't put her down, but apparently he could be just as pig-headed as she. And while an argument hung off the tip of her tongue, she knew he had a point. Calix hated seeing her in pain.

And in all possibility, he would probably hightail it to her room as soon as he returned. But what if he couldn't? What if he was too frozen and needed her warmth to thaw out? Well, she'd just put her boot on and go out there as soon as he returned.

As if Mac had read her mind, he took her medical boot when he left her room. The fiend.

* * * *

After talking to Mac, Calix trudged to the small hill between Annie's cabin and the tree line. He stopped, searched the area, and listened. Even with the snow blowing frantically, he was able to see a faint light ahead and hear the motor. Seeing and hearing his destination would have brought a smile to Calix's face if he could move his lips. Slowly, he inched along toward his destination and only fell twice. By the time he reached the porch, his face, fingers, and toes were numb, and his green coat was white with ice crystals. He crawled up the steps and grabbed the porch railing. Mac opened the door and hauled Calix inside. Mac then removed a rope from the handle of a device that had been Calix's lifesaver and the motor stopped.

Calix took a deep breath of air that did not feel like a thousand tiny slivers of ice. Warmth. He never thought he would feel it again. With stiff legs, he lurched toward the closest chair and collapsed on the seat.

"Is Annie okay?" The words came out slurred, his lips barely moved. Calix tried to get the coat off, but his fingers would not work.

"Annie's fine." Mac zipped the coat open and removed it. "You need to take your boots off so you don't get frostbite."

Calix shivered. Moving around took more energy than he ever anticipated. How did the people of this area survive such weather? He unlaced his boots, but getting them off was harder than it should have been. Mac helped and pulled them off.

"Might want to take those jeans off, too," Mac said. "I'll go get you a blanket."

With fingers that felt fat, Calix managed to unbutton and unzip the jeans. His legs were covered in ice and the jeans would not slip off. He got them down as far as his knees and had to sit to get the leverage he needed to remove them all the way. He was beginning to hate snow. At least being out in it.

Mac handed him a blanket. "Here you go. I'm getting ready to fix some hot chocolate. I started a fire in the living room. Why don't you go thaw out in there?"

Anything with hot in it sounded good to him. But a fire? In the house? When he shuffled into the living room, Mac's comment became clearer. Or Calix's brain finally thawed. The hearth was aglow. He put his hands out. Heat, glorious heat. He sat on the floor with the blanket wrapped around his shoulders, basking in the warmth. He knew what could warm him up quicker, though. Annie. She would probably appreciate the fire, too. He stood and headed toward her room when Mac blocked his path, holding a pair of Calix's pants.

"Put these on. I need to talk to you about Annie."

Calix looked past Mac down the hall. Her door was shut. His heart pounded in fear. "You said she was *fine*. Did something happen?"

"Easy, fella." Mac smiled. "She's probably a little pissed at me, but she's okay. This has nothing to do with her ankle. This has to do with the two of you."

The two of them. He kind of liked the sound of that. Made them sound like a couple in one of those books he read. After slipping on his pants, Calix sat on the couch and hugged the blanket around his still-shivering body.

Mac turned on the fan over the stove. He brought over two mugs with steaming liquid. "You might want to let it cool a little before drinking."

Calix started to warm his hands on the mug, but it was hotter than he expected and he held it by the handle instead. "Why did you turn that on?"

"So Annie doesn't eavesdrop. What I want to talk to you about, she doesn't need to know."

Calix hated how they both kept secrets from one another, but maybe that was what families were all about. "What makes you think I will not tell her?"

"I'm guessing you won't want to tell her, but if you do, no skin off my nose." Mac rubbed his chin and leaned his head back. "What are your plans with my sister?"

"Plans?" Calix still wondered what he was going to tell the sentinel, but that probably was not what Mac meant.

"You said you were here to observe. When you're done, you're going back. Right?"

"I am not going back. I already told her." Calix stared at his mug. He could not imagine being apart from Annie, even if she only liked him because the chip no longer subdued whatever it was it subdued. He just hoped she still liked him after he told her he was fertile.

"Well you can't stay here." Mac stood and paced. "This isn't your home. Eventually, you'll have to find your own place, right?"

He had not thought about that. "Does Annie want me to leave?"

"That's not the point. You are not one of us. You don't understand us. You don't understand what it means to her to live with her."

Calix put the mug on the table. "Then tell me what it means. I want to know."

"How can I tell you something you've never experienced? Do you even know what love is?"

"I have read the definition."

Mac laughed. "Yeah, but knowing what it means and actually feeling it are two totally different things. Are you capable of love?"

Before he arrived on this planet, the question would have been absurd. The word love was not even in his vocabulary. Things were or were not. But now he was feeling emotions he had never felt before. "I think I am. I care for what happens to you and Annie. Is that not love?"

"Yes, that's one form. But are you in love with Annie? And before you ask, yes, there's a difference between loving someone and being in love."

"Is wanting sex being in love?"

"No. What you're feeling is a physical attraction. We call it lust. But Annie, she's not…I mean…oh hell. Do me a favor. No more sex with Annie until we figure out what your plans are on this planet. Can you do that?"

"Even if she asks?"

"Especially if she asks. She's vulnerable. You don't want to hurt her, do you? Having sex before your living arrangements are made will do that. Do you understand?"

Calix sighed. He did not wish to hurt Annie. "I understand."

"Good. I'm going to trust you on that. Now, why don't you take her some hot chocolate before it gets cold? I'm sure she wants to see you."

"Maybe I should bring her out here instead. To enjoy the fire." Because as much as he did not want to hurt her, he did want to have sex with her. And if she indicated she wanted the same, well, he might not be able to stop.

* * * *

"You know, I could have used the crutches." Annie held onto Calix's neck as he lowered her to the couch. She didn't want to let him go. In fact, she wanted a kiss. He'd been quiet ever since Portia showed up. She never got a chance to talk to him on the drive home, since she was pretty much out of it, and now Mac was here. Would she ever get him alone?

"There is no need. I like carrying you." Calix pulled her arms free, causing disappointment to burn in her chest. He didn't even kiss her forehead.

Maybe he liked to carry her, but he didn't seem to want to hold her as long. "Are you sure you're okay? You were out there an awful long time."

"I am fine. Do not worry about me." He placed her foot on the pillows that Mac had arranged on the coffee table.

That little bit of movement hurt and caused her to wince. Not even the pills were working all that well.

"Do you need another pain pill?"

She'd like a couple of dozen, but that wouldn't be wise. "It's too soon, but thank you."

Mac brought another ice pack and removed the old one.

She nearly screamed from the pain as it shot up her leg. "Do you really need to do that? My foot is already frozen."

"Maybe you should have thought about that before walking around on it all day, because I'm sure that's what you did." He looked at the swollen limb. "If this keeps getting worse, you're going to have to see a doctor."

She grabbed the armrest as Mac secured the new ice pack. "The doctor won't do any more than you're already doing. I'll be fine."

After draping an afghan over her lap and feet, Calix fetched a mug filled with hot chocolate and handed it to her. He sat gently beside her, probably trying not to cause her any undue movement. At least he didn't feel the need to sit across the room. She might have burst into tears then.

After a careful sip, she hadn't realized how cold she had gotten until the heat of the drink blazed a trail to her stomach. What better way to spend a snowy day than with a cup of cocoa, a burning fireplace, and your best guy? And despite how he acted, Calix was her best guy. Now, if she could only get rid of her brother. Without him hanging around, Calix would have cozied up to her. Wouldn't he? Or had Mac said something to Calix while the fan was turned on? Why else turn on the fan? In any case, she was not going to get anything out of Calix while Mac was in the room.

Maybe if she got Mac's mind on his current girl, he'd leave the room to call her. "How was your date with Justine?"

He looked up from his phone. "Since when do you care about my dates?"

"Just trying to make conversation." Okay, no date talk. There had to be another way to get him to leave.

Calix placed his mug on the coffee table and looked at Mac. "Do you mind if I talk to Annie alone?"

Her heart skipped. Was him wanting to be alone with her a good thing or a bad thing? Crap. She had to stop torturing herself. Besides, didn't she want to be alone with him anyway?

"Nah. I guess I could play a game on the computer." Mac took his phone and mug and headed for her office.

Well, gee. Why didn't she think of that? Maybe the direct approach worked best after all.

She took another sip of the hot chocolate and decided to beat Calix to the conversation. "So, what did Portia say to you earlier?"

"Why do you need to know?"

"I thought we agreed. You tell me about Portia, I tell you about my ankle."

"No. Why do you *need* to know?"

"Because I know she said something to upset you. But I can't do anything about her until I know what."

"Then you do not need to know. I do not want you fighting for me."

"But, Calix…"

"No. It is not important. However, I am wondering if I gave your experiment enough effort."

Her chest constricted. She knew it. Portia did say something. Or did something. "I wish I had never thought of that stupid experiment."

His eyebrows squished together. "Why?"

"Because… Because…" *Because you're mine.* Oh, if only he were.

"Because?"

She closed her eyes for a moment. Oh, hell. "Because I don't like you being with other women, okay? I thought it would matter if this planet affected you, but I don't care."

A smile flittered briefly across his features and then he became serious. "What if this planet is not the problem? What if the problem is me, because of my missing chip? Could that be why people…women…react to me differently?"

She bit back a laugh. "I don't think your chip has anything to do with that."

"But you are acting possessively. Is that normal?"

"Did Portia react possessively? Is that what happened?"

He took a ragged breath. "This has nothing to do with her. I am asking about you."

Annie took another sip. *She* was possessive? Oh wait, she was. Damn. If not for her foot, she'd stand up and walk to the other side of the room. The close proximity of his body and the fireplace was becoming too much for her. Sweat broke out on her upper lip. She stared at her mug.

"Annie?"

"It's not normal for me." She'd never fussed over a guy like she had with Calix. No way was it his missing chip, though. That just didn't make any sense.

* * * *

Calix held his hands together. All he wanted to do was touch Annie, but touching would lead to kissing which would lead to sex, and he had promised Mac no sex until his plans were in order.

"So, if it is not normal for you, could your reaction be caused by the missing chip?" Whether the lack of his chip or the planet caused his new-found libido, he hated the fact he became aroused when Portia touched him. But he would never tell Annie. She looked for an excuse to fight, and he would not have her fighting because of something he did.

"I doubt it. The chip most likely only affected you. It could possibly send out signals to keep people away, but again, I doubt that. Instead, without the chip, you are what you really are. You're experiencing emotions you never felt before. You're not being forced to be something you're not."

"So what I—what you are feeling is normal?" He could not believe he almost told her what he felt. "You just said it was not normal for you."

"Yeah, but then I've never been this jealous before, either."

"What is jealous?"

"It's an irrational feeling you get when you don't want to share."

"And what is it you do not wish to share?"

"You."

"Me?" He almost smiled, but tried to stay serious. He truly wanted to understand. "But I do not want to be shared."

"I told you it was irrational. Let me ask you this. How would you have felt if Logan had kissed me instead of harassed me?"

His chest burned. He gripped his hands tighter, causing his knuckles to pale. Was this how Annie felt toward Portia? "I would not have liked that."

"Do you feel a little bit angry just thinking about it?"

"I feel a lot angry. Is that why you kicked him? He had made you jealous?"

She crunched her forehead. "Eww, no! Logan and I are not and never were a couple. I kicked him because of what he did to my friend."

"But you have had other men, right? Men you have tossed aside when you grew tired of them?" He regretted the words as soon as he said them. How did she do it? How did she get him to tell her what he did not wish to talk about?

"Tossed aside?" She stared at him. "What are you talking about? Oh wait. Let me guess. Portia." She shook her head. "Calix, my last…boyfriend left six months ago, and we'd been together for over a year. I haven't tossed anyone aside."

"Why did he leave? Was he jealous?"

"I wish," she mumbled. "We just wanted different things, and he wasn't willing to compromise." She bent over to place her mug on the table, but he took it from her hands and accomplished the task before she could hurt herself. "Thank you."

She took his hand. Even after holding the mug, her hand was still cool. Could he warm it up? Better yet, take both hands and warm them up? She was certainly warming him up. But if he took both hands, could he stop there? Probably not, but he continued to hold the one hand.

She sighed. "I know you don't want to tell me what Portia said. But how can I defend myself if I don't know what garbage she's fed you?"

He started to tell her he had not eaten anything when he realized she was not being literal. "Portia is your family, but you do not like her. Why is that? I thought families loved one another."

"Close families usually do. Portia and I are not close. Never have been. She thinks I stole her boyfriend back in the fifth grade. I was ten. He was just a friend. But she didn't see it that way. Ever since, she's tried to get even, although I've never really had anyone she was interested in until now. It's hard to compete. She has the perfect body, whereas I don't."

Perfect body? Portia was much too thin. He liked Annie's body. It was soft in all the right places, and he didn't feel like he would break her. "There is nothing wrong with your body."

She flattened her lips and nodded. He did not believe she agreed with him. Somehow he would have to convince her.

He rubbed her knuckles with his thumb. "Portia hoped I would be interested in her instead of you and told me to call when you became bored with me. But even if you do…" That thought pained his heart. "I have no intention of calling her. I do not like her like I like you. And I do not want you to fight with her."

She leaned back against the cushion and smiled. "I like you, too. A lot. Sorry if I'm a little jealous at the way other women look at you. But that has nothing to do with your lack of a chip, okay?"

He continued to caress her hand. She was so soft and he shouldn't be touching her, but he did not wish to let go. "Have you ever experienced love?"

Her hand clenched a bit and her arm tensed. She looked down at her lap. "Yes."

He felt hope. Was it possible she felt love toward him? "What is it like?"

She chuckled. "Again, hard to explain. But you know you're in love with someone when you would do anything just to bring a smile to their face. When their life matters more than your own. Unfortunately, one person can give too much when they love more than they are loved. If it isn't shared and balanced, love will die. And when it dies, it hurts." She pointed to her chest. "In here."

He already would do anything to bring a smile to her face. And her life did matter more than his own. Did this mean he was in love with Annie?

CHAPTER 14

Why'd Calix have to bring up love? Like, she could handle. Like was safe. Love was dangerous territory.

Annie gazed into those beautiful purplish-blue eyes of his. They almost glowed at her. If she only knew what he was thinking.

"What compromise did your boyfriend not want to make?"

Oh hell. No way was she getting into that. "It's not important."

"Do you still love him?"

She had until she saw Denny with another woman. That scene pretty much killed any feelings she had left for him. "No."

Calix smiled like a man who saw an opportunity open in front of him. "Is jealousy associated with love?"

"Not really. Jealousy stems from distrust and insecurity."

He frowned. "You do not trust me?"

"It's not that I don't trust you. I don't really know you all that well. Which leads to my insecurity. It's confusing, I know."

"So trust is associated with love?"

She laughed. "I guess you could say that. I couldn't fall in love with someone I didn't trust."

"What does it mean to fall in love? In the books I have read, couples also make love, which seems to mean having sex. What is the difference?"

"It's not surprising you're confused. Most people are confused when it comes to love. But a person doesn't fall in love with a family member, a blood relative. Just like blood relatives do not make love, have sex, with each another. Yet they love one another." She chuckled, thinking about Portia. "Usually."

He touched her cheek and stared deep into her eyes. "How do you know then? How do you know if you are in love?"

His touch set her on fire and she leaned into his palm. How could she tell him what she didn't understand? Oh, but she did, didn't she? She'd already fallen down that well and there was no going back up. "Oh, Calix. I…"

"Is it a burning need to be with that person?" He leaned in close. His lips mere inches from hers, teasing. "Or is that only a chemical reaction?"

Was he aware of the affect he had on her? Did she affect him the same way? His scent was like a drug through her system—she couldn't get enough. "Chemistry has been known to be involved when two people are attracted to each other."

"And this attraction can lead to love?" He ran his thumb across her cheek and glanced at her lips.

"It can." She so badly wanted to grab him and kiss him, but he apparently was trying to work something out and she wouldn't interfere. If he was thinking about love, maybe it wasn't so far-fetched that she could have a relationship with an alien being. Especially if he stayed.

"But trust is important," he said.

"Very."

He sat back, much to her disappointment. "Then I should tell you what I discovered today." He frowned. "Apparently, sperm has been taken from me without my knowledge and has been used to fertilize female eggs. I can father children."

Not the words she longed to hear. In fact, they were probably the worst words. But at least now her worries had merit. She placed her hand on his arm. "I kind of figured that already. So, you have children?"

"No. Just fertilized eggs. And I doubt they will turn into anything. Most fertilized eggs are destroyed and not used."

"That seems strange. I thought you could freeze embryos for…decades." She had almost gone that route but then had reconsidered. Especially since she wasn't sure she ever wanted kids.

"Why freeze when you have sufficient…"

"Donors?"

"I was thinking more along the line of stock, but donor works just as well."

She gave his arm another comfort squeeze. "Yeah, I guess it would make you feel that way. I'm sorry the news wasn't what you hoped to find."

"You are not mad at me?"

Damn, she really needed to watch her anger. Was that all he ever saw? "It's not like you kept the information from me. You didn't know. But thank you for telling me."

He leaned forward again and palmed her cheek, making her heart race. "Annie…"

The lights flickered twice before blinking off. The refrigerator's constant hum died. Mac cursed from down the hall.

The fireplace illuminated Calix and he turned toward the darkened lamp. "What happened?"

"We lost power."

Mac stormed into the living room and yanked his coat on. "How much propane do you have?"

"I don't know. It's due to be checked this week."

"Great." He grabbed his gloves and went out the back. The door slammed shut.

There were only nine logs beside the fireplace.

"Would you tell Mac we need more wood?" She hated feeling useless, but if she got up, she'd not only scream in pain, she'd get yelled at by two of the most important people in her life. Not a way to start an evening without power to distract them.

"I will help him." Calix put his gear on and followed Mac.

The door had barely shut when the generator came to life and the refrigerator hummed. The living room light remained out, the signal to indicate when the power returned since the generator only ran the essential appliances. At least she wouldn't have to store her food outside.

After three trips, the guys had a reasonable stack of wood in the living room. Mac turned down the thermostat to save fuel and they all hunkered down by the fireplace. So much for being alone with Calix.

Yet, the evening didn't turn out all that bad. Mac fixed dinner, and later he and Annie showed Calix how to play *Monopoly*. By ten o'clock, she was beat. This had to be the longest Saturday she'd ever experienced. Mac grabbed pillows and blankets and the three of them slept by the fireplace, her sandwiched between the guys.

Calix spooned her and his erection poked her in the back. She smiled knowing there wasn't a damn thing she could do about it. Maybe having Mac in the room was a good thing. She'd probably want to do something stupid like try another condom. But damn, she wanted Calix something bad.

When her period came on Wednesday, she would make sure never to miss another pill.

* * * *

By Thursday, Calix was about to venture out into the snow regardless of how cold it was. Not because he was cooped up inside a small cabin. Because he was cooped up with Mac.

The man rarely gave him and Annie a chance to be alone. Even during sleep, Mac had stayed close by. When the power had returned early Monday morning, Calix thought for sure he could sleep with Annie in her bed that night, but when Mac had given him a look—a look that clearly meant no—Calix resigned himself to sleeping on the couch.

What was even worse, she had offered an invitation. He hated declining, but she seemed to understand why he had done it. At least she had managed to sneak in a kiss or two whenever Mac had left the room.

That was until yesterday. Since then, no kisses. No smiles. Only frowning and yelling. But not at him. At Mac.

At least Calix had his data. He had spent most of his time researching what he had downloaded. He found the procedure on chip insertion. Everyone on his planet received the chip at age five. The documentation stated it was for accountability, but the procedure to insert it was very detailed and Calix had no idea what most of it meant. If it was just a locator chip, why did it matter if it was attached to certain nerves? Were they nerves that blocked emotion? If he were a medic, he would know. If he taught medics he would know. But he was just a history teacher and he had never felt so useless.

If that chip was more than a locator—as Annie had suggested—had he given Sentinel Gaylor a reason to terminate him? Again, he could find no proof that that would happen. At least not in the documentation he had downloaded. Frustrated, he had continued to search for unification.

There was nothing under processes and procedures. Oh sure, the word popped up, but it was used as if the reader should know what it meant. So, it had to be a theory. Could he search for theories and find it? That would also require returning to his ship. But every time he had suggested he go back, Annie would say it was unsafe or too cold or he would get lost without his locator. And Calix would let her convince him to not go.

Mac had said he was procrastinating. Calix had looked up the word. Mac was right. But now he needed a break from Mac. And badly. Plus, he was running out of time. Saturday was only two days away and he was no closer to coming up with a plan than he was last week. If he did not contact his people on Saturday, it would only be an invitation for them to send someone else. If they had not done so already.

That was something he did not wish to think about.

Annie marched into the living room with that clomping noise her boot made. She had been doing a lot of clomping, but this was the first time it sounded strong. As if her foot no longer hurt.

"When are you going to leave?"

Calix looked up from his laptop. His heart nearly stopped, afraid she was directing the question at him, but she stared at Mac.

He was sitting on the chair staring at his phone. He looked up and glanced at Calix. "I'm not needed at work."

"I didn't ask about you returning to work. When are you going to leave? My ankle is fine and the roads are clear. You have your own apartment. Shouldn't you live in it?" Her hands were on her hips and her cheeks turned red.

"Your ankle isn't fine. You still can't drive."

"No, but Calix can if I need to go anywhere."

Calix smiled, glad she now felt comfortable in his ability. She had shown him where to learn the rules and quizzed him. One of the few times they were able to be together in front of Mac.

"Calix doesn't have a license."

"Technically, you don't either. But that's not the point. You need to go."

"This is the thanks I get for helping? You're kicking me out?"

She lowered her head and her hands fell by her side. "You know that's not what this is about. I can't live with you, Mac. It's not healthy for our relationship."

Mac stood. "Fine. If I have to go, Calix should go with me. He can take your car and come back up here if you need to be transported. It would look better if he stayed with another guy anyway, don't you think?"

Calix gripped the laptop. No! The last thing he wanted to do was leave Annie.

Her eyes widened. "Do you really think that's necessary? His ship is here."

"Why does he need his ship? He's supposed to be observing. Aren't you, Calix?" Mac turned and stared.

Calix did not expect to be dragged into the fight, and his tongue refused to work. "I…uh."

"I think you've done all you can up here in the boonies," Mac said. "I think you'll learn a lot more in the city."

"He doesn't want to observe anymore." She turned toward Calix and pleaded with her eyes. "Do you?"

"No," Calix said. "There is no need."

Mac threw his phone onto his chair. "Oh, screw it!" He picked up his bag and started stuffing his clothes into it. "Just don't come running to me when you find out he's knocked you up."

Her face turned red and her eyes filled with tears.

The fight had gone on long enough and Calix wanted it to end. "Stop it. You are hurting her."

"I'm hurting her?" Mac pointed to himself. "I'm not the one who will be flying off when my mission is over, now am I?"

Calix put the laptop aside and stood. "How many times do I have to tell you that I am not going back to my people?"

"How the heck do you plan on staying here? There's no record of your birth. No record of you coming to the States. No record of you anywhere. How do you plan on explaining all that?"

"I will show my ship to whoever needs to know."

Annie shook her head, tears running down her cheek. She brushed them away with the back of her hand. "You can't do that. They'll take you away. You'll become one huge experiment."

"You do not know that." Calix stepped toward her, wanting to hold her, but afraid of Mac's reaction if he did.

Mac grabbed his arm. "Yes, she does. We tend to act first and ask questions later. You should know that by now. If word got out you are from another planet, your freedom would be over, if not your life. It would be best for you if you returned to your people."

Calix stared at the woman who had opened his heart. He did not want to go back. He did not believe his life was in danger if he stayed, but it most certainly was if he returned to his people. And it did not matter what he told his people. He could see that now. If the inhabitants accepted aliens, their lives could be taken over. If the inhabitants did not accept aliens, they could be annihilated. He did not wish either scenario for Annie. If only there were an easy solution. "What do you want me to do?"

* * * *

Annie rubbed her hand over her abdomen. What did she want Calix to do? She wanted him to stay and love her. She wanted him to stay and be a father. Because she was fairly certain she was pregnant. She had never been late. Never. When she stopped taking the pill for her period, her period always started. Just like clockwork. But not this time.

Could he have a life here? With her? There were people who could make up false identifications. She just didn't know where to begin looking for them. Still wouldn't save him if by some chance he got caught. Because people always got caught.

"Ah, shit!" Mac said. "Was the test positive?"

"No." She lowered her hand and fidgeted with the bottom of her sweatshirt. She hadn't told a total lie, since the pregnancy test was still unused.

"What test?" Calix asked.

Mac placed his hands on hips. "Have you even taken it?"

"What test?" Calix asked.

"The test to determine whether or not she's carrying your child."

The silence after that bomb dropped was deafening. She couldn't believe what a big mouth her brother had.

"Thanks a lot, Mac." Her face burned and she headed for the bedroom. She needed some distance or she might just do something she would regret later. Like re-injure her ankle when she kicked the shit out of her brother.

Calix came up behind her in the hall and turned her around. "You can take a test?"

She nodded. She couldn't look him in the eye. She might just burst into tears then.

"Are you afraid?"

Tears escaped anyway. How could she tell him she was afraid without hurting his feelings? It would be like saying she didn't want his children when that wasn't the case at all.

And if that realization didn't just slap her upside the head. Apparently, it wasn't just kids she didn't want. She just hadn't wanted Denny's.

He cupped her face and wiped the tears away with his thumbs. He leaned in close. "Take the test."

She nodded. "If it comes back negative, it might be too soon, though. Just saying."

"Okay." He kissed her forehead.

His warm lips lingered and she leaned into him. She wanted his arms around her. She wanted him to declare his love. But if all she got was a kiss on the head, she'd take that. For now. It was more than she'd gotten from him since the snow storm. But then, Mac pretty much put the kibosh on any kind of intimacy.

"You might as well wait in the living room. It will take a few minutes."

"I want to be there for you."

"You want to watch me pee on a stick?"

"Well…no. I can turn my back on that part."

She laughed. Why not have him there? It concerned him just as much as it concerned her. She went into the bedroom and opened the nightstand drawer. The package lay there waiting to be used. She snatched it up and headed for the bathroom. Calix closed the door behind him and turned his back on her.

"So what does the stick do?"

She opened the package. She'd read the instructions a dozen times already and knew them by heart. "It reacts with the urine. If I have a certain chemical in my system, a chemical that appears when a woman is pregnant, the word yes will appear."

"Does the word no appear if you are not pregnant?"

"Yeah, but it could also mean I tested too soon." She proceeded with the steps, feeling a little awkward with him in the room. Her bladder had never been shy before. Once she closed her eyes, she was able to relax.

He turned around after she flushed the toilet. His hair had fallen forward and she was tempted to brush it back, but he did it for her, awarding her with the sight of his beautiful eyes. Her heart clenched. When he left—and she had no doubt he would leave, because it would be too dangerous for him to stay—she'd have no proof he was here. She needed to take his picture. Take their picture together. Something to gaze at when she missed him. Because when he left, she would miss him very much.

"What's the matter?" he asked.

She brushed the tears from her eyes and sat on the toilet lid. "Nothing. I feel like I haven't seen you in like forever."

He knelt down in front of her. "I have missed being close to you, too. I am surprised Mac is not in here."

"He has been a little protective." She tried to laugh, to lighten the mood, but the realization that Calix would be gone came crashing down on her. The tears flowed and she covered her face.

"Annie."

That one word brought a sob from her lips. He pulled her in close and she clung to him. Why'd he have to be an alien? Why couldn't he have been a neighbor instead? She rested her head on his shoulder, content to stay that way forever. Or at least until she got her emotions under control.

"I am sorry if I have made you sad."

"You haven't." Her emotions were all over the place. Either she was due to start her period, or she was pregnant. And considering she'd never been late… She glanced at the clock. Moment of truth just arrived.

She reluctantly moved away from Calix and reached for the stick.

* * * *

Calix put his hand on Annie's outstretched arm. "Before you look at it, I need to tell you something first."

Her eyes were red from crying. Sadness still lingered on her face, but she stared at him with those sparkling green eyes he would never tire of looking at.

He kissed her puffy lips. Just a light brush, nothing lingering. If he had, he might not stop, and what he wanted to say could not wait any longer. He held her face in his hands. "Annie…"

A loud knock on the door startled them both.

"So, what's the verdict?" Mac demanded.

Calix closed his eyes and turned his head toward the door. "You'll find out when we leave this room. Now go away!"

His voice came out louder than he intended, but Mac's retreating footsteps told him it had worked.

She chuckled. "You're starting to sound like us, using contractions and yelling."

Yelling. So unlike him, but that was the old him. The Calix who felt…nothing. He turned back to Annie. He liked the new him. The Calix who felt…everything. Maybe his lack of the chip was responsible, but he never would have felt such joy if not for her.

He took her hand and brought it up to his lips. After their last private conversation, he had plenty of time to think about what she had said. And he had read some more on the subject. There was no doubt left in his mind what he was feeling.

"I love you, Annie. You have my heart. I did not understand what that meant before, but I do now."

He assumed she would smile or laugh, that she would be happy to hear the words. Instead, the tears returned and she lowered her head. He was not sorry he told her, though. He did love her. He would do anything for her.

She wiped at her face and looked up, only for the tears to flow once again. She lurched at him and hugged his neck. "I love you, too."

Hearing her say it made his eyes also water. But he was happy, not sad. Maybe she was happy, too? He wrapped his arms around her and squeezed, but not too tight. Just in case. Together they would figure out what to do. As long as they had each other, nothing else mattered.

She placed her hands on his shoulders and pushed away. She picked up the stick, which was not really a stick, and read it. She handed the item to him while a wrenching sob burst from her mouth.

Yes. It said yes. He smiled. He couldn't help it. She had a part of him growing inside of her. But she was crying. Did that mean she was not happy about having his child?

"You do not want this child?"

She jumped up and covered her mouth. "Oh, God, no. That's not it. Don't you get it? You'll be gone."

He rose and held her face. "Annie. I cannot leave you. Unless…" His heart nearly broke at the thought. "Do you want me to leave?"

"No!" She grabbed a tissue, dabbed her eyes and blew her nose. "It's just that it's not safe for you here."

He liked how she was concerned for his safety. It meant she really cared, really loved him, not that he doubted it. She would not have told him otherwise. But she had to know the truth of his situation.

A truth he was just now realizing. He had lost his chip and had told his people. If he had only known better at the time.

"I believe I am not safe with my people, either. I am different now. I could very well be destroyed if I go back to them, that is if they have not already sent someone out to retrieve me."

CHAPTER 15

"What?" Annie clutched Calix's arms. His words took the ground from underneath her feet, like that Spin Out ride she had despised at Magic Mountain. But instead of being plastered to the wall, she headed downward in despair. He grabbed her by the waist, keeping her from becoming a puddle on the floor.

"Mac," Calix yelled.

"No, don't call him."

Too late. The door opened. "It's positive, isn't it? Are you okay?"

She was not okay. Far from it. Her whole world was crumbling. "Calix's life is in danger."

"Because he fathered a child? What kind of messed up world are you from?"

"Like you'd want me to keep this baby. Admit it. You want me to get rid of it."

"Under the circumstances, do you think it's smart to keep it?"

"Stop," Calix said. "You destroy the unborn here, too?"

Ahh, his destroyed eggs. Apparently, that had bothered him. She cupped his face. "Some women will end their pregnancy for reasons of their own. I have no intention of doing that, okay? But why would they destroy you? You haven't done anything wrong."

"I do not fit into their perfect world anymore, and they know I no longer have my chip."

She was a veritable fountain with the way the tears kept flowing. She'd cried more in the past ten minutes than she had all year. And that included the time Denny left her. She sat on the toilet and grabbed some tissue to wipe her face. "They could put it back, couldn't they?"

His eyes widened. "I do not want it back."

"But if it means keeping you alive—"

"No! I am not even sure it would work. Maybe it would reduce my sexual drive, but I do not see how it can change what is in my head." He pounded his chest. "Or in my heart."

"He's got a point, Annie," Mac said.

She wasn't sure she'd want someone to try and control her feelings, either. "Then you need to get rid of that chip so they can't find you."

Calix knelt in front of her and shook his head. "That won't stop them from coming here. They know this planet exists. Remember, my people need a new home, and I am just one person in their way. I have to figure out how to tell them that I am not a danger to them. That the people on this planet are not a danger to them."

Mac straightened up. "They're coming here? Now?"

"Not all of them, no. But they could have sent a replacement for me, or they may wait until after I contact them on Saturday to do it. They will not give up this planet that easily. Would you?"

"Did you find out what unification is?" Annie asked.

Calix shook his head. "I could not find any documentation that they have actually performed the process, which makes sense since your planet is the first our people have discovered with sentient life. It is possibly just a theory."

"So what are you gonna do?" Mac asked. "Tell them our planet is unsuitable?"

"They already know it is suitable. They are more worried about the people living here. And they are probably worried about me. But it will be all right." Calix hugged her. "We will figure something out. Together. You have made me happy today, Annie. You have given me something I never had before. Love. A life worth living. A family."

"So I guess you're staying?" Mac asked.

"Yes, he's staying." She wouldn't trust anyone else to keep him safe.

They moved into the dining room where Mac fixed lunch as if the end of the world wasn't coming on Saturday. And maybe it wasn't technically ending then, but the time clock could very well start. Food really didn't appeal to Annie, but she ate anyway. Eating for two and all that.

"How about you tell them the air is poison?" Mac asked between bites of his bologna sandwich. "That we've polluted it beyond help."

"But they know that is not the case. I already checked in. Remember?" Calix stirred his soup and looked at her. "What is this?"

"Tomato soup, a vegetable." Or was that a fruit. She never could remember.

"But what if it's recent?" Mac continued. "Say an atomic bomb went off, or some kind of nuclear war. Tell them you're leaving, but then your ship explodes and they think you were destroyed in the nuclear blast."

Annie stared at her brother as if he'd grown another head. A stupid head. "And how would we destroy his ship? In space?"

"Does it have a self-destruct button?" Mac asked.

"It does, but they would be informed once it was activated and could deactivate it." Calix took a spoonful and smiled. "This is tasty."

The things he found delight in surprised her. She squeezed his hand. "I'm glad you like it."

"Okay, then maybe we put a bomb on it and set it off at a certain time," Mac said.

"What?" Annie would have slapped him if he were in reach. "Like you can buy one at Walmart?"

"I'm sure you could Google how to build one."

"Yeah, and in the meantime blow ourselves up while building it. No, thank you."

"It does not matter," Calix said. "They would only send out someone to investigate my claim. Someone who could very well be on their way. Thank you for your suggestions though. They are most helpful."

Helpful? How were Mac's stupid suggestions helpful? If Calix's people could only see him sitting here, eating, being all calm and reasonable, they would leave him alone. Wouldn't they? Or would they destroy him along with all the other people on this planet?

If only she had all the answers. But she didn't. She just wanted to keep Calix safe. She had no idea how to do that, but their baby was counting on her. Hell, she was counting on her.

* * * *

Doug pulled over to the side of the road and put the SUV in park. Thanks to Jay Bryant, this was the closest he'd actually been to finding proof of an alien invasion. If that second intruder inside Bryant's cabin was indeed an alien.

Ever since he was a child, the universe had fascinated him. He'd wonder which stars were homes to other worlds. And what kind of people lived on those worlds. Sure, all the signs he'd found at Bryant's place had pointed toward his creature being human. The footprints and fingerprints appeared normal, if not a little larger than the average citizen. But Doug never believed in *E.T.*-type aliens. Especially if they traveled through space. They would need the dexterity to create, to build.

So if Doug came face-to-face with this alien, he would not be surprised if it resembled a human being. Tests would uncover the truth.

The problem would be determining whether they came in peace or not. If their intentions were harmless, why the secrecy? Cloaking ships usually meant spying. And spying usually meant their intentions were not good. Until Doug learned otherwise, his creature was an enemy.

He double-checked the address on his phone. "This is where O'Shea's sister lives. Kind of makes sense, too. This isn't far from the sighting."

John peered through the windshield. "There aren't any tracks on the driveway. Think she's home?"

"Only one way to find out." Doug put the gear in drive when an older Jeep Cherokee came barreling down the driveway.

"That's O'Shea," John said.

And he was alone. Doug smiled as his heart thumped hungrily against his chest. Was this his chance to make history? Could the alien be up in the cabin? What better place to hide someone than in a place most people didn't live in during the winter. This was his lucky day.

* * * *

Calix entered the clearing of his ship. Snow-covered trees offset the brilliant blue sky and the sun shone unobstructed, reflecting off the pristine cover. Even with all that sunlight, the air was frigid and his breath fogged as he exhaled.

He squinted, reaching out one arm while supporting Annie on his back with the other. If he had his locator, he would know where to go and cautious footsteps would be unnecessary, but the last thing he needed to do was run into his ship. And he wasn't about to let her walk in this snow.

How had he let her talk him into bringing her anyway?

It may have had something to do with not being able to say no to her.

"We could have stopped to look for your locator," she said.

He had thought about it for all of two seconds. If he had stopped, he would have had to put her down, and he was not going to do that.

"I might wait until the snow melts."

"Ha! You'll be waiting awhile, then."

In that, he did not doubt her. Did this place ever get warm? He stepped into a well-concealed hole and stumbled.

She tightened her hold around his neck and he awkwardly righted himself, slamming her against his back in the process.

"Are you okay?" he asked. "The baby?" Ever since he learned of her pregnancy, he was afraid of hurting her and the baby.

She loosened her hold once he had her secured. "The baby is fine. Trust me, it would take a lot to hurt him or her right now. Do you know how long the gestation period is on your planet?"

He shook the snow from his leg. "Yes. I found the documentation. New life is introduced in two seasons' time. A little more than eight of your months. But eggs are not fertilized until someone dies. I discovered that that is what triggers the donation process. When it is my turn to donate, that is when they schedule my physical and take my sperm."

"Are you telling me that the population on your planet remains steady? No population boom? They don't kill you when you turn thirty, do they?"

He laughed. "Why would you think that?"

"A movie I saw once."

These people certainly had active imaginations. Would his own people be the same way without the chip or was that a learned ability? "Many of our people die of old age. Some die in accidents. But we are destroyed if we can no longer function." Such as a headache. *A headache!* "It never bothered me before. It is just the way things are done. I do not feel that way now."

"I'm sorry I brought that up. At least I don't have to worry about explaining having a kid in less than nine months. Or worse, longer. Try explaining that to a doctor. Oh crap. I guess I'll need to make an appointment."

"An appointment?"

"For a doctor. Just to make sure everything is okay. It's not like I can deliver the baby by myself. Do you think our people are related?"

He continued to wave his hand outward, feeling for the ship. The hairs on his arm stood on end. Getting close now. "I believe it is a possibility. We are very similar."

"And it would explain our compatibility. How else could you get me pregnant, huh?"

She made a valid point, one he had not thought of. What if their people were related? Would that make a difference in unification? Or would his people see it as a responsibility to take over?

Probably the latter.

His knuckles rapped the side of the ship. He felt around until he found the indentation for the door handle.

"I'm surprised it's not covered in snow. Wouldn't that look weird then?"

"The surface has an electronic barrier that repels dirt and dust. I guess it repels snow, too. If you put your hand out, you should be able to feel the barrier."

She reached out. "Wow. And here I thought it was you."

Chuckling, she nuzzled and kissed his cheek. He supposed she was just being silly, because he did not believe he sent out signals like the barrier, but then maybe he did. Or they did together. Her nuzzling sent a shot of desire straight to his groin. He loved the way his body reacted to her. He loved her.

Opening the door triggered the alarm. He had set it on automatic after the break-in. Just in case. He put her down inside and punched in his number. The inner door opened and the lights came on. "If you ever have to come here without me, these are the numbers you will select."

While he pointed to the sequence, she read them out loud, "4. 7. 8. 2. 5. That's what the dots say, right? That's the same as on your bag."

"You can read the numbers?"

"Sure. It's like looking at a deck of cards. But without the hearts, diamonds, spades, or clovers."

He had seen the cards and had not really paid attention, but she was correct. They were just ordered differently.

"What's it mean?" she asked.

"Technically? It is my numbering sequence. Sort of like a last name."

She entered the ship and sat on the bed. "So, does that mean you're the forty-seven thousand eight hundred twenty-fifth Calix?"

"Not exactly. Once the numbering sequence reaches 9-9-9-9-9, they will restart the numbering at 1-0-0-0-0." He closed the outer door.

She frowned. "Why that number? Why not start over with one?"

"I do not know."

She smiled like she knew she had asked what she called a stupid question. And now he understood that phrase because she most likely knew what his answer would be.

"How often have they restarted your name," she asked.

He should not be surprised she would ask such technical questions. She was a technician after all. "Again, I do not know."

"You can't even guess?"

He sat beside her on the bed. "When it comes to numbers, I am not a good guesser. I do not teach math. But maybe you can guess. There are ten districts. I believe they use the name once a year in each district. But I could be wrong."

She scrunched her brow. "If you divide your numbering sequence by ten that's about forty-seven hundred years. That's not very long. Is it? What year is it on your planet?"

"It has been 22,535 years since we restarted documentation."

Her eyes widened. "You have documentation that go back that—wait, you said restarted?"

"Yes. There was a catastrophe, called the Catastrophic Event, and we had lost all our documentation. I do not know how many years prior to that we existed. My history classes only go back that far. So do you have a guess?"

She laughed. "Okay, so just rounding the numbers, it looks like you could be on your fourth repeat. Wow. That's a lot of data. Our data doesn't go back that far."

"Yes, you are new technologically. Where we have had computers for over 22,000 years."

"Okay, now you're just showing off."

He laughed and kissed her lightly on the lips, which always thrilled him. He grew hard for her. If it were not for the baby, he would like to show her how much he desired her. He stood so he would not be tempted. "I told you, our people have been around a long time."

"So have ours, but I figured you had technology for, like, 2,000 years, not 22,000. I'm surprised you haven't taken over this planet sooner."

"We did not need it."

"So logical. I'd like to think our own people would be that way, but if you've read our history, you know that isn't the case."

Yes, he had read all about their wars. And that did worry him. No one on this world seemed to be happy being where they were. Doing what they were doing. If they could have it all, they would go for it. And why? So they could say they had it all? Did making other people miserable bring them joy? It did not make sense.

She stared at his groin and smiled. "You know, since I don't have to worry about getting pregnant, you don't need the condom anymore."

He grinned. That was indeed good news. He hated that thing. But even better news… "You can still have sex?"

"Hell, yeah." She grabbed the waistband of his pants and pulled him between her legs. Her eyes watered. "Damn hormones. If I'm this emotional now, I can only imagine what I'll be like in a few months."

He fell to his knees and held her face. "What is the matter? Are you unhappy?"

She closed her eyes. "Not exactly. I'm afraid this is all a dream and I'll wake up and you won't be here."

"It is not a dream." He kissed her tenderly on the mouth before moving down to her neck, inhaling her scent of soap and flowers. "I will do everything in my power not to leave you. You must believe me."

She tilted her head to the side, giving him better access. "I do believe you. Now stop talking and make love to me."

Exactly what he had in mind. And then some. "Annie, there are some…things…I would like to try with you. May I?"

"Things? What kind of things?"

Her breathing became restless and her eyes fluttered. He liked how he made her excited just by kissing her neck.

He smiled. "Sex things."

At the time, he had wondered if reading her books was a good idea because he had only wanted her more. But now he had her in his arms and he so much wanted to impress her and give her pleasure. He zipped her coat open and slipped it off her shoulders.

* * * *

Sex things.

Annie kept running those two words inside her head. What kind of sex things would Calix want to experiment with? What books of hers did he actually read? Had Mac shown him some porn sites? Because she wouldn't put that past her brother.

"You are nervous." He started to back away.

What was his first hint? The twitching of her eye or the expression on her face, because she was pretty sure she looked uneasy. How could she tell this guy the only time she hadn't done it missionary style was when she straddled him? She grabbed him by the coat and kept him from moving further away. "A little, yes. I'm not very…experienced. Sexually."

He smiled as he removed her coat and tossed it behind him. "Then we will learn together. I promise to stop if you tell me to."

"I know that." Little tremors skittered down her spine. Wasn't she supposed to be the teacher and him the student? When did it get turned around? If he was experimenting with what he had read, and would stop if she asked, what was her problem? She trusted him and, frankly, was getting excited just wondering what he wanted to do. "Yeah, sure. Why not?" She reached for his zipper and he held her hands away.

"Let me do this my way, okay?" He kissed her lightly on the lips. "No talking and no touching. I want to please you."

Holy shit on a shingle. How did she get so lucky? Gosh, if she didn't watch out, she'd start bawling, and that would certainly ruin the mood. She smiled and nodded.

He removed his coat before he started in on her, although she would have preferred he removed more than that. His body was pretty hot looking and would give her something to gaze upon while he went about with his plan. Whatever the heck his plan was.

Her footwear came off next—one normal boot, one medical boot. He took his time, being gentle, as if he could hurt her.

She wished he'd hurry it up just a bit. Once she got a taste of him, it was hard to go slowly. The kisses she'd given him the past few days were not enough. She'd been jonesing for him all week, but Mac hovering like a piranha made it impossible to do anything intimate with Calix. Well, her brother wasn't going to barge in now.

Once her feet were bare, Calix ran his hands under her sweater, his touch sending erotic shockwaves through her body. His fingers brushed alongside her breasts, causing her to gasp in pleasure. She raised her arms to help him remove the clothing. He stared at her pink lacy bra and ran a finger inside the top front edge.

She arched forward, wanting him to touch her more, but it seemed he had other ideas and went to work on her jeans. Who knew getting undressed could be so sensuous? Her nipples hardened and her sex clenched in the need for him, and he'd hardly done anything to her.

She leaned back on her elbows as he pulled her jeans off and added them to the pile of clothes.

He stood as if admiring his creation. "You are beautiful."

She straightened up and shook her head. No she wasn't. Far from it. Maybe if she lost ten, fifteen pounds, but even then she would look okay at best. Not beautiful.

He frowned. "I would not lie to you." He dropped to his knees and cradled her jaw in his hands. His purplish-blue eyes were dark with desire. "I would never lie to you."

Maybe he wouldn't, but how did he know who was beautiful and who wasn't? "But—"

He brought his mouth over hers in a possessive kiss, silencing her. His tongue demanded entrance and tangled with her own. She nearly swooned. If this was what talking got her, she might speak up more often.

When he broke the kiss, she felt the loss, but he quickly unhooked her bra and bared her breasts. He took one nipple in his mouth, giving her another chance at that swoon. Teeth nibbled, tongue swirled. She arched into the sensation, wanting more. Wanting him.

Damn it all. She didn't care what he said. She wanted to feel him against her. She reached for his shirt, but he grasped her wrists and put them to her sides. He stood and smiled. In one swift movement, the sweatshirt was gone and she was blessed with viewing his wonderful chest. Sitting on the floor, he removed his boots and socks and tossed them to the side. He crawled to her on his hands and knees, stopping when his face met her thighs.

Her heart roared in her chest. He wasn't thinking of doing *that*, was he?

He hooked his fingers around the band of her panties and tugged them off. He then spread her legs and looked up at her, his eyes heavy with desire, and inhaled through his nose. "You smell really good right now."

His voice sounded husky, as if he was drunk. Did she do that to him? He was certainly driving *her* nuts.

She was going to break his rule and speak. Tell him it wasn't necessary for him to go down on her. What if he didn't like it? Did she really want that kind of memory?

But by the time she was ready to voice her opinion, he grabbed her hips and licked her sex. His tongue was warm and wet and oh, so, good. Fisting the covers, she fell back as his ministrations sent her over the edge. No wonder women liked this. What wasn't to like?

"You taste even better." He dove his tongue inside her and then swirled it around her clit. She jerked when he did that, which apparently gave him another idea. He stuck two fingers inside her and sucked the little nub.

The orgasm struck hard and she screamed out his name. Glory God, she had never felt such explosions before.

Somewhere between that suck and coming, he managed to ditch the pants. He moved her so she was lengthwise on the bed and then climbed on top of her. He kissed her, making her forget about everything except wanting him in her.

* * * *

Calix never knew Annie could taste so sweet. He never knew tasting her would make him so hard. Every move he made on her was meant for her pleasure, but somehow he managed to enjoy it just as much.

While he devoured her luscious mouth, he found her breasts and tweaked her nipples. She arched into him and held onto his neck.

It would be so easy to enter her this way, but he had other plans. He unhooked her arms and turned her over. Not once did she question his motives. She completely trusted him and he would make sure not to lose that trust.

Pulling her hair aside, he nuzzled her neck. She smelled so good. He dug his erection into her backside and she moaned. Soon he would be in her. But not yet. Anticipation would make it sweeter.

He just wished he knew who was anticipating it more.

He slid his hands over soft, smooth skin and caressed her breasts, squeezing them gently, rolling the hardened nipples between his thumb and finger. Her moans brought him joy. Apparently, she enjoyed his fondling as much as he did. He kissed along the indentation of her spine, making her gasp. Leaving those soft mounds behind, he ran his hands down her sides, stopping at her hips. Gently, he lifted her bottom into the air.

How could she not think she was beautiful? His eyes knew beauty. So did his body. He fit so perfectly in her.

She brought her knees up under her, raising her buttocks, tempting him. He wanted to taste her again, but negated that idea. Right now he needed to be in her. Be connected. Be one.

He guided his penis into her warm, wet, wonder. After a few small thrusts, he was able to bury deep inside her, deeper than he'd ever been. His testicles rubbed against her pubic hair and clenched. A driving need urged him on. He pumped in and out of her, motivated by her moans of pleasure.

He could not understand why someone would do it from behind when seeing her expressions was almost as good as releasing, but there were benefits from all positions, this one providing him deeper access. Unfortunately, he was not rubbing against the part she enjoyed the most. He reached around her and found that little nub.

She jerked and shoved back into him. Her breathing became rapid and she gripped the covers. Her orgasm squeezed him and he paused for a moment to enjoy the sensation. When she pushed into him, urging him to continue, he thrust into her until his testicles tightened and his own release threatened.

He pulled out and flipped her over. There were some things he just had to see. He slipped back inside, back home, and stared at the person he cared for the most. "I love you, Annie."

His own orgasm took him over the edge.

She wrapped her arms and legs around him and hugged him tight. Against the stupid rules he had set at the beginning of this session, but by this time he did not care. He turned soft in her arms.

CHAPTER 16

Holy shit on a shingle. Annie snuggled into Calix. She'd never felt so cherished in all her life. And the sex. Holy shit, the sex. He could experiment with her any time. He was her guy. Forever.

He rubbed his hand on her belly. "Will your stomach get big like that woman from the store?"

Knowing her luck, probably bigger. "Yeah, does that freak you out?"

"No. I think it is a miracle a child can survive inside you, that it can breathe."

Because life on his planet was created in the lab. What would that be like, if her own people could do that? Probably not good. "Do you see the children on your planet or are they hidden until adulthood?"

"I am familiar with children and I have taught history to them, but I have not seen one younger than five years of age until I came to this planet. Babies seem helpless."

"They are. That's why they need their parents. To take care of them."

Calix touched her cheek. "I look forward to taking care of our child."

He kissed her, long and deep. Damn if she didn't want to have sex again. But time was running short and she wasn't helping any.

"Hate to stop a good time, but we did come out here for a reason, didn't we?" she asked.

He laughed and hugged her. "Yes, we did. But I have been much too distracted lately."

"Mmm, me too." She sat up and stretched. "But we really need to find an answer to our problem."

"I am sure there are more files I can download. If the data even exists."

She located her panties on the floor and slipped them on. "Well, if you think it's a theory, see if they document theories. It's a start, anyway." Her bra had landed on one of the portals. As she plucked it free, she stopped to gaze out and gasped. Two men were standing in the snow. One in a long overcoat and a scarf, the other in a puffy coat and a knitted beanie. Since they weren't carrying rifles, they were most likely not hunters. "Calix. We have company."

He bolted upright and joined her at the portal. "They know the ship is here. How?"

More like who? Who would be out here looking? "Are you sure you weren't detected when you landed here?"

"Yes, I am sure." His eyes widened. "Oh no."

"What? You're *not* sure?"

He shook his head. "That old man knew about this ship."

"Yeah, so? You moved it. And neither one of those guys is that old man."

"What if he told somebody? Do you think that is possible?"

Oh crap. Of course it was possible. If the guy believed he was on an alien spacecraft, he probably spread the word around. That still didn't answer her question. "Okay, say he told someone. How did those two end up here, then?"

"How do you identify people on this planet? With fingerprints, correct?"

"Yeah, but your fingerprints…" She stopped as her brain finally functioned. "Ah, crap. I thought Mac wore his gloves."

"He did, but when we got to the house, he wanted to make sure the man was still alive and he took them off. He did not put them back on until after he closed the door."

And of course, her brother had a record, so his fingerprints would have been in the system. "This isn't good. If those guys have access to fingerprints, then they're with the government. Probably some super-secret agency I don't know about." She pulled her cellphone out of the pocket of her jeans. "I should call Mac. Maybe he can distract these jokers."

"Do not bother," he said. "You cannot get a signal inside the ship. I had to wait until the door was open before I could call."

Not that she didn't trust him, but she still checked. No bars. "So what should we do?"

* * * *

Doug stood in the tree line, shivering. If he had been smart, he would have worn warmer clothes. Would have brought something warm to drink.

After O'Shea left the cabin, Doug had decided to question the sister. Make her think her brother was in trouble. But no one had answered the door.

They'd gone around to the back when John had pointed out the footsteps leading to the tree line. Whoever went out that way had yet to return. They followed the tracks and, lo and behold, the tracks stopped abruptly. Either something was there or something picked them up into the air.

John placed his hand out, as if he were a mime. "There's something here all right. And I think I found the door. Should I open it?"

Holy shit! Had they actually stumbled across the spaceship? "You might not want to do that. Remember what happened to the old guy?"

"So, what, we're supposed to stand out here and freeze our butts off until someone comes out?"

"Well, you could try knocking."

John shook his head, but he pounded on the door anyway. "Hello! Someone home?"

They either didn't hear or were ignoring them. And if it were an alien, probably ignoring them. Doug could barely contain his eagerness. Something unknown to them was here. He just couldn't see it.

Together they waited in the tree line where the wind wasn't as severe.

"What's that sound?" John was leaning against a tree and looked up as if something flew overhead.

The cold caused Doug's teeth to rattle; he couldn't hear anything else. Once he clenched his jaw, a vibrating engine sounded low. "Shit! It's taking off." He rushed into the clearing where a large patch of packed snow appeared. "Damn it! We need to get back to the cabin. I want you to move the car away, make it look like we left. Then meet me in the back of the cabin. We'll get them when they return."

"You sure they'll return?"

"I think they're living in that cabin, so yeah, I'm pretty sure." He just hoped he didn't freeze with those words.

* * * *

Calix stared out the backseat window of Mac's car, but the scenery flew by in a blur. His mind was elsewhere, figuring out how to keep Annie and Mac safe. According to Mac, the government did not like foreigners on their land or the people who hid them. Calix did not want to get anyone in trouble.

Once he had found a spot to land his ship, Annie was able to call Mac, who had come and picked them up. Unfamiliar with the territory, Calix wasn't sure he would be able to find the ship again without his locator now. He should have gotten it when Annie had suggested it.

She looped her arm under his and held his hand. "It'll be okay. They don't know what you look like. And they knew the ship left. I'm sure they're long gone by now."

Calix was not as confident as Annie. If anything, the more they spoke about their government, the more nervous he became. But he could not leave Annie. He had promised he would stay with her. A man kept his promises. Mac had said.

Mac pulled into the driveway. "Looks like Annie was right. No one is here."

No one they could see. Calix found it hard to believe the men wouldn't stick around, but the temperature had gotten colder. It was possible they were not prepared to stay for any length of time and went back for more supplies. Whatever the reason, now was his chance to get the locator before it was found by the wrong person.

"Do you have a shovel? It might help me find that locator."

"There's one on the back porch," she said. "I can show you."

"No, I want you to stay inside. Mac can do it."

"It's just the porch. I'm not an invalid."

"You are as long as you wear that boot. Please stay in."

She wrapped her arms around his waist, looked up and batted her eyes. "I will if you promise to snuggle with me by the fireplace when you finish."

"I would enjoy that." He kissed her forehead, which led to her lips. He couldn't get enough of her. But he had to do this now, before it was too late. He pulled away.

He really wanted to do that snuggling by the fire with Annie, but leaving would be better. He could stay on his ship or move to another city. Neither one appealed to him, but maybe she had a better idea. One that would include both of them. However, he needed that locator first. Then he would discuss his options with her.

Mac went to the little shed at the end of the porch and pulled out a stick with prongs at the end. "This rake should work better than the shovel." He indicated how it should be used. "Do you need any help?"

The hill between the cabin and the tree line made it impossible to see anyone out there. Of course, that meant he and Mac couldn't be seen, either. Still, he got an uneasy feeling as if someone were watching. Or waiting.

Calix took the rake. "No. It would be better if you stayed. Annie might want to help then too."

"You got that right. Not that I can always stop her."

Calix smiled as he thought about all the times she managed to get her way. "I do need you to do me a favor."

"What kind of favor?"

"If I do not come back, watch after her. Make sure she stays safe."

"You plan on going somewhere?"

"Not if I can help it. But if something were to go wrong… For her safety, your safety, I do not want either of you coming after me."

"Ah, shit. You're not asking for much, are you?"

"I love her, Mac. I need to know she will be safe. That both of you will be safe."

Mac nodded. "I'll do my best. That's all I can promise. Man, I hope it doesn't come to that."

"So do I." Calix placed his hand on Mac's shoulder. "Thank you. You are a good friend. A good brother."

"You're not so bad yourself, big guy. Go on. Hurry up, then. I'll have some hot chocolate waiting for you."

Calix slowly trudged up the hill, following the tracks in the snow. The men had returned this way, so maybe they had left. Once the tree line came into view, he crouched and waited, keeping alert for any movement or people hiding nearby. A bird chirped in the distance, but nothing else out of the ordinary. He breathed easier.

The snow was disturbed where he had fallen during that storm. Apparently, the men had also found the hole, or at least one of them had.

Calix took the rake and used it as Mac showed him. The device could not have gone far.

"Looking for something?"

Calix froze at the stranger's voice. Then his heart sank into his stomach. At a time like this, Mac or Annie might say "shit" or "damn" and he could almost see why. He certainly felt like saying something. He turned around.

The man with the overcoat, the one Calix had seen from the ship, held the locator in his hand. "As luck would have it, I fell in that hole and came across this. Would this be what you're looking for?"

The other man who wore the knit cap approached from Calix's right, holding what appeared to be a rifle. At least they hadn't shot first. Maybe if he played it innocent, these men would leave him alone.

"Yes, I am. May I have it back?" Calix stretched out his arm and took a step forward.

The man in the overcoat held a hand up. "I don't think so. Wow, I honestly didn't think you'd understand me. And while I thought you might look like us, you are rather on the large size."

Calix made a point to speak more like Annie and Mac. "What's not to understand? You're speaking English. So, may I have it back? Please?"

The man laughed and looked to his partner. "Polite, isn't he?" He nodded some kind of communication and turned back to Calix. "What is this? Some kind of ray gun?"

"A ray gun?" Calix laughed, but it came out weak and probably not very convincing. But what could it be? Not a remote control.

Then he remembered Mac playing with an old game system Annie owned. "It's the controller to my game. Now can I have it back?"

"I'm afraid I can't do that. I think this is an alien device and you're the alien that goes with it. So if you're smart, you'll come with us real easy like and we'll talk about where you came from and what your intentions are here."

The man with the knit cap started for Calix, holding the gun out in front. Calix took a couple of steps back and held the rake across his chest. As if that would stop a bullet. "An alien? Are you serious? I don't have to go with you crazy people. I have rights."

"Rights? You hear that, John? He has rights. Fine. Show me your ID, then."

"I don't have it on me."

"Of course you don't. Should we go to the cabin and get it?"

Calix looked at the gun John held. He did not want that anywhere near Annie and Mac.

"That's what I thought. So I'll tell you how it is. If you run, we'll tranquilize you. If we have to tranquilize you, I will make sure your friends in the cabin see the inside of a jail. Where they could rot, for all I care. Is that what you want?"

No. It was far from what he wanted. "Do not hurt them. They have done nothing wrong."

"I have no need for them. If you cooperate, I promise I'll forget all about the O'Sheas."

Calix took one last look toward the cabin. He could only see the top of the roof, but sent Annie all his love. At least she was safe.

* * * *

Annie paced the living room. "What's taking him so long?"

Mac stood in her way and placed his hands on her shoulders. "Will you calm down? He hasn't been gone all that long. Now sit down and enjoy the fire."

"I can't sit down. One of us should have gone with him. Will you go check on him? Please?"

Mac rolled his eyes. "He's a big guy. I really don't think—"

"Fine. If you won't do it, then I will." She grabbed her coat and headed for the back door.

Mac gripped her arm. "Whoa. Hold on there. Geez. Impatient much?"

"One of us will check on him. Who's it gonna be?"

"Well, I know he'd kick my ass if I let you go."

She laughed. "Calix wouldn't hurt you. He's too sweet."

"Oh yeah? When it comes to protecting you, there is no sweetness in him."

He had a point. Calix was even bossy with her if he thought she was doing something foolish. "Will you check on him, please? If he asks why you're out there, just tell him I bugged you to death."

Mac slipped on his jacket. "And it wouldn't be a lie, either."

Once her brother stepped outside, she pulled out a chair and sat by the door. He told her to sit, didn't say where. A few minutes later, he disappeared over the hill.

Each second felt like fifty. God, what was taking him so long? If Calix was okay, Mac would have returned right away. Well, maybe not. Maybe Calix was having trouble finding his locator. Mac would help.

Movement at the top of the hill. Calix? Mac? Only one head and the hair was long. She opened the door and stepped out on the back porch. Without her coat, she shivered, but only hugged herself instead of going back inside. Mac held the rake in his hand. What happened? Where was Calix? Why wasn't Mac running?

He was too far to hear her and she wasn't about to yell. When Mac reached the steps, she asked, "Is he hurt?"

Mac shook his head. "He's not there. All I found was the rake. Maybe he found the locator and went back to his ship."

"But why? Why wouldn't he come back here first? No, something's wrong. Do you think they took him?"

Mac shrugged. "That, or he decided to leave."

She didn't like the sound of Mac's voice. Like he wasn't telling her everything. "What do you mean? He wouldn't leave."

"He would if he thought your life was in danger."

"But he would have told me. No. Something went wrong."

He put his arm around her shoulders. "Come on. Let's go back in where it's warm."

She shrugged away. "No. Let's go back to the ship, then."

"It'll be dark soon. If he's at the ship, he'll be there tomorrow."

"If?" She clutched her chest. It felt like someone was ripping her heart out.

Mac ushered her inside where the warm air blew in her face. The cabin felt empty. Her chest felt empty.

She collapsed onto the chair. "He's in trouble, Mac. I feel it. If I cover my foot up, we can go out searching for him."

Mac knelt in front of her. "Listen, I didn't want to tell you this, but his weren't the only footprints out there."

"You saying they took him?"

"I'm not saying anything. We don't know what happened. It could have been the tracks they made after Calix moved his ship. It could have been the tracks Calix made because he saw them and ran away. Which means he could be at his ship. Let's not do anything stupid, okay? I'm sure he'll get in touch as soon as he's able."

Unless he was captured. Then how would he contact them? It's not like those men would let Calix make a phone call. "Do you remember where that old man lived?"

"Maybe."

She grabbed the table and stood. "Then let's go. He probably knows who those guys are."

Mac held her shoulders and pushed her back into the chair. "I get it, you're upset, but let's not overreact. We'll check out the ship tomorrow, okay? If he's not there, then we'll check on the old man."

"They could be torturing him as we speak. Tomorrow might be too late."

"Will you listen to yourself? They're not going to torture him. They don't even know what he is, if they even have him. But you know what would torture him? You, getting hurt."

She pounded her hand on the table. "You're asking me to do nothing, Mac. I can't do nothing."

"No, I'm asking you to wait. I'm guessing Calix is doing something to protect you, and he wouldn't be so happy if you blew that, now would he?"

She hated it when he was right, but waiting might just kill her. "You promise? We'll go out tomorrow?"

He hugged her close. "I promise."

The night looked to be long and lonely. She prayed Calix was safe. Heaven help anyone who hurt him.

* * * *

Calix pulled on the restraints that bound his wrists to the seat. The plastic cut into his skin and his constant tugging was making sores. He did not like being immobilized. He had gone with these people peacefully, so why was he bound? Did they think he would take over and fly this aircraft?

He had been taken to an airport and practically dragged up a portable staircase attached to one of the aircraft. He had seen them on the TV and the laptop, and Annie had to explain why everyone did not have one, but he had not realized how large they were. And while this one was large all by itself, there were airplanes over twice the size nearby. Once inside, he had been pushed down a narrow walkway and shoved into a seat about half-way to the back, where he was then bound. A few minutes later, they were in the air.

"You can tug on that all you want, but you're not getting free." The overcoat man, who had introduced himself as Agent Lazur, sat in the seat across the aisle. "Besides, where are you going to go? It's a long way down to the ground. Unless you're Superman. Are you Superman?"

Calix had no idea who Superman was. Probably one of those fictional characters he had hoped to read about someday. Would he ever have another someday? Probably not. And here he was afraid of what his own people would do to him. "So why bind me if I cannot get away?"

"Like I'm going to trust someone your size not to overtake us and this plane. I'm not stupid."

If only he did know how to fly an airplane, then he would try harder to get free. So, what should he do? Would telling this man the truth make things worse? Annie seemed to think so. And with the way he was bound, he was beginning to believe her. Eventually, the people on this planet would need to know what was in store for them and he was the only one—right now—who could tell them. But what if they didn't believe him? How could he fix this?

"Are you going to tell me your name or do I have to keep calling you Buster?"

The agent had tried numerous times to start a conversation, wanted to know more about the ship. Calix was sure if he started talking, he would be tricked into saying something he did not wish to divulge, in the same manner Annie had done. So he had responded each time the way Annie had instructed, this time no different. "I want a lawyer. You have no right to hold me."

"Okay. Buster, it is. You sure are pig-headed, you know? And I have every right to hold you if I believe you're a spy."

A spy and not an alien? Was that better or…worse? "What do you want with me?"

"I want to know what you are."

What, not who. As if he was some kind of thing instead of a person. "So, not a spy. An alien. Are you ever going to stop with the alien nonsense?"

Lazur smiled. "No, because that's what you are. So, are you going to talk to me now?"

"I want a lawyer first. I want to understand these rights you say you have to hold me against my will."

Agent Lazur scowled and moved to the back.

For several hours Calix was left alone. He was caught napping when the aircraft jerked him awake. It was landing. It would have been nice to witness the landing, or see where he was being taken, but apparently his captors had decided that would not be in their best interests. The windows were covered and out of reach.

Annie was correct. If this was how her people treated unknowns, how might they treat him if they knew he *was* an alien? He took several deep breaths. They would have to release him to get off the airplane. Then he would make his escape.

But would that put Annie and Mac at risk? Calix was far away from them now. He could contact them and warn them. And then he would hide somewhere else and never see them again, or his child. He would not put their lives in danger.

A great weight squeezed his heart, bringing tears to his eyes. Annie had cried when she had thought she would never see him again. Had told him she was sad. He did not like feeling sad. It hurt too much.

"Hold still." John held a weapon they called a Taser— something that would stun and not kill—against Calix's chest while he unbuckled the seat belt.

They had told him about the weapon, probably hoping it would scare him, and in a way it had. He had been shocked numerous times back home, from touching. Would that weapon be any different? Probably not. If he hoped to escape while disembarking, the last thing he wanted was to be shocked unconscious.

John cut the strips attaching the rings around Calix's wrists to the seats. "Put your arms behind you."

Calix leaned over and did as he was told. He could take John down, but his feet were still attached to the chair. Another plastic strip was looped through both rings, binding his wrists behind him. Not an ideal situation, but as soon as his feet were free, and he cleared the aircraft, he could make a dash for it. He would figure out how to get the restraints off later.

After John cut the ankle strips free, Agent Lazur tugged on Calix's jacket. "Get up, Buster."

Calix stood. It felt good to stretch his legs. The trip had been long and the area small; he would have been cramped even if he hadn't been immobilized. A prickly sensation traveled up his legs. Right now walking seemed unlikely. And he wanted to run from them?

John prodded Calix in the back. "Let's go."

Calix took his time by stumbling over his feet and bumping into the seats. Not only to make it appear as if he had trouble walking—which he did, just not to that extent—but to get the circulation back in his legs.

When he got to the exit, nightfall greeted him, as well as warmer weather. Not warm enough to go without a coat, but not that bone-chilling cold, either. Even better, no snow on the ground. Hope surged.

The wind whipped across his face; flags crackled in the distance. He took the steps slowly since the hand rail was out of reach. The last thing he needed was to fall. He thought about asking what city they had landed in, but since he had been uncommunicative with them, he doubted they would be forthcoming with that information.

Straight ahead, a building was several yards away. To his right was a lighted parking lot, and beyond that, his goal—trees. If they walked to the building, he would be able to make a dash, catching them unaware. Yes. This could work. The trees would offer him dark cover.

A long black car pulled up.

Hope crashed. John was at Calix's back and Agent Lazur opened the door. A gust of wind sent papers into the night.

"Ah, damn. Get those!" the agent yelled.

As John rushed after the flying papers, Calix bolted for the trees. His legs burned, but he would not stop.

Shouting voices. Squealing tires. He was a few feet from the parking lot when a weapon discharged. Pain flared in his arm. Did they just shoot him? He kept running.

The cars would have made great cover if there were more of them. But even a few were better than none. He did his best to keep a car between him and the enemy. Because they were the enemy. Everything Annie and Mac had told him was true.

Another discharge and more pain, this time in his back. His vision wavered as he wound his way through the parked jungle. The ground undulated and he stumbled. Must. Keep. Moving. The trees—freedom—was within reach.

He blinked and ran into the side of a car. An alarm went off. No, the trees. He needed the trees. He continued onward, but they seemed to get farther away instead of closer. Each step became a chore and his head felt heavy. He fell to his knees. *No.* Must. Keep. Moving. His breathing was ragged. He could not get his legs to work.

"Don't move," John said.

Calix fell to his side, the weakest he had ever felt. Was this what death was like? Would he just fall asleep and never wake up?

John pointed the weapon at him.

Agent Lazur appeared. "Two shots and he's still awake? Damn. Next time use bigger tranquilizers."

Not dead, drugged. *Damn.* That was a good word. Now he might never be free.

CHAPTER 17

Calix opened his eyes. His head was pounding and he was lying on his back on a bed in a strange room. He attempted to sit up, but straps across his chest secured him to the bed. His wrists were secured also. And on top of all that, he was wearing some type of gown instead of his regular clothes. Had they destroyed them so he could not run off again? Not that he could get free from the bed. Guess they had learned their lesson. No escaping today.

Thankfully, curtains covered the windows. His head already pounded. Adding sunlight to the mix would not help him any. A dimly lit lamp hung overhead and there were monitors to his left making faint beeping sounds. They seemed to be in sync with his heartbeat. At least the bed was comfortable. And there was a chair and a television, not that he could reach either.

Light spilled in from another source as the door opened. Agent Lazur entered and leaned back, shutting them in. He smiled, but it was not a happy smile. Calix was fairly certain the man was furious with him.

"Hello, Buster. Did you have a nice nap? I thought maybe you were immune to those tranqs, but apparently not. You conked out just like the rest of us would."

Calix stared at his captor. "I want a lawyer."

Lazur strolled to the chair, turned it so the back faced Calix, and sat with his arms resting on the seatback. "Listen, you're not going to get a lawyer, so you might as well stop saying it."

"Then send me back to Canada."

The agent's eyebrows rose. "Canada? That's a good one. I do have to say, you seem to know your stuff."

"Will you let me sit up?"

"No."

That one word was said with such disdain, it abolished any hope Calix had in getting out of the situation alive. He was trapped, just as Annie said he would be.

"Remember when I said if you cooperated, I would forget about the O'Sheas?"

Calix swallowed the lump that formed in his throat. "I came with you."

"Yes, you did. But you're far from cooperating. It would help if you answer my questions."

"Why? You don't believe what I tell you, so why should I answer?"

"Fair enough. Where in Canada are you from?"

Calix quickly accessed his memory. He had researched the country after Annie asked if he'd come from there. "Vancouver."

Agent Lazur nodded. "What do you do there?"

"I teach."

"Really? You're a teacher? You know, I can almost believe that. You certainly don't seem like a warrior."

That was more true than not. The only warrior he knew was Annie.

"What subject?"

"History."

"So what's a history teacher from Vancouver doing in Spokane?"

"Exploring."

"Without a passport? How did you get into the States?"

"I never said I didn't have a passport. I just didn't have it on me."

"Then tell me your name so I can verify this claim and you can go home. To Canada."

Calix stared down at his feet. *Damn, damn, damn.* Yeah, he liked that word. He would be stuck in their care forever, it would seem. Not that he had a home to go to. Annie was the only home he had ever experienced, and even that was off limits now.

"That's what I thought. So what is Annie O'Shea to you?"

My wife. My reason for living. She might not think they were married, but he did. He would have enjoyed growing old with her. Now he would be lucky to reach thirty. "No one."

The agent stood. "No one, huh? Then you wouldn't mind if I brought her in here? To question her?"

Calix closed his eyes and fisted his hands. The beeps on the machine sounded closer together. If that man so much as touched her...

"See, I think she's more than a no one. I think you care about her."

He shook his head. Afraid his voice might betray him, not that the machine hadn't already done so. He had to keep Annie out of this.

"Tell me what this is." Agent Lazur held the locator in his hands.

Calix relaxed at the change of subject. "I told you. It's my game controller."

"Sure it is. I think it belongs with your spaceship."

Calix laughed, but did not think he was very convincing. "A spaceship? What do you think I am?"

"I think you're an alien. Not an illegal alien from Canada, but the extraterrestrial type."

"Now who's joking? Do I look like a little green man to you?"

Agent Lazur went to the door. "It's not a joke, and I will eventually prove it. While you were out, we ran some tests. Took some X-rays, too. I will get to the truth, and you will be exposed for what you are."

Calix hoped Annie's theory was correct and he was the same species as the agent. "Which is human."

"Sure. We'll talk after I get the results." The agent departed and the door clicked locked.

Alone. How often had he wanted that very thing on his own planet? He missed Mac. He missed Annie even more. Knowing he would never see either again made his chest hurt.

* * * *

Annie reached the street and shook the snow off her feet before limping back to Mac's Cherokee. All that walking to and from the ship had aggravated her ankle, but she couldn't very well ask Mac to carry her.

She had really hoped she'd find Calix, but there wasn't any sign he had even returned. The only footsteps around his ship were the ones he had made when they left. Hadn't stopped her from going inside though. The emptiness she had found caused an ache in her chest that wouldn't go away.

She had to face it. Those men had taken Calix.

She climbed into the car and buckled up. "We have to go to that old man. He's gotta know who those guys are."

"If they are government officials, how much information do you think they'd give that old guy?"

"We won't know unless we ask."

Mac shook his head and started up the car. "No."

"What? You promised!"

"I shouldn't have. I'm sorry, Annie, but I won't put you in any more danger."

"No!" She pounded on Mac's arms. "You have to take me to that man. We can't abandon Calix. We can't!"

Mac grabbed her arms and held them together. "You don't know he's been taken, so cut it out."

"I can't give up. He's my life." She clawed to get free, but his grip was too tight.

"Annie, you hardly know him."

She finally yanked free, or Mac finally gave up. "I can't help what I feel. No one has mattered as much to me. Not even Denny."

"Then start thinking about him. How would he feel if you got hurt looking for him? Huh? Think about the baby and how much he wants it. You know he'd be here if he could. You're just gonna have to be patient."

Patient? God, she hated being patient, wasn't even sure she owned the gene, but what else could she do? It wasn't like she could call every government agency to see if they had an alien on hand. Still, it killed her not doing anything. She just wanted him back.

"Listen, I have to go to work today," Mac said. "Are you going to be okay on your own?"

"Are you asking if I plan on driving anywhere?" As if she knew how to get to the old man's place. "You can be a real jerk, you know that?"

"You think I'm a jerk now, how about I call Portia?"

"I hate you."

He dropped her off. "You might want to call Jen and get some legal advice."

"Like she's going to know how to find a missing alien?"

"No, doofus. But those guys will probably return. We need to know what our rights are. Plus, it wouldn't hurt to let someone else know what's going on. I'm scared, Annie. Those guys scared me."

"I'm scared too. Then don't go to work. Stay here. Help me find him."

"I can't. My court date is today. I'll see you later. And call Jen."

Of all the days to have his court date. As she clomped down to her office, she stopped at the bedroom door. Calix's chip was in there, being totally useless. She might as well carry it, just in case he came back and needed to locate her. Right? She went to the nightstand and opened the drawer.

So tiny and apparently powerful. What kind of people could put such a leash on their own? Without Calix to stop them, would they send someone else? According to Calix, they most likely had. Well, if they did, they would find her instead of him. Would it matter?

"Guess I'll find out if it happens." She slipped the chip in her pants pocket.

She didn't want to talk to Jen over the phone. If she was still on vacation, the call wouldn't matter. Annie opened the message app.

"You back from your trip yet?"

Only a few moments went by when Jen responded. *"Yep. Back 2 work 4 me."*

"Can you stop by after?"

"Sure. NP. See ya."

Well, that was easy. Annie sat at her desk. Work was a great distracter, even if her heart wasn't in it. By four o'clock her stomach growled, telling her to take a break. She flipped the light on in the kitchen and searched for some food.

A knock on the door caused her to jump. She never heard anyone drive up, but then the snow did manage to keep the gravel crunching down to zero. She hobbled over to the door and peeked through the window. Time to discover their options. If they had any.

She opened the door with a smile. "Jen! So glad you could make it."

Her friend looked radiant. California sun had agreed with her. Hopefully this visit wouldn't spoil that.

* * * *

Doug pounded his fist on the desk, sending the test results onto the floor. There had to be some mistake.

John picked up the report and placed it back where it came from. "Bad news?"

Doug stared at his partner as he sat in the chair, laid-back as if they were chatting in the backyard, eating burgers and drinking beers. Nothing ever bothered this guy. "What made you take this job?"

John shrugged. "The toys?"

Doug laughed. Yeah, they had some pretty awesome electronics. "Did you always believe in aliens?"

"Who says I believe?"

"If you don't believe, why take the job?"

"Why not take the job? Someone who doesn't believe would certainly find every reason to disprove extraterrestrial beings. It's like being a P.I., but the benefits are better. So, what got you so angry?"

Doug picked up the report. "The tests came back normal."

"What tests?"

"The blood tests. The X-rays. They say our friend, Buster, is human."

John chuckled. "Sorry, man. But I kind of figured that out already."

"Even with his funky eye color?"

"No different than Elizabeth Taylor's. Is she an alien, too?"

"Elizabeth who?"

"The actress? Man, you really need to get out more."

Like getting out mattered. Actors, actresses. What did they have to do with aliens? Doug folded his arms on the desktop. "What about that ship? Explain that."

"Okay, you got me there. But it doesn't necessarily mean it's extraterrestrial. Maybe Buster's a genius. People build strange things all the time. See, this is why it's good I don't believe. You need someone to show you the truth."

The truth? Doug knew the truth and it wasn't in the form of a genius human. That thing was an alien. "Tell you what. You go nab the girl, Annie O'Shea. Bring her here. I'll bet you anything, he'll spill if he thinks we'll hurt her."

"Hey, I didn't sign up to torture anyone."

"No one's getting tortured. I just want to scare him. Motivate him to speak."

"So how will you know he's telling you the truth, then? What makes you think he wouldn't tell you what you want to hear just to save her, if she's as important as you think?"

"I'll use a lie detector test."

"But if he's not human, do you really think you can fool him with the machine?"

"I don't know. There's something about him that's kind of naïve. I have a feeling he'd believe anything we say."

* * * *

Annie carried two mugs to the kitchen. Talk about being a chicken shit. She just didn't know how to broach the subject. So she'd suggested they watch *Sleepless in Seattle* instead.

Big mistake. She missed Calix even more.

"Okay, who is he?" Jen sat at the dining table, staring with accusation in her eyes.

"What?" The mugs slipped through Annie's fingers and she caught them before they crashed on the counter. Crisis diverted. Sort of.

"Oh, God. Are you trying to get back with Denny? Annie, do you think—"

"No, no, a hundred times no. That's over." Annie sat across from her friend. What could she say? *I met this alien....*

"Well, someone's got you down. You usually perk up after watching that movie. Is that why you invited me over? Guy troubles?"

"We have troubles. Mac and me."

"What kind?" Jen's eyes lit. "Legal troubles? What happened? Did you do something stupid to Logan?" She glanced at the boot. "Annie...what did you do?"

It wasn't the conversation she was going for, but damn it, Logan just made her so frickin' mad. "Why didn't you press charges? I saw him hit you. I could be a witness."

"You saw..." Jen lowered her head. "Shit. He slapped me, yes. After I slapped him."

"You slapped him?" God, just the thought made her giddy. "Still, he shouldn't have hit you back."

"Maybe so, but I'm not pressing charges for name-calling and slapping. God, Annie. What did you do?"

"What any good friend would. I kicked his ass. Or tried to. But Logan isn't the cause of our troubles."

"So what's going on? What kind of legal advice do you need?"

Annie slipped her hand inside her pocket and gripped Calix's chip. In a way it comforted her. A little piece of Calix in her hand, since she couldn't touch the little piece of him inside her womb. Would the baby have his eyes? God, she hoped so.

Just thinking about Calix and those two men doing God-knew-what to him brought tears to her eyes. Before she could make a fool of herself, she claimed needing to use the bathroom and left Jen in the dining room.

After splashing water on her face, Annie felt more in control. She could do this and not sound crazy, right? Because nothing about harboring an alien sounded crazy.

"Annie!" Jen yelled. "You might want to come out here. There's a big guy on your back porch. I think he just passed out."

A big guy? Calix? Her heart soared and she rushed out of the bathroom as fast as her boot allowed. But when she got to the back door, she stopped. *Holy shit on a shingle.* Not Calix. The man lying on her porch was even bigger than her guy, yet wore the same clothes. He most likely came from Calix's planet.

She slid the door open. No matter who he was, she had to help him. He was practically frozen, having worn no cap or gloves. "Help me get him inside."

"Are you sure that's wise? Shouldn't we call the cops or something?"

"I think I know who he is. It'll be all right." She hoped. The man most likely came for Calix, not anyone else.

Together, they lifted him under his arms. Either he was frozen or his body was solid muscle. He shivered and his teeth clattered. Thankfully, the man wasn't completely out of it, and getting him to his feet didn't require a forklift. He muttered words similar to the ones Calix used when he had spoken to the people from his planet.

"What's he saying?"

"No idea. He's probably delirious." And she was delirious if she thought she'd keep Calix's identity a secret from Jen now. They each slipped an arm around the man. Not as if that would prevent him from falling if he couldn't walk.

They had just made it inside when the man jerked free and landed on his butt. His eyes widened. He acted just like Calix had when she first touched him.

"Jen, shut the door and get me the afghan." When her friend departed, she went back to the stranger. "It's okay," she said, hoping he understood. "We can't shock you." At least she didn't think she could. Calix had the chip in him, but had it been connected to anything? Only way to find out if her theory was correct was to actually touch his skin. She prayed she hadn't made a mistake. The guy was way too big for them to carry to the couch.

She grabbed his ice-cold hand. He tensed but didn't pass out. Yay!

Jen returned with the afghan and draped it over the man's shoulders. His shudders seemed to quiet a bit.

"Can you understand me?" Annie asked.

"Yes."

Barry White had nothing on this guy; his voice was deep and sexy as hell. Jen let out a little moan.

Annie gave a quick glance at her friend. Jen had the decency to blush. Well, she couldn't really blame her friend. The stranger was quite stunning. Not as stunning as her guy, but still…

"How is this possible?" He stared at their linked hands and enunciated each word deliberately, like someone from another country would. Like someone who might have had a crash course in a new language.

She released his hand and made sure to speak slowly so he would understand. "I am not sure. I did not shock Calix, either."

At the mention of Calix's name, his eyebrows rose. "I must speak with him."

"He is not here." She wasn't sure if she was glad or sad. Which confinement was best for Calix? Her people or his own?

He furrowed his head in confusion and then pulled out his own locator. He hit the side as if he thought it was malfunctioning. Annie nearly laughed. How many times had she done that with the television remote?

"You probably got a reading from this." She pulled the chip from her pocket. "Would you like to sit down where it is warmer? And maybe more comfortable?"

He paused for a moment and then hugged his arms. "Yes."

She grabbed his elbow so he could stand, not that she was much help. Neither was the ceiling as it prevented him from straightening to his full height. Even hunched over, the man stood a good deal taller than Calix and probably weighed fifty pounds more—all muscle. Damn, did all the men on their planet look like Adonis? She led him to the living room. He sat on the end of the couch closest to the fireplace, hugging the afghan close.

"Okay, Annie," Jen whispered. "What the hell is going on? Who is this guy and who's Calix?"

"Calix is the reason I asked you to come. He's my—our trouble, but it's a long story. Maybe you should go. I'll tell you tomorrow."

"Oh hell no. I'm not leaving you alone with him."

Did Jen fear for her or just have the hots for him? "Fine, but I can't explain anything right now. You'll have to be patient."

Jen moved to the chair and sat with her arms folded across her chest. Annie chewed her bottom lip. Yeah, she had a lot of explaining to do.

"Calix should not have told you about us."

Annie spun around. The man stared at her with eyes a lighter shade than Calix's, but purplish-blue all the same.

She sat on the other end of the couch. "He basically had no choice. He needed my help. And now I need yours. What's your name? Mine is Annie. My friend over there is Jen."

He stared briefly at Jen, who smiled and waved. "My name is Pax. Where can I find Calix?"

"I wish I knew. Can your device locate another device just like that one?"

He looked down at his hand. "No."

Her heart sunk with those words. She wasn't even sure if Calix had his locator, but if Pax couldn't find Calix, how the heck would she?

CHAPTER 18

Pax 46013 stared at the two females. When he had been given this mission, he read the documentation Calix had assembled regarding this planet. He had not believed the inhabitants resembled his own people—no images were provided—yet he was staring at a species that, while small, could be considered his own.

But how did this species work together if they all lived apart? Or were these two females important enough to warrant a place of their own? The only quarters he ever had in solitude had been his own ship, and he made sure to be in it often.

He should dispose of these females, regardless of their importance on this planet. They already knew too much, and Calix's mission was to observe, not share. Apparently, the man was worse off than anyone knew. But until he had Calix in custody, he would use whatever assistance he could and right now that included these two.

Pax hugged the cover around his shoulders. Heat from the fire at the end of the room took the chill away. His body no longer shuddered and his bones were safe from breaking, which he was sure would occur if he could not control his shaking. He was certain he would not have survived another minute in that weather. The sooner he captured Calix, the sooner he could leave this icebox of a planet.

"Why do you not know where Calix is? Was he aware of my arrival? Is that why he departed?"

"He suspected someone was coming, but he didn't run away," Annie said. "He was taken, and I'm not sure what is being done to him."

The events were worse than he thought. "Taken?"

"Yes. That's why I was hoping you could find him with that device. It's possible he has his."

"I am only receiving two signals. His chip and his ship. There are no others."

"There's no way you can reprogram that thing to find one?"

He did not understand the words she used, but as she pointed to his locator, he assumed it was technical. "I am not a technician. I am a traveler. I do not understand."

"Of course you don't. I swear, no one on your planet can multi-task." She punched the cushion with her fist. "Can a technician from your planet fix that device from over there so it can look for a similar device here?"

"Planet?" Jen asked, her eyes going wide. "Who the hell is this guy?"

"Later," Annie said over her shoulder. She turned back to him. "Can they?"

"I do not know. I am not a technician."

"Well, could you find out?" Her voice raised and she stood, pacing back and forth, flinging her arms. "I mean, really. How hard could it be? It's just a freakin' program."

He had never seen anyone so agitated before. Was this what the documentation meant when it stated they were prone to violence? He must tread carefully. "Why is Calix important to you? Have you been performing experiments?"

"No. That's not to say the men who have him haven't. We need to save him."

"But why do you…want him?"

"Because I love him." Annie covered her face with her hands.

Jen gasped, her hand went to her mouth.

Apparently love was important. Pax had noticed the word in his learning, but had no reference to understand its meaning. "What does that mean?"

Jen stood and wrapped her arms around her companion. It still amazed him how freely they touched. "It means she'll do anything to find him." She spoke to Annie, "I wish you had told me. I'm so sorry."

"I just want him back, Jen. I know the government took him. I'm afraid."

"Did they take him because he is violent?" Pax asked.

Annie looked at him, the whites of her eyes now red, her cheeks wet. "He's not violent. Well, unless he thinks someone is hurting me. Even then he's only being protective, because he loves me. I really doubt he would hurt anyone."

There was that love word again. And his headache flared. He rubbed his temples.

Annie moved to stand in front of him. "I know you don't understand that word. It took Calix a while to understand it, and he probably had an easier time without that chip." She pointed to his temple. "The chip in your head takes away your humanity, your emotions. It's turned you into a virtual robot."

More words he did not understand. "Robot?"

"Yeah, you know. A machine controlled by man."

"I am not a machine. I control my own actions."

"You control what your people want you to control. That chip prevents you from caring, from feeling."

"The chip, as you call it, is only a device to account for our people. Nothing more."

"Yeah, sure. I'll let Calix explain it to you *after* we rescue him. We need to return to your ship so you can find out if your locator can be re-programmed."

Return? In that weather? Pax shivered.

"Annie, do you think that's wise?" Jen asked. "Look at him. He's still half-frozen. Maybe in the morning, once the sun comes up?"

The sun sounded good and warm. It was nice to have one person on his side. Even so, he would still have to dispose of her.

* * * *

Annie scowled at her hot chocolate. Pax refused to go back to his ship and Jen agreed. She almost called Mac to come help her convince those two, but figured he'd only take their side. Besides, he was on a date with Justine and probably wouldn't come over even if she begged.

"This drink is tasty," Pax said. "And I like the warm."

"That's why it's called *hot* chocolate," she said.

"Annie, behave," Jen said. "Pax, do you have chocolate on your planet?"

"No." He sipped at the hot liquid.

"Wow. Can't imagine never having chocolate. It's uncivilized."

He frowned. "We are civilized. More than the people of this planet."

"Hey!" Annie interjected. "You don't know anything about us."

He turned those purplish-blue eyes her way. "I know you live in the woods. How is that civilized?"

Before she could respond, a vehicle pulled into her driveway. She went to the front window.

Holy shit on a shingle. Mac had tried to convince her that Calix had just left on his own, but she'd known in her gut that wasn't the case. And now she had proof. The man who wore the knit cap back at the ship was now in her driveway. But what was he doing here if he had Calix? Maybe Calix had escaped. She needed to talk to that man and now.

"Who is it?" Jen asked.

"He's one of the guys who took Calix. I saw him earlier today." Annie spun around. "He can't see Pax, or he'll take him, too."

"No one will take me. I can prevent that."

"You can't hurt him. He has information I need. We need. You two go back to my office. Jen, text Mac and let him know what's going on."

"And what are you going to do?"

"Whatever I can. He's my ticket to finding Calix."

Jen grabbed her arm. "Annie, be careful. You have no idea how dangerous that person is."

Annie smiled with the first stirrings of hope. "I'll be fine. Now go hide. He can't know anyone's here."

Pax stood. *Thunk.* His head hit the ceiling. "Oww."

"Sorry about the ceiling. I wasn't expecting any giants." Annie nearly snickered, but controlled herself. Pax wouldn't understand, but Jen might scold her again.

She waited near the door while Jen and Pax disappeared down the hall.

Thunk. "Oww." Pax apparently didn't duck.

"Yeah, you might want to watch out for the doorways, too," Jen said.

Annie smiled. Served him right. She'd like to do more damage to the stubborn man, especially if she didn't need his help. Oh, who was she kidding. She did need his help. And Calix would, too, once she rescued him.

The stranger knocked on the door. She opened it up to what she hoped were her answers.

"Hello, Miss O'Shea? My name is Agent Harper." He flashed some kind of identification. "I need to talk to you regarding this man."

She might have asked to see that ID again except he held out a photo of Calix. Pain sliced through her chest and tears threatened to fall as she gazed upon his pale face and closed eyes. She grabbed the picture. "Oh my God! You killed him?"

Agent Harper snatched the photo back. "He's not dead. We took this when he was…asleep."

"Asleep? You mean unconscious, don't you? What did you do to him? And why are you here?"

"Can we discuss this inside?" Agent Harper shivered and huddled inside his coat.

She couldn't have this man spot Pax or Jen, no matter what the weather. "No. You had no right to take him. Where is he? I want to see him."

He stuffed the picture back inside his coat and smiled. "I think that can be arranged."

"It can?" Holy shit. Finally, she was getting somewhere. It might just be the worst mistake she ever made—not just for her, but her baby—but what other option did she have to free Calix? He was alive and she was being taken to him. That was more than she had a moment ago.

* * * *

Mac slammed the door to the cabin, rattling the windows. "Annie! Where are you?"

He had left sweet Justine just before he was about to get lucky. Now he'd be lucky if she ever spoke to him again. What kind of game was his sister playing anyway?

Jen appeared in the hallway. "She's not here. I told you that on the phone."

"No, you said she was leaving with some stranger. I told you not to let her go."

She placed her hands on hips. "And how the heck was I supposed to do that and not be discovered? Besides, she's determined to find Calix, who, by the way, she never did tell me about."

Damn it. Why'd Annie have to be right? And why did she have to go off and do it all by herself? The woman was certifiable. "Did she take her phone?"

Jen shook her head and pointed to the dining room table. Annie's purse was there.

He rummaged through it and found her cell. "Great! How the hell am I supposed to find her?"

"I can find her."

The deep baritone voice had Mac spinning around. A huge man ducked out of Annie's office, continued hunching as his head nearly touched the ceiling, holding one of those locator devices in his hand.

"Who...who—"

"That's Pax," Jen said. "Now I *know* I told you about him."

She had. She just failed to mention the guy was a giant.

"So how can *you* find Annie?" Mac asked.

Pax held up the device, showing a blinking red light. "She has Calix's...chip."

Had she done that on purpose or just forgot she had it? While she was smart and all that, his guess would be the latter. Still, it was good news. "Then we should go after her. Where's your ship?"

"She is moving slowly, so there is no need to follow at this time. When she has reached her destination, then I will depart."

"Damn it!" Mac threw his coat onto the chair. Now he knew how she felt about going after Calix. The wait might very well kill him. If the government or this alien didn't do it first.

* * * *

For the last five minutes, Calix had yelled for help from his darkened room. Eventually someone would arrive if just to shut him up. He had hoped to put his plan into action two hours ago, but fell asleep waiting. Would the building and surrounding area still be as empty at five in the morning as it was at three? It sounded quiet.

This had better work. If he failed, he was at a loss as to what to do next. He had no other idea.

The door opened, spilling light from the hallway.

"What are you going on about now?" A small woman in a white uniform stood in silhouette. Her voice had an edge to it. Maybe his yelling had gotten on her nerves.

"I need to use the bathroom."

She started to turn and then stopped. "Number one or number two?"

"What?"

She placed a hand on her hip and let out an exasperated sigh. "Liquid or solid?"

He almost laughed. They numbered their bodily functions?

"Both." That should get him out of this bed.

She nodded and left. Good. When she brought the keys back to release him, then he would make his escape. Most likely no one was around with a tranquilizer or any other type of gun. He hoped.

Moments later the woman returned. Instead of carrying a set of keys, she held a large roundish object.

She raised the top part of the bed—causing him to sit up better—pulled the covers down and nudged his bottom. "Lift."

"What are you doing? I need to use the bathroom. Is it not in that other room?"

"That is for people who are not restrained." She held up the item. "This is your bathroom."

"Nooo."

"Yesss."

He pulled on the restraints. "What kind of place is this where a person can't use the bathroom in private?"

Granted, he never had such privacy on his own planet, but this woman didn't know that.

"Trust me, you'll get all the privacy you need. I'm not sticking around to watch."

Apparently, the bossy attitude was not working. "Please," he begged. "It's not like there's a window in there, is there? Where am I going to go?"

"You're more than twice my size. Do I look stupid? Either you go in the bedpan or you don't go. Your choice."

"I want to use the bathroom."

"Fine." She took her bedpan and headed for the door.

"I will keep yelling."

"You do that." She went out the door and it clicked shut.

"Damn, damn, damn!" He yanked on the restraints as he screamed out his frustration.

CHAPTER 19

A shaking pulled Annie out of one awesome dream. She and Calix were at a beach. He looked so sexy in his swim trunks.

"Wake up," John said. "We're here."

"Where am I?" She tried to open her eyes, but the blindfold prevented her from doing that. And she would have removed the covering if she could reach it. Once her head cleared, and that lovely dream disappeared, she remembered.

When the plane had landed, the agent had cuffed her wrists behind her and blindfolded her, which had made getting off the plane without breaking her neck more difficult than it needed to be. He then practically shoved her inside the vehicle, most likely an SUV if the height was any indication. He might as well have stuffed her in the back. Didn't he realize she wanted to be here?

The door beside her opened and someone, probably John, grasped her elbow, placed a hand on her head, and tugged. "Watch your head."

She swung her feet around and slid to the ground. "What the hell? Some help you are. I can't see shit. Why the blindfold? Are you the mob?"

He laughed as he helped her stand. "Sorry, just following orders. Blame your friend."

John had called Calix that many times, never using his name. Either Calix hadn't shared that information and John hoped she would correct him, or he just didn't like using Calix's name. Well, whatever the reason, she was not sharing information Calix apparently didn't want shared.

"So what's the weather like around these parts? It doesn't feel cold enough to snow." Heck, it felt balmy compared to Spokane. Which meant they had to have travelled south. But how far south?

"Can't tell. It's too dark out."

While he continued to hold her elbow and lead her to Calix—or so she presumed—she kept with the inquiries. "Air isn't humid enough to be Florida. Not that I've ever been. Only heard about it. We're not in Florida, are we?"

John laughed. "No. We're in Virginia."

"Virginia?" Not Ohio? Wasn't that where all the alien investigations took place? Or was that New Mexico?

He stopped. "There are three steps in front of you."

She toed each step with her good foot before taking it, shaking the pins and needles out of her injured one while it was airborne. "So what did…my friend do to the government to cause me to wear a blindfold?"

"He tried to escape."

"He did?" Ah, way to go, Calix. She wasn't sure he had it in him.

"Is there something you two have against us knowing his name?"

"I don't know. What do you want with it?"

He sighed. "Just makes it easier to communicate, don't you think?"

The whoosh of an automatic door sounded in front of her. Heat rushed at her face. They were indoors now and the blindfold came off.

She blinked at the bright lights as they stung her eyes. "What is this? A hospital?" She assumed Calix left peacefully, but maybe he had fought them. "Is he hurt?"

"He was fine when I left." John unlocked the cuffs and freed her wrists. "The doors are all locked. You'll need a card to exit, so if you run, you won't be able to get far. Not that you could with that boot anyway."

She hadn't planned on running until she got Calix, and he would most likely carry her, but that bit of information put a crimp into her plans. How the heck would they get out? Maybe she could pull the fire alarm.

John ushered her to the elevators. They went up to the third floor. As the doors opened, someone's yells echoed through the hallway. The person must have been at it awhile. His voice was hoarse.

"You torture people in this place?" she asked.

"No one's being tortured."

"Yeah, sure. Tell that to the person yelling."

A small nurse rushed up to John. "You've got to do something. He's been doing this for the past hour, and I can't find anyone to get permission to sedate him."

"Where's Agent Lazur?"

"I have no idea. He's not answering his cell. Can you give me permission?"

John glanced at Annie for moment before turning back to the nurse. "Let me try something first." He tugged on Annie's arm. "Come on."

"Where are we going?" The yelling got louder as they walked down the hall. Goosebumps formed on her skin as she came to recognize the voice. Calix?

John unlocked and opened the door to the source of the screams and pushed her. The door clicked behind her, sealing her inside a darkened room.

Her eyes needed to adjust to the sudden darkness, but the screams stopped. Either she was with the man she loved or that agent just put her on some stranger's menu.

* * * *

The light from the hall was brief, but enough for Calix to recognize the woman who had been pushed into his room. But how could it be her? She was supposed to be in Washington. She was supposed to stay put.

"Annie?" His voice was raw from all the yelling and it came out more like a whisper.

"Oh, thank God." A light came on and she rushed to his bed. "Oh sweetie. What'd they do to you?"

Damn. It was her. Now how would he protect her? "What are you doing here?"

"I came to see you. What else?" She pulled on the two-inch strap across his chest.

"Unless you have the key, I am stuck here. You need to leave before it's too late."

"Don't have the key and I think they locked me in." She cupped his face in her hands. "I missed you so much. Are you hurt?"

As badly as he wanted her gone and safe, he reveled in her touch. It felt like years since he'd seen her, and he shouldn't be seeing her now. He shook his head. "Why are you here? Mac was supposed to keep you safe."

"Don't blame Mac. They came and got me."

"I am sorry. I did not intend for you to get involved. They told me if I went with them they would leave you alone."

"Yeah, that sounds about right. Liars. Every one of them. But you should have known I don't give up so easily. They *did* come for me, but I kind of invited myself."

His laughter held no mirth. The one time he wanted her to fight and she didn't. "Oh, Annie. What are we going to do?"

"I know what I want to do." She climbed on top of him, hugged him the best she could, and burrowed her nose into his neck. "I'm not hurting you, am I?"

"No." He just wished he could hold her, but he would settle for this. Her body was soft and warm against his and she smelled like home.

"What have you told them?" she whispered.

"That I'm from Canada and want a lawyer," he said loud enough for anyone to hear. He was sure the room was being monitored. Especially now. She apparently thought the same since she kept her voice low.

She chuckled. "Anything else?"

"No. Telling them anything will not get my freedom, so I tell them nothing." He took in her scent and spoke low. "Now that you are here, I may have to rethink that. I am afraid of what they will do to you."

"They aren't going to hurt me, they just want you afraid. They're only using me for leverage, so don't tell them anything because of me. They have no right to hold you here. Or me, either."

"So what should we do?"

The door opened. "Yes, Miss O'Shea. Do tell."

Damn. The listening device must be beside his bed if they heard that. She stiffened. The overhead lights came on, causing him to squint.

Slowly, she turned and looked over her shoulder. Doug stood at the foot of the bed, smiling while the nurse wheeled in some equipment.

John grabbed Annie around the waist and pulled her off of Calix. What little comfort she had given him was snatched away. Would he ever feel her body again?

"Hey, let me go!" She shrugged free or John released her. Either way, she scowled at the man as she gained her balance.

Doug extended his hand toward Annie. "We haven't been properly introduced. I'm Agent Lazur."

She stared at the hand as John pushed her toward Lazur, but she did not shake it. "What are you going to do to him?"

Doug lowered his arm. "I don't want to hurt him. What is it with you people? I'm not the bad guy here."

"Sure you are. You kidnapped him when he hasn't done anything wrong. Why can't you go harass some criminals, huh?"

He smiled at Calix. "I can see why you like her, Buster. She's got a fire in her, doesn't she?" He quickly grabbed her around the waist. "Now maybe I'll get some answers."

No. Calix thrashed on the bed, cold fear filling his veins, straps cutting into his raw wrists. Something ripped. Whether he was finally getting through the restraints or just destroying the sheets, he did not know. He pictured tearing off the agent's head. When this was all over and he lived, he might get his wish. "Don't hurt her!"

She clawed to get free, but failed. "I thought you said you weren't the bad guy."

"I'm not, but he might be." Doug stared at Calix. "The nurse is going to wire you. I'm going to ask you some questions and you're going to answer me truthfully. I'll know if you're lying, so if you do, I'll zap her with this Taser." He pulled the device from his pocket and poked it in her side. "You want her unharmed, cooperate and answer the damn questions."

His heart nearly slammed out of his chest. Zap her? Not if he could help it. Threatening Annie was too much. To think someone would stoop so low to get information made him sick. "Leave her alone. You win. I'll tell you everything."

"No!" Tears filled her eyes. "He doesn't mean it."

"It doesn't matter, Annie. You matter more. You will always matter more."

Doug released her. "Glad you came to your senses." He looked to the nurse. "Leave us."

The nurse let out a huge breath and departed, leaving the equipment behind.

Annie came to him, wiping at her wet checks. "You don't have to do this. We'll figure out another way."

There was no other way. He could see that now.

"At least remove his restraints," she said to the agent.

"I don't think so."

"Then he's not talking."

"Annie… It's okay," Calix said.

"No. They can't treat you like this. If they can't be nice, there's no reason for you to be."

Doug reached into his pocket. "Fine. But only the arms." When Annie brought her hands to her hips, he amended, "for now." He started toward Calix, then stopped and held the key out to her. "Maybe it'd be better if you did the honors."

Smart man.

As soon as Annie freed the first wrist restraint, Calix grabbed her hand and brought it up to his lips. She smelled wonderful and helped anchor him. The anger that had boiled inside simmered.

She eyed the chest restraint and Calix tugged her chin to look at him. He shook his head. If she even attempted it, Doug would no doubt zap her. She nodded and squeezed his hand before freeing his other wrist. Once he was free, he promptly took her into his arms. It felt good to hold her close. To know she was safe. He would not let her go.

"You okay?" she asked.

He was angry at himself for getting her into this mess. He was disappointed it had even gotten this far. Maybe it was his inexperience, but he highly doubted that. It was her people. They feared the unknown, and he was one big unknown to them.

He hugged her close. "I am fine."

Agent Lazur dragged a chair by the bed. "The keys, please?"

Annie tossed them to him. He must not have trusted her. Calix could not blame him; she could be sneaky at times. John stood in the far corner watching with what looked like interest.

"Why don't you start by telling us your name?" Doug asked.

"My name is Calix."

"Now, was that so hard? Calix. I say, that's an unusual name."

"My sister's son is named Calix," John said. "Greek origin, I believe."

Doug glared at John before turning his attention back to Calix. "Where are you really from?"

Annie tensed in his arms and he hugged her. She was still afraid they would hurt him, but at this point, he was more worried about her and the baby. He hoped his cooperation would earn her freedom. His freedom was pretty much done for. "I came from a planet in the galaxy you call Andromeda."

"Holy shit!" Doug jumped out of his chair and paced. "I knew it. I told you, John. There is other life out there."

"You believe him?" John asked. "How do you know he's not just saying what you want to hear?"

The man wasn't too far off. The truth did sound crazy to anyone who didn't believe.

"Because of his ship. You can show it to us, right?"

Calix nodded. "It's back in Washington." And if they were stupid enough to take him back there, he would find a way to get him and Annie free. Only problem with that plan: he didn't think they were stupid.

"So, what brings you here? What's your mission? Why haven't you tried to contact our leaders?" Doug acted as if this were a pleasure visit. He sat in the chair, crossed his legs, and held the Taser in his lap.

"Really, Doug?" John asked. "Did you really expect him to say 'Take me to your leader'?"

Annie snickered. Apparently, it was a common joke.

"If you can't have an open mind, maybe you should leave."

"Oh no. Someone has to stick around and make sure you don't go off the deep end. For all we know, he's a spy from another country. There's no way anyone could travel from the Andromeda galaxy and live to tell about it."

Calix was more than happy to let them argue about it. But was being a spy any better? Probably not.

Doug stood and approached John. "That's enough. I want to hear him out. That's our job. And until we get some information, I would appreciate you staying out of this."

John raised his palms out and retreated to his corner.

Doug returned to the chair and took a deep breath. "Shall we continue?"

"No," Annie said. "Who are you anyway? What authority do you have to hold us?"

"We are Homeland Security. And I have every right to hold someone who is a potential threat."

"Then shouldn't we have a lawyer?"

Doug shook his head. "Is that where he got that from? Aliens from another planet don't have rights."

"It's okay, Annie," Calix said. "I am tired of hiding. I want a life here. Maybe they can give me one."

Annie eyed the agent. "Can you give him asylum?"

"That depends on how cooperative and truthful you are. And if we determine you are not a threat."

Calix relaxed. If they believed him, maybe they could get out of this unharmed after all. "My planet is in the path of a comet and will be destroyed in about seven years. I was sent here to see if your people were still alive. And if so, if you would be willing to accept our people. But I see now that your planet is much too crowded to accept us. Much too skeptical, or rather, not willing to share. And I am not sure what our people would do if by some chance we are given acceptance. If I tell them the planet is not suitable, I doom my people. If I tell them they are welcome, it is possible I have doomed your people. I just do not know what to do."

"How many people are we talking about?"

"We maintain an average population of 200 million beings."

Doug's eyes widened. "Okay, that's a lot of people for just one country to handle. But what do you mean, doom our people? Are we going to be attacked?"

"I do not know. You are different from them. I am different from them, now. Will they see that as a threat or a challenge? I am afraid it might be the former. People they cannot control are a threat to their perfect system. I see that now. But since I am locked up here…" He tugged on the strap to emphasize his point. "I cannot contact my people today. Not that I have an answer for them anyway. If they haven't already, they will send another traveler to come get me since I refuse to return home."

Annie cleared her throat. "Um, Calix? I hate to tell you this, but they've already sent somebody."

CHAPTER 20

Annie closed her eyes. What had she done? Only invited the enemy inside her house, that's what. Because Pax was definitely the enemy.

"Are you sure?" Calix asked.

She toyed with the lock on his chest restraint. "Yes, I'm sure. Last night he showed up half-frozen on my back porch. Said his name is Pax. He was looking for you."

"Another alien?" Agent Lazur asked. "Damn, John. I thought you were monitoring the skies. How come we didn't get any readings?"

"Our ships are resistant to discovery," Calix said. "You did not find mine through your electronics, did you?"

"No," John said. "But then we had that solar storm. It kind of fucked up everything we had. Nothing worked for days. Shit. To have spacecraft that is undetectable… That can't be good, alien or not."

"Wait," Doug said. "Why is he looking for you? You said your deadline was today."

"He's probably been told I am damaged." Calix caressed Annie's cheek and stared at her with sadness in his eyes. "I never had a chance, did I?"

"We can explain it to him." Although she was pretty sure that was useless from the little time she had spent with the man.

"He will not care what I have to say. He will only do what he is told. That is how he functions."

"And you don't function the same?" Doug asked.

"Not anymore."

Thank goodness she had never seen that side of Calix. She couldn't imagine him being any other way than the caring person he was.

"So what changed you?" Doug asked.

"I had hoped it was your planet, because if it was, there would be no problem. Either my people prepare to face the changes I went through or would find a more suitable planet. But it turns out it is not your planet at all."

"I don't get it, then. How did you change?"

"All of my people have a locator chip implanted in their temple. At least, that is what we are told to believe. But I lost my chip after I landed. I started feeling emotions. Curiosity." He caressed her cheek. "Love."

"And this Pax guy, he's more like what, a Vulcan?"

"Are you referencing a television show or is there such a species?"

"TV," Annie said. "Actually, from what I've seen they're more like androids. They'll do what they're ordered regardless of who gets hurt."

"You should be safe from Pax," Calix said. "Seems he was sent to capture me, and since he can only track my chip and ship, which are still in Washington, he has nowhere to go."

Annie fisted her hand and never felt more foolish. "Ummm…"

"What?" Calix, Doug, and John asked in unison.

She pulled the chip from her pocket and held it out in her palm. "He's probably on his way here."

* * * *

Pax sat at his dashboard and rubbed his temple. This mission was making his head ache worse. It should have been a simple job. But he soon discovered that nothing on this planet was simple. Oh, to be finished and return home. But first, he needed to complete his mission. It had taken several hours before the chip stopped moving and now he was finally on his way. He had planned on making this trip solo, but so far none of his plans were successful.

He turned in his chair and stared at the man who sat on the edge of his bed. Mac had insisted he would be needed if they found Calix first. And since Pax had no idea how Calix acted without his chip, it seemed logical if Mac's presence would keep Calix calm.

Keeping Calix calm would ensure a successful mission. That is all that mattered.

"Are all your ships this size?" Mac asked as he looked around the room. "This is identical to Calix's."

"Only the solo traveler ships." Pax turned back to the dashboard. He would prefer quiet, but this human liked to talk. Sharing information was forbidden on this mission, but since he would have to follow Directive 23—eliminate the risk of exposure—upon Calix's capture, it did not matter. He should have taken care of the female Jen, but then Mac might have been a problem. From the little he had witnessed, these people seemed to have some kind of bond with one another and it had nothing to do with any job. How bizarre. He would go back for Jen later.

"How long have you been an explorer? I bet it's a fun job. Flying around space. Seeing other planets."

"I was trained for this position since I was young. It is what I excelled at."

"Do you like it, though?"

"What does liking it have to do with skill?"

"Nothing, I guess. How many other intelligent life forms have you discovered?"

"Depends on what you consider intelligent." Before he would let Mac ask another inane question, he went back to his mission. "The signal is in that building up ahead. Be prepared to land." Not that he would have difficulty landing, but he just wanted Mac to stop talking.

Mac sat on the floor and held onto the bed leg. "We're here already? How far did we go?"

Apparently, nothing would stop the man from talking. The area around the signal was fortified with an electric barrier. He found a suitable site and landed the ship. The outside temperature reading was many degrees warmer than his previous location. Still not warm, but better than a food storage unit.

"We have traveled to the other side of this land mass."

"What? Man, that was fast. Imagine what we could do with this kind of travel. From L.A. to New York in minutes instead of hours. Mind boggling!"

If they wanted to travel faster, could they not? They had satellites around the planet but inefficient travel. They should be further advanced than that. But that was not for him to dwell upon.

His mission was to retrieve Calix and return him home. He would document his findings and let those responsible do with it as they would.

"Do these ships come smaller? You know, for everyday, stay-within-the-planet's-atmosphere use? Like our cars?"

Pax massaged his temple. He did not know what a car was, but he was finished with the talking. He touched the weapon. Would he need it to capture Calix? It was an efficient device for threatening species. One squeeze at the low or medium setting could disable his opponent; the high setting would destroy them, a requirement for Directive 23. A new directive, at that, and probably created for Calix's mission. If Calix spotted the weapon, he might run off. Pax left it on the console and picked up the locator device. He stood and towered over the puny man. "It is time to find Calix."

* * * *

Calix rubbed his wrists. Amazing what could happen when Annie suggested a second alien's arrival was imminent. He was free from the restraints, out of that gown, and back in his own clothes. If only that would solve his problem. Or rather…problems.

Doug handed over the locator. "So, your chip is a homing device?"

Once Calix started cooperating, Doug's attitude had changed. Now that his questions were being answered, he no longer held the Taser, but had given it to John, who, standing by the door, held it out, ready to zap if the need arose. John needed more time or proof to believe, apparently.

"I do not understand homing," Calix said.

Annie squeezed his thigh and looked at the agent. "Yes."

Calix turned on the locator and his stomach churned as he stared at the results. "You were right. He's here. Above us."

"He's on the roof? Already?" Doug looked up as if he could see through the ceiling. "How exciting."

He couldn't fault the agent for his excitement. This was certainly all new experiences. But caution was called for here. "You cannot capture him. That will not solve the problem."

"A problem you say we have. I want to believe you, but how do I know you just don't want to escape and go back to your people?"

Calix stood and shook his head. How many times did he have to say it? "Even if I wanted to—and I do not—I cannot return. They will destroy me."

Annie took his arm and pulled him back to the bed. She rubbed her hand along his shoulders and back, easing his frustration. His fear.

"So we protect you," Doug said. "Put you somewhere without that chip so Pax can't find you. I can't imagine he will stay here indefinitely. Eventually he will realize he cannot complete his mission and go home. Won't he?"

"I do not know how much time he was allotted, but yes, it is likely that he will return home if he cannot find me since that is his mission. But the next traveler or travelers they send will have a different mission. Do you really want to see your land invaded by another species? A species who thinks the people here are violent? We may look and test as human, but we are not the same."

John moved away from the door. "Excuse me. Now you're talking alien invasion? Are you for real?"

Doug spun around. "I understand you want to be the voice of reason here, but can't you see he's afraid? I'm sure if I can talk to Pax, make him understand—"

"Oh great. You believe he's an alien, yet you don't believe him when he says his friend is a threat."

Calix interjected. "He is not my friend, and he is not here to be yours, either. He has one mission and will do anything to succeed."

Doug scratched his head. "You want him to leave voluntarily without you, right?"

"That would be ideal, yes. But I do not know how to do that besides letting Pax think I was destroyed. How would that solve stopping a possible invasion?"

"Let me talk to him. Surely, as an explorer he would—"

"He will not talk to you." Just how many times did he have to say it?

"If I show him I'm not a threat, why not talk to me?"

"But you *are* a threat. If you were on a rescue mission, would you stop to talk to the abductors?"

"He's got a point," John said.

"What other option is there?" Doug asked.

"Well…" It was just a fleeting thought, but if he didn't voice it and it was possible… "Do you have the ability to move or destroy a comet? Then my people wouldn't need this planet."

"Your people can't do that?"

"I was told we could not."

"You're trying to tell me that you have all these spaceships and no ability to move a space object? How do you take off into space?"

"With my ship?" If only he taught the sciences instead of history, he might understand the question better.

Doug shook his head. "Don't you have to blast off? To keep gravity from pulling you back down?"

Ahh, he understood the question now. Still, his knowledge was limited. "I do not know how it all works, but we do not blast anything. It just…goes."

"Sounds like they found a different solution to gravity," John said. "Man, wouldn't that be neat?"

Neither Doug nor John said they couldn't move a comet. Did that mean they could? Was this all about bartering? "I can share the documentation. I am sure it is somewhere on the file server. But can you build something to move a comet?"

"We have rockets," Doug said. "We've nudged asteroids. I don't see why we couldn't do the same to a comet. But how will that get Pax to leave?"

Since being abducted, he had hope. Hope for a solution to their major problem. A problem Pax probably didn't even know about. "I will need to talk to him. Tell him what is happening."

"Nooo," Annie wailed, gripping his arm. "Pax doesn't want to talk to you. If you go up there, he'll only take you away."

Maybe, but what choice did he really have? He told them about Directive 23.

* * * *

Mac strained his neck as he looked up at the giant. He scrambled off the bed and stood, but that didn't help with his perspective any. Pax was huge and the ship was small, in a hotel room kind of way. Even if he had a weapon, would he be able to surprise the guy? All of a sudden his idea of taking Pax out seemed impossible.

"So, what's the plan?" He'd already scanned the small area for any kind of weapon to bop Pax over the head, but the only things he could find weren't big enough to do damage to a rat. "If the area is fortified, then there are probably guards outside, too."

"It is not fortified to keep out wild animals?"

Mac nearly laughed, but refrained since the alien was being serious. "We don't use electricity to keep out wild animals. A simple fence would do that. I'm guessing this is a government facility designed to keep unauthorized people out. Which means we'd need ID, I mean, identification, to get in."

"But we are already in."

"Yeah, but different people have different levels of access. We won't be able to just enter the building."

"But we are on top of the building. Can we not enter it from above?"

On top? Damn, this guy was good. "Show me where we are."

Pax let out an exasperated breath and punched on his keyboard. The monitor came on and an image of a rooftop came into view.

"Damn. Now, see, I never would have thought to land on the helicopter pad. Way to go, dude." Mac held his hand up for a high-five before he realized who he was high-fiving.

"Dude?" Pax stared at Mac's hand.

Why did he get the impression he wasn't being asked a definition? As if the alien would understand slang. Mac just lowered his hand instead and asked a question the man might understand. "Can you scan the area?"

The view moved, showing dishes and antennas, but nothing he could use as a weapon. Then a set of double doors appeared and, beside them, a stack of lumber. *Holy shit.* Now there was something he could use.

"The roof is monitored." Mac pointed to a camera mounted above the doors. "They can probably see anyone up here, if they're bothering to look, that is." What were the odds a security guard manned the helicopter pad if there wasn't a helicopter around?

"I can disable their cameras."

"Yeah, but then they'll be on alert and you want to go in unnoticed, right? Maybe we should just take our chances they aren't watching."

"How likely is that?"

"Unless they are expecting someone to arrive on the roof, not very. But we'll have bigger problems if someone decides to land here."

"Agreed. All the more reason to hurry." Pax picked up his locator and opened the door.

Mac followed, and while Pax secured the ship, headed over to the lumber. His hopes crashed. For one thing, the two-by-fours were too long. For another, they were secured with metal ties.

"What are those?" Pax asked from behind.

Mac jumped. "Damn. Sneak up on a guy, why don't you? It's wood. I guess they're getting ready to build something up here." Okay, he would leave the disabling to Calix. He just wasn't cut out for this kind of crap and Calix was more Pax's size. "Can you tell how far down we have to go?"

"Approximately twenty feet."

"What is that? Like, two floors?"

"I do not know, but I will know when we reach it."

Mac put his ear to the door, but no sound came through. Either no one was manning the area or the door was too thick. He turned the lever and it was unlocked. With his heart ready to punch an exit through his chest, he slowly poked his head inside. Empty. An elevator was straight ahead and the stairs leading down were to the right. The door didn't appear to have any kind of security lock, which was a good thing. Wasn't like anyone could escape from the roof. No other buildings were close by and the only way down was to jump.

"Mac?"

Mac jumped and his heart gave up pounding for a couple of beats. It was Calix! And he was coming up the stairs. Mac ran up to him and grabbed his arms. "Dude! My God! I thought we'd have to scour this place to find you. How did you escape? Where's Annie?" A hundred other questions were cut off by Calix's quizzical look.

"What are you doing here?" Calix asked.

"We came to help rescue you, you big ox. Figured you'd need me to make introductions. Calix, this is Pax. One of your countrymen." Mac noticed the locator in Calix's hands. "But then I guess you know that already." And then a serious thought slapped him upside the head. "Are you turning yourself in?" Annie would have a fit if that were the case.

Calix palmed Mac's shoulder in a reassuring way. "It's okay. I'm not here to turn myself in. I'm here to talk. I just didn't realize you came with him."

Yeah, it was probably not a good idea. But he was here now. Man, he was starting to act like Annie: act first, think later.

Pax pushed the door open all the way, tilted his head, and cleared the entryway. He then spoke in a language Mac did not understand. And it sounded like some kind of order. Like, "Come with me now," but with a lot more words. Oh shit. That couldn't be good.

Mac backed up into a corner, feeling like one big chicken. Would there be a fight or would Pax go away willingly? And where the heck was Annie?

* * * *

Calix swallowed down his nervousness. He'd never experienced it before today, and if not for Annie, wouldn't know why he felt the way he did. His chest was tight. His hands shook. She had told him it was normal to be nervous since he had no idea how Pax would react. Annie was nervous, too. So much so, she had wanted to accompany him, but he had insisted she stay behind. He didn't want to spook Pax any more than necessary. And now that Mac was involved, he needed to be extra careful.

"I am here to take you home," Pax said in their language. "We must depart now."

Take him home. Right. Pax was certainly being polite about it. Then again, he didn't understand their situation. Calix played it dumb, but spoke in English, not just for Mac's sake, but for Doug's too, since he was hiding in the stairwell. "Why? My mission is not complete."

Pax scrunched his forehead. According to Annie, he spoke English. Or was it the mission part that confused him? He pointed to Calix's temple. "I was told you were injured. And Annie said you were abducted. Did they do something to you?"

His scar. Of course. At least Pax was speaking in English now. "Yes, I was injured. I fell and hit my head on a rock the day I landed here. But I am well. I told Sentinel Gaylor that, too. And yes, I was abducted, but they have not harmed me. In fact, it appears they can help me in my mission. Is that not the important part?"

"What is your mission? Maybe we can complete it together."

Helping was good. Or was it a ploy to get him to leave? Probably the latter. He would not let on, though. He continued to act as if the missing chip had not changed him. "I am close to completing it now. I was to observe the people here. See if they would accept us. Allow us to move here."

Pax scrunched his forehead again. "Why would we want to move to a planet that is not suitable? What is wrong with our own planet?"

If Pax knew what was going on, he would not have asked the second question. But his first question was intriguing. "You think this planet is unsuitable? Why?"

"It is colder than a food storage unit and the people of this planet have nothing to offer us. They are violent, unstable creatures."

"Hey." Mac's eyes widened. "Sorry. Never mind the violent and unstable creature here."

Calix nearly laughed, which would not bode well for his plan. "Who has been violent to you? Annie?"

"No. She was most accommodating to my situation. I am referring to the report."

"That report was written nearly 200 years ago. These people have changed. But that is not the issue here. You asked what is wrong with our own planet. Sentinel Gaylor swore me to secrecy—"

"Secrecy?" Pax interrupted. "The sentinel told you to disobey Directive 1?"

"I asked him the same thing. He said I would not be disobeying anything, but that I would be obeying him. Did he tell you anything about what is to happen to our planet?"

"I was told you were injured and I was to bring you back home. That is all."

And of course Pax wouldn't ask why. Their people just didn't do that sort of thing. "If I allow you to complete your mission before I complete mine, we waste precious time. Time we cannot afford. Our planet is in the path of a comet. I just found out that it is possible to change its trajectory. That the people on this planet know how to do that."

"Dude!" Mac interrupted. "That is great news. Was it a bomb like I suggested?"

"No, not a bomb. A rocket."

"Oh, yeah. That makes sense. Still, awesome news." Mac gave a thumbs up then waved his fingers. "Continue."

"What are you talking about?" Pax asked.

"That I have found a solution to the comet. You need to tell Sentinel Gaylor. Let him know we do not need this planet."

"Are you telling me our planet will be destroyed?"

"Yes, that is exactly what will happen if we do not move the comet."

"You are not thinking clearly. These people are beneath us technologically. How can they possibly do something that we cannot? You must return with me so you can be repaired."

"I am not broken!" Damn it. Could he blame his anger on the atmosphere? Better to not dwell on it at all. He took a deep breath. "I understand your confusion. But they have different abilities than we do. They go into space differently than we do. Like with rockets."

"Rockets? What are rockets?"

"Something that uses a lot of energy to blast away from the planet."

"Their ships do not just go?"

Okay, now Calix didn't feel so dumb when Doug asked how they left their own planet. Apparently Pax didn't know any differently, either. "No. I told you: different. But that difference can be our salvation. I cannot go back right now. You need to tell Sentinel Gaylor that I am finalizing a plan and will contact him when I return to my ship. Once he understands the mission has changed, that there is a solution, you will be released from your mission and allowed to go home. Without me. I am sure of it."

"We should go tell him together. Come with me to my ship."

"No."

Pax's forehead scrunched again. "You are different."

"I am. This planet has…changed me. The people here have accepted me. Our people will no longer accept me, I know this now. If I go with you, you will just take me away and then there is no saving our planet. Is that what you want?"

Pax took what felt like forever to answer. "I understand. I will relay your message."

He understood? He understood! Was this finally over? Excitement shivered all through Calix's body and for once in his life he had the urge to jump with joy. But he refrained for Pax's sake. Talking calmly had never been so difficult, but he needed one more thing from Pax, and he was pretty certain Pax would agree. "I suggest you leave the area now unless you want to be bombarded with questions. The people on this planet are thirsty for knowledge. And you know more about space than I do. Unless…you wish to speak with them?"

Pax rubbed his temple and reverted to their own language. "No. They are frustrating creatures. I just want to be free of them."

No, they were not frustrating creatures. They were wonderful beings and now it seemed he would be one of them. His life was finally turning around and all he could do was stand there calmly until Pax left.

CHAPTER 21

As soon as the door closed behind Pax, Calix let out a ragged breath. He did it. He actually did it.

Mac emerged from the corner. "Whoa, dude. You did some mighty good convincing. I was sure he was hell-bent on capturing you."

"And yet you still came with him. Why?"

Doug trotted up the stairs, but Calix paid him no mind. Mac could have been seriously hurt. Or worse, killed.

"Because I thought maybe I could, you know…help." Mac chuckled. "Not sure how much help I could have been, though. I'm really glad you two didn't fight it out." He put up his fists and pumped one arm out while jumping side to side.

"My people do not fight like that." What was the need? They just did what they were told, no questions asked. He turned toward Doug. "Thank you for allowing me to handle this."

The agent smiled. "We'll see if I regret my decision or not. When can we have that talk?"

Mac grabbed Calix's arm. "Talk? What's going on? And where's Annie?"

Calix introduced the two men. "Annie is fine, and I promised Doug I would tell them everything I know in exchange for that rocket."

Mac's gaze flitted between Doug and Calix. "Just talk? They're not…experimenting?"

"Not if I can help it," Doug said. "I know our methods are intimidating, but we have no way of knowing if our visitors are friendly or not, or if they're actually visitors. And until we do, we must protect ourselves, our country, our people. I wish to communicate with other life forms, not dissect them."

Calix grasped Doug's shoulder. "And I believe you. Will Annie and Mac be allowed to return home?"

"I have no need for them. We might all go together, though. There's that ship of yours I'm dying to see. Data to retrieve. Right?"

"Right." But he would make sure he had something definitive before he gave up all his documentation. Annie would probably insist on it, too. "If you'll excuse me, I wish to tell Annie the good news."

"I suppose I can wait a few more minutes." The agent looked at Mac. "You came in with Pax, right? Why don't you tell me what that trip was like?"

As Calix rushed down the stairs, Mac's animated voice echoed along the walls. Silence greeted him once he exited the stairwell. He felt free. Liberated. Soon he would be able to live an actual life without fear of being discovered, and he couldn't wait to get started.

He stopped at the doorway and stared at the woman he loved. His future would not be possible without her. "He's gone."

Annie sprung off the bed. "What?"

"That easy?" John said.

"Well, not that easy." Calix told them what had happened, and John departed to find Doug.

Annie rushed into his arms. She felt so good against his body. He bent down and gave her a kiss, wishing they had the privacy of her cabin. Or his ship. He ended the kiss before he lost control.

When they broke apart, she looked up at him. "I want to be happy, I do, but are you sure he left? That seemed awfully quick and easy."

"Of course I am sure." He pulled out his locator. "See? It shows he has already left the atmosphere."

"Yeah, but he could come back."

He tossed the device on the bed. "He does not work that way, Annie."

She scrunched up her face. "But you were so sure he would take you."

He ran his fingers through her silky hair and stopped before he went any further. And he definitely wanted to go further. "I was wrong. It helped that I might have hinted that the atmosphere on this planet changed me. And once he contacts Sentinel Gaylor, he will see I wasn't lying about the comet. Why are you frowning? This is good news."

"Because good things don't come that easy."

"Maybe some do. You don't have to fight for everything. Have a little trust."

"People take advantage of those who trust easily. Fighting is the only way to get your point across."

"Fighting is not the only way. If I had not listened to you, those agents would never have brought you here."

She backed away. "What are you talking about?"

"You told me that your government would harm me. They only harmed me when I fought them. Once I cooperated, they have been nice."

"Of course they're nice. They're getting what they want. You. I still have to figure out how to get us out of here."

"You don't have to figure out anything. We are allowed to go home. Once I get my rocket and they get my documentation, they will have no need for me. I will be free."

She folded her arms across her chest. "Now that's just being naïve. They're taking advantage of you because you don't know any better."

Her words caused a pain in his chest. "You think I'm stupid? That I don't know what I'm doing?"

"No, of course you're not stupid. But you don't know my people like I do." She lowered her arms and paced the room. "I still think Pax is up to something."

"But Pax is my people. Not yours. So according to your reasoning, I should know him better."

"True, but he's a traveler and has probably seen more than you have. Plus, he still has his chip."

"Oh, so because I'm a teacher, that makes me naïve?" His position never bothered him before, but she made him sound weak.

"No, but—"

"Or am I stupid because I am no longer controlled?"

"I don't—"

"I know more than you think." He would not let her finish. He would not let her get her way this time. "Face it, Annie. You were wrong. Fighting wasn't the answer. If I had cooperated at the beginning, none of this would have occurred."

* * * *

Annie froze. Gah! He wouldn't let her speak. Every time she'd opened her mouth, he kept on talking. What happened? How had he managed to twist her words, her actions? "I was only trying to help."

"Like you helped your friend by fighting her fight? How is your ankle by the way?"

"Why are you being like this? I took care of you. I took you into my home."

His eyes widened. "So this all stems from guilt? You felt sorry for hitting me?"

"That is not why I took you in. And I didn't hit you."

"No. Technically Mac did. So…you were protecting Mac."

"Yes, I was protecting my brother. Just like I tried to protect Jen. Like I'm trying to protect you. You are too optimistic. Especially toward Pax. He will not leave without you."

"You do not trust me."

"This has nothing to do with trust." Hell, she trusted him with her life. Didn't he know that?

"You don't believe me. My words mean nothing. You think I'm naïve. How is that trusting me?"

He was twisting everything she said. How could she get out of this? "Listen, once we get home, and have time to calm down, we can talk about this."

"What is there to talk about? How can I live with someone who doesn't trust me?"

Annie's heart ached. "What are you saying? That you're not coming home?"

"I have no home."

No home? What about her and the baby? The pain that slashed her heart was worse than when Denny left. But she wasn't going to be that woman to throw a child at a man to get him to follow. Damn him for thinking everything she'd done for him was out of guilt. Served her right for believing in the impossible. She reached into her pocket, pulled out the chip, and threw it at his chest. He flinched. "I guess I don't need that anymore then, huh? Have a good life, Calix."

She stormed out of the room and swiped her eyes. Damn it. How did she end up this way? All she wanted to do was help him. All she'd done was love him.

Heading to the elevator, she emerged into what used to be a nurses station and stutter-stepped. Mac was leaning against the counter. "What are you doing here?"

"What, Calix didn't tell you? I came with Pax. Now I need a ride home."

Calix might have told her if she hadn't just insulted his intelligence. What the hell had she done?

John was sitting behind the counter in front of a computer monitor. "I was told to take you home after you sign this agreement stating that everything you have seen or heard regarding this whole alien issue is not to be repeated anywhere. If you do, you can be charged with treason."

"Treason?" Mac said. "Kind of extreme, isn't it?"

"We still don't know who or what Calix is. Until we can confirm that he hasn't come from another country, this is being treated as a security measure. And if you want to go home, then sign the form."

Mac signed where indicated. "When do we get to leave?"

John typed some and stared at the monitor. "The flight's leaving in four hours."

"Four hours?" Mac asked. "I thought you had a plane at your command."

"We share it. Four hours."

Mac slid the document over to Annie. "So is Doug talking to Calix now?"

Annie shrugged. "How should I know?" She blinked back the burning in her eyes as she signed the form.

"Hey, what's the matter?"

"I need some air. Can I go outside now?"

John looked up. "Yeah. The doors are unlocked. I'll be down in a bit."

Instead of waiting for the elevator, she opened the door to the stairs, wanting to put as much distance between her and Calix as soon as she could.

"Hey, wait up." Mac followed. "Shouldn't you take the elevator with that foot of yours?"

"You can take it. I'm walking." She needed to expend some energy and the stairs seemed the best bet. Maybe she'd reinjure her ankle, but she didn't care. The ache in her ankle could distract her from the pain in her heart.

After they exited the stairwell, the door slammed shut. She was surrounded by silence. Apparently, no one worked on the first floor, not even security. She hobbled over to the exit and shoved the doors open. The cool air felt good against her skin, her eyes.

The outside was just as quiet. Didn't anyone work here on the weekends, or weren't aliens important enough for that? A breeze kicked up, sending an errant paper up along the building. The sky was grey enough to hold snow, but with the warmer temps, maybe it only held rain. It just didn't smell like rain, though.

The parking lot only held two cars, both black SUVs. Doors were locked on both. She leaned up against one, wishing she could collapse on a bed. It had been too long since her last honest-to-goodness sleep.

Mac folded his arms as he stood in front of her. "Okay, what's going on?"

Her eyes watered, but she refused to cry. "Nothing."

"Don't give me that. Spill."

Maybe Mac could explain what happened better. "Were you up there with Calix and Pax?" When Mac nodded, she continued. "Don't you think Pax caved in a little too easy?"

"He didn't exactly cave in, and it wasn't all that easy. But Calix convinced him. I thought for sure there would have been a fight, but then again, they don't touch. It was very civil. Except for the one time Calix raised his voice."

"He raised his voice? Why?"

"Pax said Calix could be repaired. Calix yelled that he wasn't broken."

Yeah, that would bother Calix. "But don't you think it was strange the rest of their conversation was civil? Could Pax have tricked Calix by pretending to believe him?"

"How the heck should I know? Pax was very quiet on the trip out here. I think I did most of the talking. But he seemed kind of reasonable, too. Why wouldn't he believe Calix? Especially since he can verify Calix's story."

She shook her head. "But he wanted Calix. He was very adamant back at the cabin."

"Yeah, but he didn't know about the comet. Calix convinced Pax that he was needed here to secure a plan to change the comet's trajectory. That if Pax took him away, he would ruin any chance of their planet's survival. I can't imagine anyone risking that. Especially since it can be verified."

Calix was right. And she went and called him naïve when it was more like the other way around. "Oh, crap. I'm such an idiot."

Mac leaned up beside her and nudged her in the side. "Tell me something I don't know."

She punched him in the arm. "He was mad, Mac. Thinks I don't trust him."

"Do you? You didn't believe him."

"You would be on his side. You think he'll forgive me?"

"You're kidding, right? The guy loves you. Of course he'll forgive you. Besides, now he can experience make-up sex. I hear it's really good." He gave her another nudge.

She gave him another punch in the arm. "This from a man who hates to discuss sex?"

"I don't hate to discuss it. I hate to… Oh shut up."

She could make this right. All she had to do was grovel. And she would if it would get Calix back. "I have to talk to him. Before we get on that plane. I'll be right back."

"You are leaving with me." Pax's deep baritone voice came from behind them.

Annie spun around. Her heart rate kicked it up a notch or a hundred. Damn it, why'd she have to be right this time?

Mac pulled her behind him. "Hey, Pax. I thought you left."

"I am not leaving without Calix." Pax stepped around the car and headed for Annie. "I need you to come with me." He looked at Mac. "Tell Calix I have her."

She grabbed onto her brother, her heart hammering away. "What, so you can trap him into going back with you? No. I'm not going."

"Sorry, dude. She's right. You'll need to come up with another plan."

He pointed a small device at Mac and pushed a button. Mac cried out and fell against the car before collapsing to the ground.

"Mac! Mac!" Annie screamed. He didn't move. Damn Pax. She would make him pay. So what if he was more than two feet taller than her? The man hurt, possibly killed, her brother. She charged and reached for the weapon. "You animal! You had no right. He did nothing to you."

Ripping pain seized every muscle and it felt like her insides would explode. She fell to the ground as her world went dark.

* * * *

Calix picked up the chip. His chest hurt and it had nothing to do with Annie throwing the chip. It was her words. And they stung. He now knew there were other ways to fight that did not require fists or feet. But unlike the physical kind, there was no winner here.

What had he done? Losing that chip and meeting Annie were the best things that had ever happened to him. But her words hurt more than he thought possible and he had just wanted to hurt her back. So he had twisted her words around and spit them out. Claimed she didn't trust him, when the truth was he didn't trust himself.

Had Pax gone along too quickly? He'd been sent on a rescue mission. Nothing Calix said should have changed that. Annie had seen it. Why couldn't he?

Now she probably thought he no longer loved her, that he no longer wanted the baby, which was far from the truth. Did she still love him or had he ruined it all?

The door opened behind him and he turned, hoping, but it was only Doug.

"We have a few hours before we have to be at the airport. I set up an office to record our conversation. Would you please come with me?"

"I will, but can it wait? Annie left rather angry and I would like to talk to her."

Doug's shoulders slumped. "Why do I get the feeling you're only stringing me along?"

"I do not know what that means, but I do want to talk, just not now." Then an idea came to mind. He handed the chip to Doug. "If I give this to you, can you find out what this actually does?"

Doug's eyes lit up. "You're giving it to me? Why?"

"I have no need for it. But I would like to know what its function was before we have to destroy it."

"Why destroy it?"

"It is a beacon to me. Once the comet has been moved, I do not wish for my people to locate me."

"Let's not be hasty. Maybe my people can just disable it."

Calix nodded. "That would be satisfactory, then. Do you have people who can do that?"

"Yeah, sure. I know someone who might be able to figure that out. Thank you for this opportunity."

"Now I must talk to Annie." He exited the room, but the hallway was empty. So was the nurses' station. "Where is she?"

"Hold on." Doug pulled out his cellphone. "John might know." His brow furrowed after several moments. "That's funny. He's not answering." He pocketed his phone. "Come on. Let's go see if they're outside."

Calix secured the locator in his pocket and joined the agent in the elevator. They rode it down in silence. He had to make this right. He couldn't let Annie continue to think he did not love her. That he did not consider her his home now. Her and the baby.

When the elevator doors opened, Calix gasped. John was lying outside by the front door. What happened? Where was Annie? Calix dashed to the door. No sign of Annie, but Mac was lying on the ground beside a car.

Calix stormed through the doors and ran toward Mac. "Annie!" Nothing. No sound whatsoever. His heart clenched in pain. Mac was motionless. Calix wasn't sure if he was alive or dead. How did one check?

Doug appeared and knelt beside Mac, placing fingers against his neck. "John is alive, just out cold." He paused as if listening. "So is Mac. What do you suppose happened?"

Calix covered his face. He knew exactly what happened. Annie was right. Pax hadn't left.

Mac's eyes fluttered open. He moaned in pain. "What the fuck?"

"Mac," Calix said. "Where's Annie?"

"Oh…my head. What the fuck kind of weapon was that?"

"The translation would be something like a destroyer or eradicator, but it does not always kill. Did he take Annie?"

Mac sat up and held his head. "I think so. He wanted her to go with him. Shit! I feel like every muscle has been twisted."

Calix helped Mac stand and they followed Doug back to John, who was starting to come out of it. He also complained about his head. A weakened Mac sat on the ground and leaned against the wall.

"I saw him take Annie," John said. "Before I could tell him to stop, he hit me with something. Damn, that thing hurt. Worse than any Taser."

Calix had never been hit with any weapon except the tranquilizers, so he had no idea what those two were experiencing. He was thankful the device was not set to destroy, which only meant one thing. "He took Annie because of me. He wants me." He pulled out his locator. "Pax is back on the roof. I have to go get her."

* * * *

Doug had read his fair share of books where the hero would stop thinking logically when it came to saving their loved one. It even happened on *The X-Files*, his favorite show. And it never turned out well. So it was up to him to stop Calix from making a huge mistake. But how did a person go about stopping someone whose main objective was to save their loved one when they had eight inches and a hundred pounds in their favor? Answer—very carefully.

The alien headed for the doors to the building and Doug grabbed his arm. "Whoa, whoa, wait a minute. You can't just go barging on up there. That's what Pax expects."

Calix glared with those strange indigo eyes of his. "You just want to keep me here. You do not care about Annie."

"That is not true. I was only pretending I'd hurt Annie so I could get you to cooperate. But if you go up there without a plan, what's to say he won't kill her anyway?"

"He's right, Calix," Mac said. "I want Annie back, too, but we have to be smart about this."

Calix paced in front of the doors. "Pax only wants me. He does not care about anyone else."

"Which means Pax won't think twice about following Directive 23, right?" Doug asked.

Calix stopped pacing and shook his head. "I do not want that."

"Neither do we. And if you go up there, what's to stop him from zapping you and then following through?"

"Nothing." He leaned against the wall and slid to the ground. "I do not want anyone to die. I just want her safe."

At least the alien was seeing reason. Doug crouched in front of the big guy. "I know that. We all do. But we need to disable him first."

"But how? I am just a teacher."

A teacher who traveled in space. The man clearly underestimated himself.

John stood on wobbly legs. "I think I know of a way to do that, but I need my computer and Calix's locator." He took a step and promptly collapsed to the ground. "Annnnd maybe a wheelchair."

CHAPTER 22

Pain greater than anything Annie had ever felt sliced and diced her brain. And her neck. And shoulders. And...heck, everything hurt. What the hell happened?

Mac. Was he with her? Wherever that was.

She slowly opened her eyes and tried not to move her aching head. Mac was nowhere to be seen inside the ship, which resembled Calix's with one exception—Pax sat at the controls.

"You cannot leave, so do not try," he said.

So much for trying to be stealthy. She wasn't even sure she could stand, let alone escape. "You're not very nice. I took you into my home. Kept you from freezing. And this is the thanks I get? What did you do to Mac?" His collapse kept playing over in her head as if it were on some kind of video loop, bringing tears to her eyes. She had to think clearly. If she were alive, then he should be, too.

And the baby?

"I told you I came for Calix. That has not changed. Mac should recover."

Should? Her heart ached. "I'm surprised you didn't kill him with your Directive 23. Isn't that your plan? To kill us all?"

"I see now you are not a threat to our people. You cannot travel like we can. Which means I do not need to enact Directive 23. But if you become an obstacle, I will enact it on you."

Oh, great. "Where are we?"

"On the roof. I expected Calix to arrive by now." He stood and towered over her but held no kind of weapon. "What kind of experiments did you perform on him? Or did you inject him with poison? I need to know so we can reverse the damage."

She laughed and regretted the movement. What she wouldn't give for a few hundred aspirin. "No experiments. No poison." Just a lost chip, but Mr. Robot here probably thought it was just a tracking device like Calix had, so why bring it up? "There was no damage so there is nothing to reverse."

"We shall see." He headed back to his chair.

"Why can't you just leave him alone? Why must you take him back when he doesn't want to go?"

Pax stopped and turned around. "He does not know what he wants because he is not thinking clearly. He claimed his mission was to determine if the people on this planet would accept our people because our planet is in the path of a comet. Yet I cannot find any documentation in our files."

"Could it be that your people hid that information?"

"Information is to be shared. It is how we learn. It makes no sense to hide it."

Unless, of course, they didn't *want* their people to know. Even accidentally. "Maybe you're looking in the wrong place. Calix had problems—"

"I know how to search for documentation. It is not there."

Hmmm… He almost seemed insulted that she'd implied otherwise. Maybe their emotions weren't totally gone, just subdued. A lot. "Have you contacted your sentinel? Confirmed Calix's story that way?"

"I am not to contact the sentinel until I have captured Calix."

That sounded about what a robot—or programmed person— would say. "So, you're not even going to try?"

He shook his head. "Calix is ill. Our people will take care of him and make him better."

"And if they can't make him fit to your specifications? What then?"

"I do not understand. Why would he not get better?"

"Because he isn't sick." Trying to get through to this alien was worse than explaining physics to a five-year-old.

Pax turned back to the console. She stuck her tongue out at him. Not that he could see her, but it made her feel a little better. Movement on the monitor caught her attention. A set of doors were on display and one opened slowly. Her heart leaped when

Calix emerged from inside the building, the locator in his hand. The ship must be camouflaged as he held the locator out, probably to find the opening, but Pax—who had also seen Calix—eliminated the need by pushing a button, opening the door.

Calix looked to his left. The ship's opening was pointed away from the building, or rather, away from the camera above the roof doors. She guessed someone—like John—was monitoring that camera. But if they had hoped to see inside the ship, they were out of luck. Calix glanced over his shoulder, but no one followed him out. It probably killed Doug to let Calix loose. Then again, maybe Doug was waiting for the go ahead to help. The ship's camera was set at some kind of wide angle and showed a good portion of the roof. Calix took tentative steps toward the opening of the ship.

Pax pushed another button. *Zap!* A beam of light from Pax's ship shot the handle off the door leading to the stairwell, causing Calix to jump.

Crap. If Calix were waiting on backup, they wouldn't be able to come now.

Pax stood in the doorway, facing Calix but pointing the weapon at her. "I knew you would come."

"Where is Annie?"

She wanted to warn Calix to leave, but with that weapon staring at her she had to think of the baby first. Maybe one zap didn't harm it, but another might be the tipping point. Sitting up was too much of a chore, that weapon had really drained her dry—it must have also caused her bladder to spring a leak as her crotch was wet—so she remained on her back. "I'm here."

"Bring her out, Pax."

"You need to come inside. We must go."

Calix shook his head. "You want me, bring her out here."

Pax pointed the weapon toward Calix. "Do I need to subdue you?"

If Pax pulled the trigger, there would be no hope of escaping. She had to get that weapon away from him. Maybe if she tried a little harder she could sit up. It was either that or roll to the floor. Ooh, that gave her an idea. But could she do it? And would Calix take the opportunity? The man knew nothing about fighting.

"If you must subdue me, then do it. But if you want me to cooperate, I suggest you let her go."

"You are damaged. How can I believe what you say?"

"And you are programmed to rescue me. Why should I believe you?"

"I am not a program. I do my job."

They could go like this forever. But now that Pax no longer pointed that thing at her and his attention was focused elsewhere, she took that opportunity and rolled.

Who knew something she'd done a million times as a kid would take so much energy? Or hurt so much? She landed on the floor with a thud. Her head and stomach both objected to the abuse. Lying on her side, she brought her knees up and prayed she'd have the energy to follow through.

* * * *

Calix fought to stand his ground. Emotions were running amok, especially after hearing Annie's weak voice. He wanted to rush inside. Save Annie. But Pax was armed and had no intention of sparing Annie. If Calix had followed his instincts, instincts he was still trying to understand… Well, he did not wish to find out how foolish that would have been.

Instead, he tried to follow the plan: distract Pax and wait for help who would subdue Pax with the tranquilizer gun. But with the door now sealed shut, no one would be coming to Calix's aid. There would be no subduing now.

Pax turned toward the bed. "What are you doing?"

He walked out of sight. What had Annie done?

She cried out and then so did Pax. He fell backward, past the opening, doubled over, holding his crotch. Calix rushed inside and fell on top of Pax, who was screaming in pain, his face several shades pale.

"Calix! I'm so glad you did that," she said. "I wasn't sure if you'd take the opportunity. Not that I think you're stupid. I don't. I swear. Oh God, Calix. I'm so sorry. I trust you, I really do."

Calix smiled. It was nice to know she was no longer mad at him. However, he was a little confused about her statement; he hadn't done anything yet. He pulled the plastic strips Doug had given him from his pocket. "What did you do to him?"

"I kicked him in the nuts. He should be glad I didn't use my boot. I thought about it."

"The nuts?"

"His testicles."

"And it hurts that bad?" He knew they were sensitive, but for a kick to cause that much pain, and from someone small like Annie, it was hard to fathom.

"Apparently. You should have seen Mac this one time…oh." Her voice hitched. "Is he okay?"

He turned to speak to her and tried not to show his alarm at the paleness of her face. She needed reassurance first. "He is fine."

A flood of tears left her eyes. "Thank God."

Calix secured Pax's arms behind his back. He was curled up into a ball, moaning and unmoving. All from getting kicked in the testicles. Calix would make sure no one ever did that to him. As he stood, he found the weapon under the console and picked it up. Just in case.

He put the weapon on the bed, sat beside her on the floor, and pulled her into his arms. He hugged her tight. "Did he harm you?"

She grabbed onto his shoulders. "My whole body feels scrambled from being zapped, but I think I'm okay."

"He shot you?" That explained why she was still lying on the floor instead of sitting on the bed. Mac and John still were trying to recover from Pax's blast.

"Why do you do that?" Pax asked.

Calix turned toward Pax. "Do what?"

"Hold her. What has she done to you?"

Calix broke the hug, held her face, and stared into her eyes. "I love her." He touched his forehead against hers and lowered his voice. "And I am so very sorry for making you angry."

"My fault. I was going to—"

He kissed her before she could finish. He didn't care who was to blame, only that they were no longer mad at one another. "I love you, Annie. I will always love you."

"And I love you, too, but can we get out of here? I'd really like to clean up."

He would love nothing more than to get her alone again. "We may have to wait for someone to open the door. Can you walk?"

"I think so."

He stood and offered his hand, but when she hoisted herself up, her legs gave out. He grabbed her around the waist before she fell to the ground.

"Okay, maybe I can't walk. I'll just wait here."

He scooped her up to place her on the bed, but the spot on the covers caused him to stop. "What is that? Is that blood?"

"No, I just had an—" She looked at the bed and her face paled even more than before. "Put me down, put me down, put me down."

He sat her on the mattress and knelt on the floor. "You are injured."

"I don't think so. I mean, I hurt everywhere, but more like muscle pain." She looked down at her crotch. "Oh crap. I thought I peed, not… Oh God, Calix." Thick tears dropped from her eyes and she clutched her stomach. "I think I'm losing the baby."

Those words nearly stopped his heart. "What? How?"

"I don't… Oh God. I'm so sorry." Her tears left big wet spots on her jeans as she kept her head down.

How could he miss something he had never seen or touched? He had never understood crying, but the loss hurt him deeply and now his own eyes watered. How could such a terrible thing happen? She had said Pax had zapped her.

Zapped her.

The weapon did this. And Pax had discharged it. On Annie. On their baby. That was the only explanation. Anger and grief took possession of his senses. He wanted to punch something. Some…body.

Pax sat up. The damage to his groin must have been superficial. Calix was tempted to make it worse.

He stood in front of Pax and clenched his fists. "You killed our baby."

Pax's breath came out in gasps. "What are you talking about? She had no baby with her when I took her."

"She was pregnant. Our child was growing inside her."

"Calix, you are talking nonsense. Babies grow in the laboratory."

Calix lifted Pax by the collar and slammed him against the wall. "Why couldn't you just leave without me? Why must you ruin my life? Why?"

Pax's eyes were wide. He did not even try to get free. His aversion to touch was not only embedded in his mind, fighting man-to-man was unfathomable for their people. "I have not ruined anything. They have altered you. Once you are back home—"

Calix punched Pax in the jaw, cutting off his words. Pax collapsed to the floor while Calix rubbed his knuckles. They stung, but he felt better in a strange kind of way. "My. Home. Is. Here."

Doug rushed inside, brandishing the tranquilizer gun. "Calix? Sorry I took so long. Damn door wouldn't open. Everything under control?"

Calix wasn't sure if he would ever be in control again.

CHAPTER 23

Annie lay on the bed, snuggled against her best guy. She loved being in Calix's arms more than anything else. Made her feel wanted, precious. Of course, once Calix realized she could have prevented getting zapped, she wasn't so sure he'd want to hold her again.

Doug had been shocked to learn she was carrying Calix's baby. She hoped she was still carrying his baby. This stupid hospital wasn't staffed for much. Not that an ultrasound would have picked up anything yet. Instead, a nurse had taken a blood sample from her arm and had taken the mess she'd made in the ship to a lab. In the meantime, an OB doctor was on the way from another hospital and all they could do now was wait.

Wait to see if something she had grown to love in such a short amount of time had been ripped from her. All because she attacked Pax. When would she ever learn?

She didn't want to think about what the doctor might say and needed something as a distraction. The hard, warm body surrounding her was a good start. She might as well enjoy it while she could.

"You should sleep." Calix ran his hand up and down her arm.

"I can't." She took his hand and kissed his bruising knuckles. "I can't believe you hit Pax. You, who advocates against fighting."

"Someone told me that fighting is the only way to get your point across."

"Yeah, well, I should have said *sometimes* fighting is the only way." It certainly didn't work for her or their baby. She blinked back the tears. Until she heard otherwise, there was still hope, and she would hold on to every little bit she could.

"You did more damage than I did. Promise me you will never kick me there."

His shocked expression had been pretty comical at the time, but after living in a no-touch society he wouldn't have known about that defensive move. "Don't worry. I would never hurt you like that. Well, not unless you turned into some kind of beast on the full moon and it was the only way I could defend myself."

"I will keep that in mind." He ran his fingers through her hair and then touched her cheek. "How are you feeling? Honestly."

Mentally or physically? She wasn't about to lie, so she stuck with the physical. "Like someone ran over me several times." She couldn't tell if she was sore from being zapped or from miscarrying. Would she even feel the miscarriage if she were, indeed, miscarrying?

He kissed the top of her head. "I am sorry."

"Not. Your. Fault." She tapped his chest on each word, knowing where the blame really lay—on her. "So, where is Pax anyway?"

"Doug has him secured in another room, where he is most likely bombarding Pax with questions, and knowing Pax, he is refusing to answer." He chuckled. "That man just doesn't give up."

"Which one? Pax or Doug?"

He thought for a moment. "Both."

"What's going to happen now? Are you going to talk to Pax again?"

"I have to. He is afraid of me now, which is probably a good thing. But if he doesn't see reason, we cannot send him back. We will just have to prepare for another visit. And I can guarantee they will not send just one person."

The door opened and a man wearing a white lab coat entered. He stared at Calix for a good long moment.

"Are you looking for someone?" she asked.

"Oh, sorry. I'm Dr. Vaughan." He looked at Calix. "I've seen the test results. If I wasn't told otherwise, I'd say you were human. You're really from another planet?"

Calix sighed. "That's the rumor."

Annie covered her mouth just as a snort escaped. Who knew he had a sense of humor? And a dry one at that?

"I am assuming you are here for Annie. So please, do not make her wait any longer."

Okay, no beating around the bush for her fella. But would he still be her fella after... Oh shit. She took Calix's hand and closed her eyes. *Please be good news, please be good news.* If she said it enough times, maybe it would come true.

"I'm sorry, but the news isn't good. I'm afraid the embryo has aborted. We found the remains on the bedsheet."

The air seemed to be sucked out of the room. She grabbed onto Calix. What had she done? Would he ever forgive her?

* * * *

Calix stared at the sleeping woman in his arms. He had never cried before this day and now he had done it twice. When the doctor had given them the horrible news, he found grief so severe he could not stop the tears. Together they had cried and eventually she fell asleep. An emptiness radiated in his chest, but as long as he had Annie, she would help fill it.

He quietly slid out from beneath her and covered her up. He hated leaving her, but he still had work to do. The corridor was eerily quiet. Pax was being held only two doors down and Calix expected noise of some sort. If not from Pax, then from Doug.

Doug stood when Calix entered the room. "I heard the news. I'm sorry for your loss."

A loss that shouldn't have happened if not for Pax. But Calix couldn't even blame the man for doing what he did. Their people just didn't know any better.

Pax was sitting in a chair with one wrist secured to the wall. Surprisingly, his face lit up at Calix's arrival. "Will you tell this...man," he said in their language, "I have no intention of answering his questions? He does not listen to me."

"What did he say?" Doug asked.

Calix clasped a hand on Doug's shoulder. "That he has no intention of answering your questions. You might want to take a break. I need to speak to Pax alone."

"Please get him to talk. Why bother exploring if you don't plan on sharing? Doesn't make sense." Doug kept on mumbling as he left the room.

Except Pax wasn't here as an explorer. He was here to retrieve and nothing more. It was up to Calix to get Pax to do something more. But how? As Pax rubbed his temple, Calix thought of a way. Just how many of their people suffered with the chip in their head?

"How bad are your headaches?" Calix asked in their language, hoping to put Pax at ease.

Pax stopped rubbing and eyed him warily. "I do not have headaches."

"Sure you do. I see you rub your temple. How bad are they?"

"This is from your hit. I told you. I do not have headaches."

"Then why are you not rubbing your chin? That is where I hit you." Pax's denial came as no surprise to Calix. He'd lost track of the excuses he'd used to explain the nagging pain. Apparently, running into a doorway three times within a week was another way to be sent to the dispensary. "When I lost my chip, my headaches went away."

Pax sat up straighter. "You had headaches?"

"Every day. I thought something was wrong with me. Last year, a fellow teacher confessed to the manager about his head hurting and was sent to the physician. I waited to see if they could help him before I admitted my own. But I never saw him again."

"That does not mean anything. People are reassigned all the time."

"He died." When Pax's eyes widened, Calix continued. "I do not think they meant to destroy him. I truly hope they did not. Most likely he died while they tried to fix him. I only know about him because I knew his name and I could look up the information."

"Why would you do that?"

Calix chuckled. Oh, how much he had changed. There was no word in their language for curious, another trait losing the chip brought about.

"What is that noise you are making?"

"It's called…" Hmmm, they had no word for it, either, so he used the English word instead. "Laughing. It is something a person does when they find…" Another word that did not exist. Their language really was stilted. He went another way. "When they find themselves in an unusual situation. In this case, I just realized I am thinking in their language now. But what it all comes down to is that I needed to know what I would face if I returned to our planet because I have seen other headache complainers disappear. Have you?"

"Yes, but that does not mean—"

"It is the chip. I am sure of it. It does not belong and the headache is our body's way of warning us. It is a wonderful feeling to wake up in the morning and not have my head hurt. I feel alive, awakened. I do not want my old life back, if it is even possible. If I go back, they will try to fix me to their standards or I will be destroyed. Why can't I just stay here? Who am I hurting?"

Pax seemed to think it over, giving Calix cause to hope.

"What would I tell them? I will not lie."

"I am not asking you to lie. Together we will contact the sentinel. I will explain how our planet can be saved. I will need to stay behind to make sure the rocket is made in time for you to return home and bring back a larger ship for transportation."

"And if he asks if you will return home then, what will you say?"

"I do not believe he will ask that, but if he does, I will not lie. I am not going back. My home is here now. I just need you to not bring up the subject. Can you do that?"

"If he does not ask, I can do that. Provided Sentinel Gaylor agrees to your plan."

"Oh, he'll agree. He will do anything to save our planet."

Pax tugged on his restraint. "Will they let me leave?"

How much could he trust Pax? He'd been tricked before. "If you follow through with our plan, I will make sure of it. Until then, you will have to be subdued in some way. Do you understand?"

"Yes. If Sentinel Gaylor can confirm your story about the comet, I will have no issues following your plan."

"Good. I will go find someone to release you. After we speak with the sentinel and you are free to go, I would like to take Annie back home as easy as possible, and your ship would be a lot quicker."

"Their travel is barbaric."

"Yes, but it works."

* * * *

Doug finished his letter and hit print. Loose ends. He never thought he'd have any to clean up.

251

John entered the office and collapsed in the chair across from Doug's desk. "I'm surprised you let them go. I figured you'd have Calix on some kind of leash."

Unfortunately, a leash would not gain information. Trust would.

Doug picked up the chip. "I think Annie was just as surprised as you. Strangely enough, I trust Calix. And he needs to know I trust him or he won't share anything. How are you feeling by the way?"

"Remind me never to get zapped with that weapon again. I swear, it must have twisted every muscle in my body. What have you got there?"

"His chip."

John leaned forward. "What? How'd you get that?"

"He gave it to me. Just temporarily. He'll need it when Pax returns, but after that, he said I can do whatever I want with it, but only if we can disable it. If we can't, then he prefers it be destroyed. For now, we can study it."

"Wow. Guess your conversation went well then?"

"It did. I would have liked to have talked with Pax, but that man's more stubborn than Calix was."

"So what's next?"

"Besides getting a rocket ready for his people to nudge a comet? We'll have some files to go through. Calix said he would download all the documentation from his ship and translate what he can for us. But that will take months, if not years. He said there's a lot to go through. It will certainly keep him busy."

"That's it?"

"Hell no. He's bringing his ship back here. Said he'd take me up for a ride. Can you believe it? I'll actually be up in space."

"Well don't forget me. Can you imagine the goodies that are on that ship? Damn. I'm salivating just thinking about it. Do you think he'll turn it over to us? In exchange for that rocket he wants?"

Doug stared at his partner, amazed at how quickly he had become a believer. "That's exactly what he wants to do, but he's not sure his people will go for that."

"Yeah. I'm assuming they'll want their ship back. So, what's the deal?"

"Well…that depends. If Calix is allowed to remain here and his ship can be used as payment, nothing. We get the ship. If they insist Calix return with his ship, then after Pax or whoever leaves with their rocket, the ship will meet with an accident. With Calix inside, of course."

"Wait a minute. We're gonna destroy it? Kill him?"

Doug shook his head. Didn't his partner have any sense? "Staged, idiot. It's gonna be staged. Something Pax or whoever they send will need to witness, somehow. We haven't come up with all the details. But it's not like we don't have time. Plus, it *is* Plan B. They could go for Plan A and we won't have to do anything. In the meantime, Calix asked for an identity so he could live here. Legally."

"That should be easy enough."

"Yeah. The difficult part was his other request. He asked me if we could buy his gold."

John sat up straight. "Gold?"

"Yeah. Seems his planet has plenty. He knew it was used as currency back in the 1830s and he brought some with him. He just doesn't know how to go about getting cash for it. I'll talk it over with the higher-ups on Monday. If they agree, then we'll buy it from him."

"Just how much gold are we talking here?"

CHAPTER 24

Lying in bed, Annie stared at the clock. If she wanted to actually show up for work today, she had to get up and get ready. But the bed was comfortable and warm. The man beside her, too, although she had her back to him.

The past week had gone by in a blur. She had taken vacation days instead of working from home, unsure she could focus on anything but her loss. Calix grieved, too, but he had important things to keep him busy. The government wasn't just going to go away. Calix promised and his promise was bond. It was one of the many things she loved about him.

She could have kept working, and maybe that would have been smarter, but her work would have suffered. She was not about to let anyone discover what had happened. Not even Jen. Since she never knew about the baby, there wasn't anything to tell.

Annie still hadn't told Calix the whole truth. Such a wimp. He deserved to know her part in the miscarriage. If she had only kept her anger in check. If she had only gone along with Pax.

She swiped at the tears in her eyes and took a deep breath. If she couldn't control her emotions, she'd show up at work with red eyes. Then everyone would suspect something was up.

Calix's arm came around her. "I think I have given you too much space. I have missed you."

She clicked the lamp on and turned to face him. His hair had fallen into his eyes and she brushed it away. "Are you done with your little missions?"

"No, but that is not what I meant. You are still sad. Mac said you would get over it, that I should give you space, but I don't see you getting better." He wiped the tear from her cheek. "Is something else wrong? Do you need to visit another doctor?"

She closed her eyes and relished his touch. Everything was wrong. Besides losing the baby and wondering if he would stick around once she told him the truth, she got a strange feeling he didn't need her anymore. And if he didn't need her and he couldn't forgive her—and how could he when she couldn't—what was to stop him from leaving? Nothing, that's what. She would tell him today, just not now. She had to survive work first. "No, I'm fine. Just not looking forward to going into work."

He kissed her lightly on the lips and then climbed out of the bed. His nakedness surprised her. She really must have been out of it not to have noticed. Would they ever make love again?

"I have a surprise for you today. Are you really going to work? Or have you changed your mind?"

"I'm going. It's time." She sat up. "What kind of surprise?"

"If I told you, then it wouldn't be a surprise. Can I meet you for lunch?"

"It's too far for me to drive up here for my lunch hour."

"No, no." He patted his chest. "I will come to you. Would that be okay?"

"But how?"

"I have a ride."

"Mac still isn't legal, so don't—"

"Don't worry about Mac. Trust me, okay?"

His grin was suspicious, but she couldn't say no to him. "Fine. Give me a call when you get there."

That was one of the first things they had done when they returned home—got Calix his own cellphone. He'd never used technology as a toy before and had been having fun with it ever since.

He zipped up his jeans and slipped on a sweatshirt. As he grabbed some socks, he paused, then returned and knelt beside the bed. He gave her another kiss. One more demanding, possessive. Oh, how she loved him. If he left her, she might never recover. He was her one and only and she had to go and blow it. She returned the kiss and held him tight. She wanted to hold him forever.

"I have really missed you," he said, his voice cracked with desire. "I have to go, but I will see you at lunch."

Maybe by lunch she would grow a spine. He deserved to know the truth.

She climbed out of bed and got ready for work. On Sunday, she'd gone the day without the boot and met with success. Her ankle was practically as good as new. It was so nice to wear something other than her athletic shoe, but she would stick to flats. For now. Why jinx it?

When she arrived at work, she remained in her car a moment. It felt like forever since she'd been in that building. She still had that anger management course to attend, but instead of regretting it, she looked forward to it. Maybe it would teach her something. Like how to be more like Calix. He was the most laid-back person she knew.

He was also the most forgiving. But would he be able to forgive her?

* * * *

Jay opened the mail box and pulled out the advertisements. Junk, junk, and more junk. Oh, look, a bill. No one ever wrote to him anymore. Then again, most of the people he knew were dead. Talk about depressing. He trudged back to the cabin while Buster ran off toward a tree, doing his sniffing and peeing—as if any other dog had ever come up here and covered his territory.

Jay opened the door and ushered Buster inside. The cold had managed to seep into his bones even with that short trip and he relished the heat of the cabin. Good thing he had a nice supply of wood, the fireplace would get a workout today. He tossed the mail to the table. A letter slipped onto the floor and he picked it up.

How'd he miss this one? It had an actual stamp, well, a metered stamp, not one of those bulk-mail kind. No return address, though. Jay ripped the envelope open. The stationary was plain and white, no name or address imprinted at the top or bottom. Like someone had taken a piece of copier paper and printed the letter.

Dear Mr. Bryant,

I want to thank you for your help regarding your extraterrestrial sighting. While I would like to tell you we had an alien visitor, I'm afraid that just wasn't the case.

As I suspected, the people responsible for the ship you found were just people from another country trying to get into ours illegally. We have since caught them.

I know how excited you were about the finding. I was excited with the possibility. Maybe one day we will get that alien visit. I hope it happens in our lifetime.

Anyway, I just wanted to let you know where things stood. If you ever come across another sighting, please keep me in mind. I would love nothing better than to prove other intelligent life forms exist.

Yours truly,
Douglas Lazur

"Bull patties!" Jay dropped the letter to the table. He didn't believe a word of it. The government was covering up the find, that's all. Probably afraid the general public couldn't handle an actual visitation, if that's what it was about. Well, how could they, when every sighting was covered up?

He would keep watching the sky like always, because where there was one, there would be others.

* * * *

Lunchtime approached and Calix's text indicated he was on his way. Annie put her coat on and stepped outside. Dreary, grey clouds hung in the sky, matching her mood. Even at noon the temperature hadn't risen all that much. Was it going to snow again? She should have checked the forecast. The groundhog predicted spring was around the corner. She hoped the little bugger was correct. She'd had enough of winter.

She searched the parking lot. No sign of Calix or Mac's Cherokee, assuming he used her brother's car. Maybe she came out too soon?

A bright green Jeep Sahara four-door pulled up. Calix waved from inside. In the driver's seat. *Holy shit on a shingle.*

He climbed out and ran around the vehicle, stopping at the passenger door. He opened it. "Surprise!"

"What, is this yours? Where did you get it? How did you get it?"

"Get in and I will explain."

She hoisted herself into the vehicle. The seat was warm. Holy moly, she could get used to this. While she buckled up, Calix climbed in. He was grinning and bouncing around like he was about to burst.

"So explain."

"You like my car? Mac helped me pick it out, but if you don't like it, I can get another."

Well, that explained the Jeep. Mac seemed to have some kind of obsession with the make.

"It's very nice." In fact, it suited his large frame. Her car was a bit tiny for him. "But how could you afford this?"

"That's the surprise." He reached between the seats and pulled out a large manila envelope. "Doug was able to get me official papers. I'm now a citizen of the United States of America. See? I have a social security number, a driver's license, and a birth certificate."

She took the certificate from his hands and laughed. "Doug has one sick sense of humor. This says you were born in Roswell, New Mexico."

"What is sick about that?"

"Look it up on your computer then ask me that question. And your name is Calix Martin?" Wasn't there a television series with a Martian that went by the name of Martin? Doug was just having fun, wasn't he?

"I wanted O'Shea, but he said Martin was a common name."

She lowered her arms and stared at him. "You wanted my name?"

The smile lit up his face and jerked her heart. "Yes. I like your name. But Doug also said people might think we were related, and with us being together, that maybe we should avoid any questions."

Oh God, she had to tell him. She opened her mouth to do just that, but chickened out. "Okay, so you have an identity. That doesn't explain how you bought this car."

"I sold my gold." He pulled out another paper. "See?"

Gold? She vaguely remembered him mentioning something about gold what felt like ages ago. She took the paper from his hands. It was a bank statement showing a balance of... "Holy shit on a shingle!"

He laughed. "I have never heard that curse before. Is it new?"

"Calix. This says you have over ten million dollars."

"I know. Doug says I will need to move some of it to other accounts, to make sure it's secure, but that we should be able to live off the interest. I do not know what that means, but I will look it up. That's good, though, right?"

"Yeah, it's good." For him. Now he really didn't need her.

* * * *

Calix stared at Annie's frown. Something had to be wrong or else she'd be happy for him. He should have spoken with her earlier, or taken her out for dinner. Anything to have gotten her out of bed before now and put a smile on her face. He thought coming back to work would have helped, or his surprise, but if anything she looked sadder than ever.

She lowered her head. "I have to tell you something. I should have told you earlier, but, well, I've been kind of scared. Now…I…well…I'm still scared, but you need to know." She took a deep breath. "It's my fault we lost the baby."

Her fault? He knew her sadness had come from the loss, but not that she thought she had caused that loss. If he had not listened to Mac, if he had done what he had wanted, she would not be feeling this guilt. A guilt she had no reason to be feeling. He took her hand. "It was no one's fault, Annie."

"But it is. I haven't told you everything."

"I know what happened. Pax told me. I understand."

She looked up with moist eyes. "How can you understand? If I had just gone quietly with him…"

"No! No!" He had to fix this. "It was not your fault. You thought he hurt Mac. You were protecting him. And you were trying to protect me. To keep me from being destroyed. Yes, we lost something in the process, but we could have lost so much more. Because of you, I am here. We are here. Alive and well. I do not blame you for the loss of our child. I do not blame Pax, either. He was only doing what he was programmed to do."

"You know and yet, you're still with me?"

"Where else would I be? I love you, Annie. That hasn't changed. Unless…" Could it be her feelings had changed? He had been so excited over his new identity and his ability to provide for her, he never even thought that maybe she only cared for him because he was the father of her baby. Or that maybe his presence caused her more grief. What if he was the reason for her sadness?

"Unless what?"

He touched the lump in his pocket. Doug had helped him with that, since he'd been afraid Mac would tell. Suddenly, his mouth went dry. Fear would not get him what he wanted. The only way to find out how she really felt was to do what he had planned from the start. He would deal with the rejection later, if need be.

He pulled out the box and opened it. "Annie? If you still want me, will you be my wife?"

She gasped and hesitantly touched the ring. A pretty, shiny stone Doug had called a diamond. Calix had already determined she was his wife, but apparently paperwork was needed for that, too. Along with her permission.

"Do you know what you're asking?"

He knew he never wanted to be without her again. "I love you, Annie. And I want to spend my life with you. Is this not how you show that?"

Tears ran down her cheeks and she nodded. "Oh, Calix! Of course I'll be your wife. Of course I still want you." She palmed his face. "Kind of knew you were the guy for me when we found you on the road. I will always want you. I will always love you."

He never knew such words would bring joy to his whole body.

She pulled his face to hers and kissed him. Brief, but wonderful.

"You have made me so happy." With fingers that had never felt fat before, he fumbled with the ring several times before he managed to get it out of the box. She held out her hand and pointed to the correct finger. After he slipped it on, he reached out to hold her and continue with that kiss, but the console was in the way, as well as the steering wheel.

"Hold on." She unbuckled her belt, climbed out of the vehicle and circled around the front. Before he could ask what she was doing, she opened his door and sat on his lap.

"See? You always know what to do." He kissed her deep and grew hard for her. Too bad she wore slacks. He now saw the sense in skirts and dresses. Better access.

"So, where are you taking me to lunch?" she asked.

"Mac suggested the Davenport Grand. Said something about make-up sex? So I reserved a room, but if you'd rather have food…"

"Hotel sounds great." She kissed him again and he felt her smile against his lips. "But we'll order room service. I've always wanted to eat naked."

Naked. With Annie. Forever. Life couldn't be any sweeter.

Thank you for reading *Alien Desires*. If you liked this book, then be on the lookout for book 2 in the Loveable Alien series: *The Alien's Change of Heart*. That will be Pax's story. I'd tell you more, but I'm still writing it. Yeah, I don't outline. Probably why it takes me longer to write a book. But I do what works. And what is more enjoyable. Gotta make it enjoyable. Right?

If you're interested in what I'm writing or what book convention/signing I might be at, subscribe to my newsletter. I don't send them out as often as I should, so you definitely won't be bombarded by me. You can find a form to join on my website, http://www.stacymckitrick.com. Joining will also entitle you to a free short story. Yay!

And while you're waiting for book 2 to be released, check out my other series: Bitten by Love and Ghostly Encounters. You can find all my books and buy links on my website. I try to show up everywhere.

Finally, if you are so inclined, please post a review from where you purchased this book. It would be most appreciated. Since this is a new series, in a different kind of genre (I still see it as paranormal, but that's apparently just me), reviews will help give this book some cred.

Happy Reading!

ABOUT THE AUTHOR

Stacy McKitrick always had stories in her head; she just never knew what to do with them. Then one day she decided to give writing a try and discovered the passion she'd been looking for all her life. She waved goodbye to accounting and now spends her time writing romance featuring vampires, ghosts, and aliens. All with happy endings, of course. Born in California, she currently resides in Ohio with her husband. They have two grown children. You can learn more about Stacy at her website www.stacymckitrick.com

Books by Stacy McKitrick

Lovable Alien series:
Alien Desires

Ghostly Encounter series:
Ghostly Liaison
Ghostly Interlude
Ghostly Protector

Bitten by Love series:
My Sunny Vampire
Bite Me, I'm Yours
Blind Temptation
A Vampire Wedding
Biting the Curse
Finding the Perfect Mate

Short Stories in the Following Anthologies:
Home for the Holidays
Love's a Beach